Outlandia

GEORGIA ANGELIS

BLACK lace

First published in 1993 by
Black Lace
332 Ladbroke Grove
London W10 5AH

Reprinted 1994

Copyright © Georgia Angelis 1993

Typeset by CentraCet, Cambridge
Printed and bound in Great Britain by
Cox & Wyman Ltd, Reading, Berks

ISBN 0 352 32883 5

This book is sold subject to the condition that it shall not, by way of trade or otherwise, be lent, resold, hired out or otherwise circulated without the publisher's prior written consent in any form of binding or cover other than that in which it is published and without a similar condition including this condition being imposed on the subsequent purchaser.

Black Lace novels are sexual fantasies. In real life, always practice safe sex.

Outlandia

GEORGIA ANGELIS

Chapter One

In 1800 England was ruled by the sporadically mad king, George III; child labour was about to be abolished and the steam engine was only a few years from its unveiling. America had fought for and achieved Independence, and France, having lost its monarchy, was being moulded into a militarily superior nation by Napoleon Bonaparte, whose sights were on expansion and conquest in Europe.

Meanwhile, in an uncertain longitude and latitudal position somewhere in the South Seas . . .

The wind howled, a shrill and uncomfortable sound. The sea raging, waves of twenty foot and more breaking over the listing bows of the barquentine *Lady Luckington*, swallowing the ship and then spitting her out again more bedraggled and broken than before. She carried no sail now, was swept forth at the mercy of the sea, her captain lashed to the wheel, which was in turn lashed to the rail of the poop deck, was sodden and chilled beneath his oilskins. His barked orders to the skeleton crew on duty at that dark time just past midnight, could scarcely be heard above the ferocious workings of the storm. Carrying them out didn't seem to matter anyhow, the hurricane was in command and took them where it would.

Below, in passenger cabin number three, the scene was much cosier.

Iona Stanley sighed and shuddered as the man she'd picked out to make love to her – a fellow passenger, Jack Savage – unbuttoned her burgundy linen evening dress and kissed the exposed nape of her neck.

Oh *yes*, that was *so* good, so longed for. She'd thought, sensed, that Jack Savage might know how to make a lady sigh, had been watching him for days and thinking about him – it. Jack Savage automatically made a woman think of *it*. And she wasn't alone. She'd observed the other women passengers mentally devouring him whenever he joined them at table in the evening for the ship's one reasonably good meal of the day. There was Miss Harker and her charge, Abigail Cosgrove, who was being transported back to England from His Majesty's antipodean colonies. She was being sent home to school, to receive the polish to her education and suchlike that life in Australia just couldn't possibly furnish.

Miss Harker stammered whenever Mr Savage had cause to engage her in conversation, while young and demure Miss Cosgrove blushed crimson and had to keep wiping her clammy hands in her satin skirts.

So what was it about the man that had them so in thrall?

Firstly, and most importantly at the outset, he was handsome. Though not in a way that showed itself to best advantage in a drawing-room. His looks were sharp, unpolished, his face dark tanned. Rather short in the legs and burly of torso, the pricey clothes he wore took on a careless elegance. His cravat was always rakishly askew, rather than immaculate; his blond hair dragged back and secured, its pigtail ribbon knotted rather than fancy. He was a gentleman and yet it was evident that he didn't strive to appear as one; he had no desire to make a statement of rank or breeding.

Secondly, he was a mystery. Despite his residing for several months in Sydney and having spent more than two years in Australia travelling, he'd given away little about himself. He'd been selective in the invitations he accepted to social events and had been backwards in coming forwards with any information.

When asked what business he was in, he'd say, 'In nothing very interesting, ma'am', or 'sir', and say it in such a dismissive, bored way that no one had ever felt comfortable about pressing the matter further.

He was likeable, you see, and so people trusted him, made up their minds that whatever business he was engaged in must be legitimate and above board.

Thirdly, he was wealthy. No one quite knew to what degree, but the style in which he dressed, lived and travelled, made the fact plain.

Many were the unattached females foisted upon him at dances and social gatherings, by mothers eager to bring such dash, wealth and obviously good breeding into the family.

But after two years of Australia, Jack Savage had grown tired of the lack of true companionship, the military and diplomatic populace and the chained gangs of convicts. He'd booked passage for home. England, Bristol.

They'd both drank well of the passable Italian wine with their dinner, but neither was drunk. Rather they were intoxicated by the sudden and explosive sexual desire that each had aroused in the other and which, this evening, had come to a head.

Seated next to each other at dinner, Jack had known the shock of surprise and amused excitement as her dainty hand had strayed beneath the tablecloth, played upon his thigh enticingly, issuing an unmistakeable invitation.

Having watched her appreciatively for a day and

more, Jack wasn't about to act the total gentleman and ignore such signs. She seemed to know what she was doing, what she wanted. She was her own woman. He knew something of her past; that she'd left her husband, was going back to her family home in Norfolk, guessed that she was an independent-minded woman who could well take care of herself. And she seemed to want him, for a casual dalliance presumably, some fun to relieve the tedium of the voyage, without any strings. That suited Jack just fine. He didn't want to make a commitment to anyone either, he was as happy being free as she was.

She dropped her dessert fork. 'Oh my, how clumsy. Would you be so kind . . .?' she asked of Jack, staring down at the floor between them.

'Certainly, madam.' He grinned, bent, groped with his hand.

She caught his hand at the wrist, brought it between her legs, whilst all the time carrying on an inane conversation concerning crochet stitches with Miss Harker.

Jack blinked with surprise but gave no other visible reaction as his hand was drawn up beneath craftily hoisted skirts and tafetta petticoats, to slide up a thigh, glide over a mound downy with soft curls.

'More wine, Mister Savage?' queried the purser, with an eye on the hovering waiter.

'Why thank you, yes,' answered Jack, a finger slipping into Mrs Stanley's warm little slit.

She drew in her breath noisily, his touch sending a shock right through her, even her toes curled.

The finger stroked leisurely, circling and teasing her bud, stroking down purposefully and just, only just, entering her, then swept up again, getting wetter with each passing moment.

She was trembling so greatly by then that Iona couldn't trust herself to hold her glass steadily enough to drink.

The captain was talking, pontificating upon the

matter of standards aboard certain vessels and she nodded in agreement. 'Yes, oh yes, yes,' very breathy indeed as Mr Savage's finger tortured her clitoris, swept down and plunged into her, again, then again, exquisite, bringing her the kind of pleasure she had never known in all her years of marriage.

'Yes, oh God *yes!*' she exclaimed, drawing all eyes to her, as, for the very first time ever, she experienced an orgasm.

Her startled expression totally perplexed the other passengers. Jack was grinning.

The captain looked at her as if she was a jibbering imbecile. 'Yes? What do you mean *yes*? Surely, madam, you don't condone the piracy on the China Seas?'

Raggedly, licking the perspiration from her upper lip, she had shaken her head adamantly, 'No, of course not. I only meant, well . . . Oh, I don't know. Overlook my comment, please, sir.'

'Its rough on deck tonight,' said the husky Jack, 'I wonder if you ladies will permit me to smoke down here?'

The misses Harker and Cosgrove nodded instantly. 'By all means, sir.' 'Yes, do. I love the smell of fine tobacco.'

He looked to the flushed, still heavily breathing Iona. 'And you, madam?'

'Smoke by all means, sir,' she permitted, her breath catching anew as he crooked the finger that had pleasured her so thoroughly, and which still glistened from her juices, and took it slowly into his mouth, to suck at it thoroughly.

Suddenly she wanted him again, properly, madly; wanted the considerable length and girth of that member she had glanced a finger over earlier, thrust deep inside her. She trembled at the thought.

When dinner had finished she'd left the saloon, looking back at him just for a second as she disappeared through the mahogany louvred doors. He'd finished his brandy and cigar and followed shortly afterwards, employing the utmost discretion. A man would have to be a bounder not to guard the reputation of so charming and generous a creature.

And she was handsome, he thought again, now, as she pressed him back into an overstuffed armchair and sat across his lap, kissing him while he tried to get to grips with the laces of her baby-pink satin corsets. The bone panelled garment was fiendishly difficult to master, though. Eventually he gave up, bent his head and nuzzled at the swell of breasts pushed enticingly high by such feminine apparel. She shivered appreciatively, rubbed her bottom against his swelling manhood, arousing him greatly through her soft layers of white, lace-edged petticoats.

Her mouth locked with his in a hot kiss, she wiggled some more, enflaming Jack. He ran a hand up beneath the petticoats, found her, caressed, groaning lustfully at the feel of her warm moistness, forgetting the rules that called for gentling, persuading and exciting. Iona Stanley needed no such preliminaries. She was making that only too plain. He moved expertly, his manhood poking up beneath her skirts as if sprung, as he unbuttoned the fly of his breeches, and in an instance he was inside her, to the hilt, the lady moaning softly with delight and grinding down upon him.

Like animals, the act was over in a matter of moments, quick, violent and devastatingly passionate.

Sitting astride of him, her breasts had pressed to his white, cravated dinner shirt. Iona had moved against him, devoured him, kissing him and making small noises by his ear that had the most sensuous effect upon Jack. He'd thrust up and up with mounting savagery, holding her down upon him at her waist, forcing his willing partner to take all of him with as much power as he could put behind each stroke of possession.

The intensity of his actions had shocked even him, worldly Jack. And she had loved it, urged him on, clutched at him with her thighs and hugged him deliciously about the neck, her breasts squeezed against him as he thrust and cried out, thrust and growled, taking them beyond any bounds of passion they'd hitherto known.

Panting, she collapsed against him, a joyous look upon her face, her blue-green eyes fever bright.

'God Almighty, Mister Savage,' she said, breath coming in quick gasps, 'that was lovely. Lovely. You know, I always guessed it could be like that, though I never knew for sure.'

His eyebrows quirked. 'But what about with Mister Stanley, your husband? Surely – '

'Mister Stanley could never make it last for more than a minute . . . with me. He didn't care for women who were, shall we say, average. His appetites were larger. I never interested him in bed, was led to believe that it was my failing,' she said, tersely.

Intrigued, both his eyebrows raised at that. But Iona wouldn't speak further of her husband. The time was inappropriate and she knew better how to spend it.

Easing herself off her now calmly breathing lover, she got to grips with the corded silk ties of her corsets, easing them open and dispensing with them. Beneath she wore a fine lawn camisole that went to a deep 'V' between her ample breasts.

She kicked off her evening shoes, rolled off her silk stockings and threw her garments into a far corner almost distastefully. Then she dropped her petticoats one by one, pulled her camisole over her head in a fluid movement and stood quite naked before a dazzled Jack.

He swallowed embarrassingly, could feel his manhood growing rigid again with unheard of swiftness. This Iona Stanley behaved like no other female he had ever met. She almost overwhelmed him. But not totally. He felt, wrily, that he was up to any challenge she might care to issue. He'd certainly give it his best shot!

'Oh, I almost forgot,' she giggled, alabaster arms extending upwards to her hair, pulling out the pins and letting the russet tendrils fall. It was perhaps her most admirable physical attribute, a legacy from her Scottish ancestors. Thick and gleaming richly, it fell in a burnished veil to her waist.

She went to the bed, threw back the covers and laid herself down, curling her legs beneath her and reclining seductively on an elbow. She laughed as she suggested, 'Maybe we could snuggle up and keep each other cosy on such a wild night? The storm doesn't seem to be lessening.'

Jack was already on his feet and undressing, the violent sway of the ship making him do an involuntary jig as he tried to climb out of one leg of his breeches. 'It would be churlish of me not to offer comfort to a lady under such circumstances,' he joked, almost ripping off his shirt in his eagerness to join her abed.

The oil lamp burned low, illuminating the intimate little scene in shades of ochre and amber.

'God, there's no bloody room in here,' Jack cursed, kneeling in the squashed bunk beside her.

She laughed, threw off the covers, drew up her knees and let her legs fall open, displaying herself fully to him. She was pink and ripe, glistening and swollen at her bud from his masterly usage.

His penis grew and reared, pearling on the bulbous tip at the sight of her.

She laughed.

'Do you know what I'd like to do?' he growled huskily, his tongue darting forth and flickering.

'Oh, Jack, no! I don't think I could stand it. I'd explode. Just the thought . . .!'

He dived at her, burying his head between her legs, tasting the soft, salty folds of her, flicking his tongue over her clitoris.

'Sweet lord!' she gurgled, fingers tearing at his hair. 'Stop, Jack, for pity's sake, or I shall die!'

But he knew that stopping was the last thing she wanted. He plunged into her, his nose rubbing up and down her sex-lips as he ravaged her with his tongue.

She was coming again, throbbing around him, arching against him, crying out, and almost immediately, he was pulling her legs over his shoulders and taking her hard, his penis battering at her very womb, stabbing, thrusting, filling her with its considerable girth.

He was too much. He was killing her. She clawed at his back, as savage as he, like a lioness too little gentled by the king of beasts before the mating.

The pain spurred him on, sharpening his thrusts. He caught her at the hips, rammed into her, thrust, thrust, her head banging against the wooden panelling at the head of the tiny bunk alcove.

Her face was intense with a savage joy. Another climax was fast approaching. He could tell. Her look was sublime. She was grinning. As the spasms of pleasure shook her and he plunged into her that final time, spurting his seed forth in a hot rush, his flanks quivered.

She murmured dreamily, 'Jack, you're a bloody marvel.'

He laughed, kissed the inside of her thigh before lowering her legs and laying down, cramped, beside her. 'I don't believe in false modesty, so I'll not deny it. But even I need to recuperate now; let's get some sleep.'

They were both asleep within seconds, Iona happy and at peace, her miserable disappointment of a marriage somehow erased a little from her mind by the loving ministrations of Jack Savage. He'd shown her how wondrous it could be between a man and a woman, how sadly lacking her marriage had been in both passion and love. She hadn't made a mistake; walking out on Horace and sailing out of Sydney had been the right thing – the only thing – to do.

Jack felt wet.

It wasn't the pleasant warm, sticky wetness of making love. This was the chill wet of death. He came awake suddenly, roused by panic, shaking Iona who lay snugly beside him in the cramped bed, like a fellow sardine.

'Quick! Get your camisole and petticoats on,' he commanded, thrusting the white lawn cotton scraps at her and jumping out of bed and in to two feet of water. A chamber pot floated by, clunked into the chest of drawers as the ship pitched violently.

As she got up to dress, the water lapping about her legs and saturating her clothes roused Iona better than any words and she cried out incoherently, not understanding, or maybe not wanting to. Terrified.

They hurried out into the companionway. Water rushed down the stairs towards them, knocking the pair into a swinging door of an empty cabin from which Miss Harker and Miss Cosgrove had long since fled.

The ship had been abandoned, they realised, while they slept sated by lovemaking, oblivious to any warning knock on their door or directive to abandon ship, and now they were all alone and in mortal danger, abandoned by a panicking crew.

Some two hundred yards from the ship the jolly boat was tossed and overturned by a huge foaming wave, crew and passengers emptied pitilessly into the sea. Iona made a small noise of distress.

A bucket and holystone cluttered past, hit Iona on her bare feet. She yelped, hopped. Jack urged her on, almost dragging her when fear threatened to paralyse her.

The great ship went nose down, lightning striking and catching the foremast alight, its furled sail dropping flaming scraps of canvas about them. Then the deck was awash and the bowsprit went under, the vessel protesting with much creaking and mournful groaning of timbers, horrendous gurgling noises like death throes erupting from its depths.

'We have to jump,' cried Jack, holding Iona's hand tightly, his words barely audible in the lashing rain carried by the hurricane.

'No!' she whimpered, terrified. She'd never learned

how to swin, and not even a swimmer stood much of a chance in that black, broiling ocean. She was going to die and she didn't feel brave.

Jack caught her about her waist, lifted her protesting, squirming form over the rail and, kissing her as if to instil courage, jumped with her into the spewing ocean.

He clung to her despearately, trying to bring them back to the surface. But his struggles were in vain. She'd gone limp, like some sleeping mermaid in his arms, lifeless, murkily beautiful, her red hair floating about her weedily.

His lungs felt like they were bursting, his grip slackened. The dark become black, blacker still.

Chapter Two

*I*ona's head was lifted by the up-rush of water, then painfully dropped onto a rock of the headland, clunk, as the wave receded. Another wave, another clunk. She groaned, couldn't quite bring herself to consciousness. Her cheek scraped on the black volcanic outcrop but she remained oblivious to the bleeding, too.

Brown faces peering hard at her through the poor light of a rain lashed, windy dawn, found her highly interesting. A hand lifted a tendril of red hair, rubbed it experimentally between thumb and forefinger. Other hands turned her over, studied the pale, wet face, blue-tinged with cold.

Words were spoken, decisions made and Iona, groaning mindlessly, was hoisted up between four strong men and carried away.

Their leader, a man resplendent in black feather costume, walked beside her, too important, it would appear, to do so menial a task as carrying, but who took the liberty of curiously touching a wet breast through the torn shreds of her camisole, its erect little nipple having captured his complete attention. She groaned again and he laughed loudly.

* * *

The early morning sun struggled through a broken patch of continuingly stormy sky and played on Jack's eyelids. Behind them his eyeballs moved restlessly, on the verge of opening the shutters, waking. He felt a stabbing pain in his big toe, sat bolt upright, immediately awake, his yell of surprised hurt quite spontaneous.

'Yowch!'

There, clinging to his toe with a monstrous fighting claw was a stalk-eyed crab. Jack had to make more than one attempt before he managed to shake it off. Then he came up onto his knees in the wet bleached white sand and stared about him.

Much to his surprise he realized that he was still alive. Alive and on dry – well almost dry – land. He felt a chuckle of joyous laughter flourish in his chest but it died quickly. He was alive, but he was alone. Scanning the length of sandy shore to its far distant limits, he saw no one, no living thing. There was just him, troubled sky, sand, sea and coconut trees. Iona hadn't made it.

Profound sadness crushed down upon him. Then a hopeful thought struck him. She might be alive after all. It was a slim hope but he clung to it. If *he* had been lucky, why shouldn't she be also?

The thought spurred him to action.

He got up resolutely and, after walking oddly for a few yards while he got used to the uncomfortable feel of his wet breeches, marched off down the beach, eyes peeled.

But it was the *Lady Luckington*'s first mate and the Able Seaman he spotted far off on the beach and only just distinguishable. There was no sign of Iona. Inwardly Jack sighed. At least, though, they were familiar faces. He was no longer alone.

His pace quickened and he called out to them, waved. The wind swallowed up his cries however and they never knew of his presence. Considering what happened next, it was just as well. Even as Jack raced towards them dark figures were moving stealthily down from the fringe of coconut trees, carrying war clubs, knives and spears.

Jack stopped dead in his tracks, looked about him, feeling, suddenly, very exposed, and started up the beach, through the heavy-going, dry sand, into the trees. He thought his heart would burst right out of his chest. He watched in horror as the two unfortunate seamen spotted their attackers all too late, were chased a little way down the beach, then caught and butchered on the spot.

'Dear God,' groaned Jack, sickened by the sight of such savage and gleeful blood-letting. He clutched his stomach and leant into the sleek trunk of the tree he hid behind, trying to control his urge to vomit.

What happened next ensured that he did so.

The heathens dragged the dismembered bodies up past the tide line to where the sand was smooth and dry and set about lighting a fire from driftwood. This done with enthusiasm and speed, they began cooking choice cuts from their butchered victims, the First Mate's huge, dark liver spitted and roasted as a tasty treat which they devourd first, and with relish. His decaptated head sat in the sand, grey-white and bloodless, the eyes turned up in their sockets, showing nearly all white. It looked, Jack thought in horror, his stomach giving another violent churn, as if the Mate watched the feasting on his own flesh; a silent, passive spectator.

Mosquitoes bit him and bugs stung, but Jack stayed where he was, hidden by the trees, with no idea of what to do next, in dreadful fear of his life.

Chapter Three

When Iona first awoke, with a thumping headache and double-vision, she thought it was night-time so dark were her surroundings. But as her eyes travelled with slow confusion about the walls of the building she found herself in, she could see patches of faint light between cane poles and woven grass which constituted the walls.

From beyond came a low and rhythmical chant that was irritatingly repetetive, grew to a crescendo then died, only to start and build all over again, more passionate than the time before.

What was happening? Where was she? How had she got there? She thought she had her answer when the door to her shed-like accommodation was thrown open with the faintest of squeaks and her dull, empty little space was invaded by several brown-skinned native youths whose loins were barely skirted by fringes of blue-black and green-black feathers.

Horrified, she sat up, drew up her knees, trying to cover her nakedness. She wished she was back in the water with Jack. She wished she was dead.

They dragged her up, clutching firmly at her upper arms and hauled her out. She didn't go willingly, biting an arm, kicking a shin. But they only laughed, certain of their masculine superiority, finding her pathetic show of spirits amusing.

She was being lead through a village of huts. Some were squalid, some tidy.

As Iona was prodded forward, through an assembled crowd of natives, the chanting intensified, the faces leered, laughed, foretold her doom.

Before her, rising up from the village and reached by some thirty or so rough hewn ancient steps, was a terrace in the heavily vegatated mountainside. A group was assembled there in all their black feathered finery, waiting, downheartedly, she knew, for her.

Thinking of her nakedness made her groan with shame. But there was nothing she could do. And soon it would no longer matter, she decided fatalistically.

At the bottom of the huge steps the chant from the crowd took on a much more purposeful cadence; it gave Iona the creeps.

It took some effort to climb the tall steps but her escorts were happy to help propel her up between them.

The sky had changed from splendorous red to night purple. Torches were lit, illuminating the scene on the lofty terrace, filling Iona with a reluctance to go further.

'No,' she said firmly, heart beating wildly in her throat. 'No, thank you-very-much.' But her escorts only laughed at such ground out words, and dragged her up over the sill of the terrace with renewed enthusiasm.

A stone altar stood before her, natives, in skirts of black feathers, flanking it like a guard of honour. Further back, set within a great niche in the densely vegetated mountainside, was an imposing, man-made skull hewn from the black volcanic rock. Torches burnt in the vast eye sockets. And in the 'OO' shaped nose cavity a clay vessel was being worshipfully intoned to by someone positively druid-like.

In her mind's eye Iona saw it all, guessed at what was to be her fate. This whole scene reminded her of the sacrificial ceremonies of the Aztecs. She'd read about them in books secreted from her father's library when a child. Bloody tales of still beating hearts being snatched from the skilfully cut open chests of breathing victims, had satisfied her childish need for gruesome detail and gore. Now she wished she'd spent less time filling her head with such dubious snippets of history. In the circumstances, thinking she *knew* her fate was probably worse than going to it in terrified ignorance.

They lifted her up onto the altar slab, just as she had expected, and held her squirming body there while the attendants bound her at neck, wrists and ankles, spreadeagled. She couldn't move, knew that awful moment when the feeling of utter hopelessness washed over her. *Oh God . . . God. Help me*! she silently prayed.

She turned her head (the only part of her still mobile) to the altar and watched the back of the black figure cloaked so splendidly in feathers. His arms were lifted, his words and gestures directed heavenwards to his gods.

Then the tall, black maned and cloaked man at the altar turned and she felt a new panic rise and accumulate atop of her already considerable terror.

He was naked save for his cloak, gleaming and darkly muscular, and sporting an erection so large and rigid that Iona's eyes popped. Her horrible suspicions rearranged themselves forthwith. It seemed that she wasn't to die after all. Or at least not straight away.

She cried out, 'No! Nooo!' in frustrated rage, then went helplessly quiet, knowing her words were wasted, closed her eyes against the assault which was doubtless to follow. The towering dark figure advanced.

Her cheek was patted, her head lifted by the hair, a clay vessel pressed to her lips. She tried to avoid it, clamped her teeth together. The black-maned man caught hold of her chin and forced her mouth open. She swallowed against her will, gurgling and choking on a liquid too sweet and fruity for her liking.

Standing now at the foot of the slab with his arms raised to exalt the heavens above the summit of the volcano, the villagers below joined with him, shouted, as one, the words of incantation. It was all a terrible nonsense to Iona.

A youth hovered, gracefully tipping a metal jug over her breasts and belly to discharge a modest flow of heavily scented oil. The black-maned man let his hands glide through the lubrication, circled her breasts, stroked her midriff and belly, then slid down further to that russet haven she could do nothing to defend. His fingers stroked, invaded, to the now sensuously soft chant of the crowd.

Whatever she'd been forced to drink had drugged her, Iona decided. That could be the only reason that her body was acting so, why she was contracting around the finger which pleasured her. And it *did* pleasure her. She couldn't deny it. Tied down she might be, and at the mercy of this dauntingly physical man, but he wasn't hurting her, brutalising her bound body in some barbaric ritual as she had envisaged. He was wooing her, lulling her, readying her. But for what?

She mused with horror that if she hadn't been tied down and incapable of movement, she might well have raised herself to meet his masterfully thrusting finger.

Almost she wanted him. It was horrendous to admit it to herself. But she did, right there, even with everyone watching. What would Horace have said to that? Suddenly she wanted to laugh almost as much as she wanted sex. Horace would have been disgusted. He would have said it was better to die than submit to such a vile thing, hypocrite that he was. Well, in this instance he would have been wrong. Her anticipation of that which was surely to happen next beat death any day.

A handmaiden stepped slowly forward, each step taken to the beat of the drum, carrying a strangely carved object. Iona looked at it long and hard, trying to puzzle out its function here at this primitive ceremony.

It was long, perhaps nine inches, and carved like a serpent, right down to the serpentine undulations and forked tongue. And its girth was four, maybe five inches, she gauged, watching it in puzzlement as it advanced, carried reverently by the girl in flowing robes.

As it was held over Iona's taut belly the boy with the anointing oil appeared again and ceremoniously dripped a few drops onto the fat head of the ebony serpent.

Iona watched this and felt a mounting disquiet. The black-maned man with his enormous penis riding up his belly did the same dipping and diving motions with his finger inside of Iona as the wooden serpent in the hands of the skilled handmaiden. Then as Iona watched, spellbound, the man stepped aside, the wooden phallus manoeuvred between her legs and teased her opening, waiting until the man's fingers withdrew then held her open by the lips of her sex, and sacrificed her to a hard and unfeeling object.

She felt it at her opening, felt it slide in, well-oiled but uncomfortably large, making her wince as it took her, filled her, made symbolic love to her before a mass audience.

Iona was well aware of the indignity. But even more so, she was aware of the growing sensation of pleasure she was feeling. Almost she welcomed the feeling of being vanquished, humbled by too strong a sexual force.

Abruptly the black wooden shaft was withdrawn and carried back to the skull altar. Then a solitary drumbeat startled her. She looked into the ebony, seemingly pupil-less eyes of her ravisher and felt the corners of her mouth twitch with the glimmerings of a smile she couldn't suppress.

The dusky man smiled back, which teeth flashing, and found her most intimate spot with his thick, hard manhood. The drum beat again and he entered her with an exquisite stroke, filling Iona, much more so than the impressive dildo. It was all she could do to stop herself sighing with delight. The drum took up a steady beat and the man performed perfectly in time.

Filling, withdrawing, the oil between them helping him to glide superbly.

The drumbeat quickened. So did he. Iona had never seen such physical control. She was impressed, excited, most thoughtfully serviced. There was no denying that she was enjoying it. It was plain to see on her face. And she really didn't care. Whatever they'd given her to drink had left her without any inhibitions. She groaned, urged him on, called out for it to be over, for him to take her to that place she'd visited with Jack Savage . . . to the Realm of Bliss.

But he wouldn't be hurried, kept perfect time with the drum, growing quicker by gentle degrees, maddening her. If she could have she would have clutched him hard to her, dragged him into her and kept him there, forcing matters to a climax. She knew how. Years of marriage to Horace had taught her how to bring a man to quick fulfilment, the sooner to find peace.

She was sweating in the warm night air, her oil glistening body on fire as the drums took up the final frenzied beatings and the raven-haired, black-eyed man rammed into her for the final dozen or so times, making her cry out, squirm despite her bonds and pulsate about his seed shedding shaft.

He roared – a heathenish cry of victor over vanquished – pushed into Iona, hard, harder still, staying there until the last shudder and quiver had passed through him. When he raised himself and withdrew, standing back from the altar to have his cloak replaced by a handmaiden, his people chanted some phrase that was gobbledygook to Iona and fell down before him, prostrate and full of reverence. His loins now covered by a splendid skirt of black feathers and oyster shells, he slowly descended the steps, all heads bowed in deference, everywhere hush.

Iona turned her head and watched his departure, bemused. Why was he treated so special? What was it about him (beyond the fact that he could physically love a woman so damned expertly) that had everyone so in thrall? They acted almost as if he was a god. She might well have found it rather amusing if she hadn't been so worried once more about what was to happen to her.

Assisted into a sitting position, she was accoutred with a black feather cloak, not dissimilar to the one gracing the back of the man who now walked slowly through his humble throng of prostrate subjects to the largest of the village dwellings.

Before she even had to try to put one foot in front of the other, her own personal transport in the shape of an open sedan-type chair arrived alongside and Iona was cordially invited to fit her bottom into the woven reed seat.

How different was her descent and the general demeanour of the people about her now. She didn't understand it one jot. But she took comfort from it. That man's possession of her body had suddenly changed their regard and her status; she guessed and hoped, for the better.

Chapter Four

For two weeks Jack had been creeping furtively around the tree-ed area near the shoreline, growing hungrier and more desperate with each passing day.

There were wild pigs in abundance, the curly tusked older beasts to be avoided at all cost. They were quick, tricky and lethal. But their piglets were smaller, succulent looking. Studying them made poor Jack's mouth water. He determined to kill himself a pig. How he would cook it afterwards without giving away his presnce to the cannibals was a problem he wouldn't even let himself begin to think about. In his present state he could only deal with one problem at a time.

He scoured the ground for likely looking rocks, praying for a smattering of flint somewhere on this Godforsaken speck of ocean-locked land. But there was not, nothing that could be knapped into a spear- or arrowhead. On the shore the shells were no more adaptable. He decided to make a club, to find a stone heavy enough to deliver a good, stunning clout, but light enough for him to wield without too much trouble.

Thus armed, he lay in wait for his prey, having determined the pigs' location from several days of observation.

At the right moment, poised comically in the undergrowth with an intensely concentrated look upon his face, allowing parents to go ahead of their offspring, Jack pounced, caught the instantly squealing, wriggling, speckle-backed feast on legs and wielded the club.

The pig squeaked, his parents U-turned and Jack watched disgustedly as the stone head of his club fell clean off, hanging there stupidly by a tangled network of vine, leaving him weaponless.

The piglet gave him a nasty bite, taking Jack so by surprise that he let the beast's leg go and then, like a double menace on remarkably quick little legs, the parents charged him.

Jack shinned up a coconut tree and stayed there, clinging on for dear life while the irate pig family launched themselves unsuccessfully at him from below. He was exhausted and perilously close to falling before they gave up and wandered off, foraging.

Disgusted with himself, his luck, everything, Jack picked fruit and berries instead. But even then his choice wasn't so very good and he made himself ill.

Still recovering from that annoying bout of illness, Jack found Miss Cosgrove's body washed up on the shore two days later. It was a sorry sight; grey, fish-nibbled and its eye sockets gruesomely empty. He was just wondering (under cover of the trees) whether to wait until nightfall to bury it – taking the hours until then to hopefully fashion himself some kind of primitive shovel – when the natives arrived on the scene and took the matter out of his hands.

With naked brown toes they nudged at the body without any visible emotion, deliberated, and then hefted her up and carried her away.

They were a large group – men, women and several children. They chanted something in a sing-song fashion as they went, brown bodies splendidly attired in red-dyed pigskin. The men and women wore loinclothes and skirts accessorised by strings of shells about their chests. The children were stark naked and ran about playing at the rear of the group, one of them trailing a torn strip off Miss Cosgrove's dress behind him like a streamer, the others trying to catch its tail with giggles and shouts.

They climbed up high onto the jagged black promontory as the tide came in, incanted *en masse* for perhaps a minute and then hurled Miss Cosgrove back into the sea from whence she'd been disgorged.

He watched as they climbed down the rock face, reassessing them. Then he had to flee before them, forced upwards through rock and dense vine networks by the sheer impenetrability of vegetation. When he felt as if they breathed down his neck, panic seized him and Jack dived for cover amongst a patch of ferns and giant red blooms, breath catching, heart thumping fit to explode.

It semed they were upon him and passing before he'd had a chance to do more than still his body into a dread-filled lump of stone.

They talked conversationally, thrashing through the undergrowth surrounding him, not because they in any way suspected that there was an alien being on their island, but because they always did it, the habit ritualistic. Sometimes such thrashings unearthed a pig which they speared and cooked on reaching home, sometimes a bird rose up with a panicked flap of wings and they brought it down with a well aimed stone, sticking its tail feathers in their hair.

This evening, with the sun sinking over the horizon, they knocked Jack on the head – *clunk* – but, luckily for him, were talking so loudly as they went, the action so absent, that they didn't hear the audible noise or the faintest of 'Ows' that followed rapidly.

The children, or at least all but two of them, had finished chasing the bright streamer and followed behind their parents, quiet, tired and apparently ready for bedtime. Jack began to register relief, he could feel the danger passing. He'd even begun to rise from his hiding place when the last two children came crashing into view. A boy had one end of the streamer, a girl the other and they were laughing uproariously as they tried to wrest it from each other. They knocked into the trees, fell into the ferns, almost at Jack's feet – making him draw in his breath apprehensively – and then, oddly, they were gone. Not the way of the others, but swallowed up in the descending darkness amongst the treacherous jungle, with only the faintest of surprised noises to accompany that disappearance.

Jack felt uneasy. They *were* of an age where they might have been taken by a sudden urge to indulge in some sexual horseplay, yet he doubted it.

Something was wrong.

He told himself it was none of his business. Gingerly he got to his feet and started creeping back towards the beach. Then he heard them again, calling from some distance, clearly distressed.

'Damn!' he cursed, low and gruff. 'Children are always bloody trouble.'

He tried to maintain a deaf ear, shut out the voices, the unquestionable pleading. It didn't matter that it was in a very strange tongue; he knew cries for help when he heard them. And he couldn't – though he knew he'd likely regret it quick enough – ignore them. He homed in on the voices.

They'd fallen. That much was evident as he climbed down from a precarious ledge to a barely existent sill in the glacial face of rock, aided by several strong looking vines, which were rooted (and well rooted he hoped) further up the ravine, and which he twisted together for greater strength.

He could see them now not too far below him, called down to them even though it was obviously pointless. 'Hang on there. Don't be frightened.'

They were. And especially of him when his pale face was caught by a dying shaft of sun spearing through the vegetation. But they were more frightened of the sheer drop below them and certain death that undoubtedly waited there in the form of shattered bones and pulped flesh. They whimpered and wiggled, each wanting to be the first to be rescued.

'Don't move!' warned Jack, noting how precarious their position was.

Still clinging to that length of skirt, they'd fallen over the edge of the ravine in the darkness and were now hanging, like two equal weights on a thread, from an upwardly thrusting knub of rock that marred the otherwise glass-smooth rock face. Luck – if that's what one could call it under the circumstances – was with them. Below them was a drop of some seventy feet.

He lay down and could take a firm hold on the cloth once he'd mastered the tricky business of wriggling his fingers between it – pulled tight and fraying – and hard rock. He sighed, began to pull it up with the considerable burden it carried swinging at its ends. The muscles in his arm screamed out, insisting that they'd strained quite enough even while he expected more of them, pulled harder, face reddening, a snarl of exertion escaping his mouth. By moving his position then, Jack was able to get to grips with both hands and within moments the children were able to stretch up and reach the ledge either side of him and scramble their way to safety.

Panting, he collapsed into a heap, his back resting against the rock-face. His muscles relaxing, hard strained sinews smoothing out, he voiced his relief with a breathless sounding 'Whew!'

Then he looked about for the children, and smiled thankfully to see them climbing safely up out of the ravine with the aid of the twisted vines. Evidently they weren't confident enough about him to hang around.

Jack laughed, couldn't blame them even as he snorted wrily to himself.

'Well, that's gratitude for you! Buggered off without so much as a thank you.'

After recovering a while, he began the climb himself.

Chapter Five

*H*e expected them at any time.
Though when they did come, things didn't turn out anything like he'd imagined. They didn't attack him, butcher him, or eat him, as he'd always anticipated. Indeed they did nothing disagreeable.

The first sign of their discovery had been earthenware bowls at his feet when he awoke one morning, cold, damp with dew, and as hungry as ever. He sat up, took a furtive look out of his untidy blanket of loose dried fern fronds and actually by-passed the bowls at first with a casual look of dismissal. Then his gaze shot backwards with alarm. He was discovered. A shiver ran through him. His eyes shot from the bowls to the vegetation surrounding him, up trees, around bushes, but if anyone was there, observing him, he couldn't see them.

Curious, he knelt up, leant over and surveyed the bowls' contents. One of them still steamed unnervingly, telling of visitors not long gone. He sniffed it. Pork! *God Almighty, real food*! His mind shouted joyously, while his stomach gave an instant growl of hungry anticipation. Evidently they were better at catching the island's pigs than he was. Better cooks too. Beside that dish was a vegetable accompaniment of odds and ends that looked like wild rice, wheat and berries, all cooked into a kind of porridge which had been cooled until it set in a pale and heavy lump. The last bowl contained a drink of some kind, its colour an attractive amber, its smell, as Jack let his nose hover over it experimentally, pungent and maybe a little bitter.

Throwing caution to the wind, he ate like a ravenous hog, belching and chomping, the wine downed in gulps to wash a path for the next crammed mouth full.

God, its grand, he thought, luxuriating in the feel of something substantial hitting his stomach for the first time in ages. A royal banquet couldn't have been finer. Meat had never tasted so succulent, wine so full-bodied and fruity.

He devoured the lot, then sat back, stuffed, his back against the base of a coconut tree, his belly a hard lump of fullness. He cradled his hands about it, sighed contentedly and enjoyed one of the most pleasant moments he could ever remember.

They hadn't eaten him. They'd fed him instead. True, he might be being fattened up just like the Christmas goose, but Jack couldn't have cared less at that moment. It was wonderful not to be hungry.

Chapter Six

Iona tried to help with the domestic chores but the other women of the household wouldn't hear of it. Tiku's wife didn't work. Tiku's wife rested, enjoying the servility of others and kept herself beautiful and ever ready for her randy husband. Iona didn't understand all that they said but she got the gist of things. And she wasn't so stupid as to complain.

Time passed and she adapted, but still she couldn't come to terms with the fact that she'd probably never leave this island – Wahwu was how the islanders pronounced its name – would like as not die here. She missed England. Often she thought of Jack Savage. But she rarely spared a thought for Horace.

Her marriage to Horace had never been a momentously romantic event in her life. Her parents, Norfolk landowners come south from Scotland, had arranged the match despite her objections, had told her confidently that in years to come she'd be grateful for their hand in things, their wise selection. Being an obedient daughter – for to be otherwise was unheard of in those days – she had reluctantly gone along with their plans. She'd just wished that it had been someone else and not Horace. He'd been such a miserable, sanctimonious wretch of a man. No fun at all. And even if she didn't believe in love, she did believe in having a good time.

Things had only livened up moderately with Horace's diplomatic posting to Sydney, Australia. Sydney was like a raw imitation of some British city with a residing military academy. The people therein thrived upon protocol, on old world habits and rituals. They dressed for tea, for dinner, for church, for receptions. Everything was done with the greatest of care so that standards shouldn't slip just because people were temporarily far from home. They were British. They would act as such.

They had weekend shooting parties and lavish balls beneath imported chandeliers. They carried on just as if they were back home, with great determination, the social structure adhered to, even the damnably hot weather stubbornly ignored. Everyone knew their place.

From the moment she arrived there Iona knew she wasn't going to fit in. The obstinate Scot in her began to surface, the fiery side of her personality to assert itself.

She didn't do any particular thing to irritate or anger Horace. Yet anything and everything began to annoy him: her unladylike rolled-up sleeves; the fact that she wouldn't nap in the afternoon like the other ladies of the colony, but lazed instead in her little garden, ruining her complexion with freckles. He didn't care for her little garden either, because she liked to tend it herself instead of allowing a servant to do it. And she helped the servants, actually making the beds and cooking instead of just giving the orders, she liked cooking. He thought it appalling, took her to task frequently.

The list of her shortcomings went on and on, growing by the month.

Iona began to hear more and more about the *perfect* Lady Jemimah Swinton, began to loath her. She had nothing in common with the excessively fat, supercilious Jemimah, whose main occupation in life seemed to be the slavish following of fashion and devout adherence to etiquette and manners. But Horace couldn't praise her highly enough and was forever adding her name to lists for functions hosted by the Stanleys, from which Iona had left her off on purpose.

Standing in the pantry one hot afternoon, the door ajar to afford some air, her cotton underwear sticking to her uncomfortably, Iona counted the sacks of flour and cones of precious sugar, unlocked and checked the contents of the tea caddy. They were getting low; she'd have to send out for new stock. With quill and paper she made a list.

Biddy, the Irish laundry maid, came in from the back garden where she'd been hanging out the wash, singing. She was a plump little thing with luxurious chestnut hair and brown-black eyes, had sailed all the way to Australia to be with her lover who was nearing the end of his term of penal servitude for having killed a rival for Biddy's affections while in a drunken rage. Unfortunately, a fortnight before the ship which carried Biddy dropped anchor in Botany Bay, her beloved perished of a tropical fever.

She'd had a variety of domestic positions since then and now, for a while at least, it seemed, appeared happy enough to take charge of the Stanley's dirty washing.

Iona held her tongue between her teeth, eyebrows knitting as she concentrated on her list.

The back door opened again and John the gardener entered, an arm through the handle of a fully laden trug. He was a full-blooded native, wily, sure of himself and thoroughly condescending towards Biddy.

Iona looked up, unobserved, could see them both clearly through the crack in the door, her eyebrows shooting up on her forehead at the sight which she beheld.

Evidently they were on very good terms. Iona had never suspected. She watched them, amused. Billy had set down the trug on the long pine table that ran through the centre of the kitchen and Biddy brought him water, handing him a pitcher while she wiped his sweaty torso down with a cool, wet cloth. Iona suddenly felt like a spy witnessing an wholly intimate scene. He was black and gleaming, not a spare ounce of fat upon him.

He drank absently – while she wiped his chest, circling around nipples – as if it was a quite common occurrence. And when he'd finished his water he gulped down the slab of fruit cake she proffered.

He licked his sticky fingers. She took the hand between hers and finished the job, taking his fingers into her mouth one at a time and sucking them clean, her tongue gliding expertly about them.

Iona was glued to the spot, eyes popping, heart racing a little. She was greatly moved, couldn't understand the warm ache that gripped her belly.

John lifted Biddy up, firm hands set sure around her ample waist, perched her on the edge of the sturdy pine table. Then he unlaced his breeches and let them drop, showing a penis that stood rigidly to attention, black and silky, the head a dusky pink hue and glistening.

Iona's breath caught. It was a glorious sight, so much more stirring than her few snatched glimpses of Horace's unimpressive wedding tackle. She watched, hardly daring to breathe, eyes unblinking, as John caught the hem of Biddy's cotton skirts and drew them up. Up over black, serviceable boots, and holed black cotton stockings, up over knees rough from kneeling and scrubbing floors, and plump thighs, until they lay bunched about her waist, exposing a triangle of springy brown hair.

'Open, girl,' said the aborigine coaxingly. 'Y'know John Boy, give y'what y'want. Spread those fat white thighs, woman, and let this black shaft in. It wants y'so bad. Ooh *so* bad,' breathed John.

Biddy was panting, did as she was bid, exposing a

slit, russet lips and borders of dark hair, leaning back just a little and bracing herself on her arms.

Iona's hands had gone clammy. This was absurd. She couldn't stay where she was. Shouldn't watch. Yet she couldn't walk out either, not then, not with them both in such a state of undress and arousal. She'd have died of embarrassment. Better to stay where she was, keep still, quiet, perhaps close her eyes in a show of delicacy. But somehow she couldn't. The sight was too compelling.

Biddy moaned softly as large, black, work-roughened hands crept up her inner thighs and toyed with her, stroking, circling, slipping into her wetness. She took John's member and caressed it from base to tip, cupping his balls and gently squeezing, stroking him right around to his buttocks. His legs twitched. He stepped forward, let her guide the swollen head of his black shaft to her moist opening.

The table was just at the right height and he reared into Biddy with such delicious precision that Iona had no doubt that they'd done this more than once before.

He cupped her buttocks, rammed at her to the hilt, held tight within her, loins fast to loins, belly to belly when she wrapped her legs about him.

Iona wanted to groan with longing as she watched their quick and furtive coupling, wanted someone like John to love her that way, wanted someone who could make her feel, desperately needed something more than the cold unfulfilment she knew with her husband.

By the time John thrust home through the final dozen strokes of ecstacy, Biddy was calling out, her bottom thudding on the table, the whole structure shuddering beneath them.

That's passion, Iona had thought, *and that's something I've never known*.

The final chapter of their disastrous marriage had been played out at a Christmas party hosted by the Stanleys at their retreat just outside of the city sprawl.

Convict labour tended the gardens. Bonded servants slaved in the house. It was a handsome building: new and ostentatious. Iona had never liked its fussy plushness though, irked by the fact that the choice of all the furnishings and furniture had been taken on by Horace, that she hadn't been so much as asked for an opinion, let alone properly consulted. Everything he did was for himself and outward appearances. He didn't give a fig for what Iona thought, never sought to please her. He knew best. Always.

The last of the guests had either departed for the city or taken the stairs to bed and Iona was just giving last minute instructions to one of the sullen servants when the front door bell was pulled. Skirting past the boy who was lowering the chandelier to extinguish the candles, Iona answered the door. It was a clerk from Horace's office with papers that had to be signed and on the England-bound barque within the hour.

She took the package, pointed to a row of chairs along the hall wall. 'Take a seat while I go get them signed for you. My husband has already retired.'

'Thank you, ma'am.'

She ascended the stairs, down the corridor and around the corner, to the other side of the house from her own room. Horace and she never slept together. He visited her occasionally to do his husbandly duty but even then returned to his own bed afterwards.

She knocked and entered. It was difficult to say who was more embarrassed – they or she. Probably them. Certainly everyone was surprised.

Iona stood, stunned, on the threshold, the most absurd picture meeting her eyes.

Upon Horace's bed, illuminated by oil lamps on small tables at either side, lay her husband, his slight, pale body tied at wrists and ankles to the four posts with leather straps, his mouth gagged with a fresh white kerchief.

Straddling his torso was the huge, white Lady Jemimah, her great luminous buttocks seeming to fill Iona's vision. She wore nothing but a black lace and whalebone corset, and an arrangement of black feathers pinned fashionably in her hair. In her right hand was a riding crop and, even as Iona burst out laughing, Jemimah was flaying him on the thighs and chest, his thin arms and the sensitive soles of his feet. So absorbed in their pleasure were they that they hadn't even noticed the door open.

Horace's little penis was wagging and rearing, Jemimah's chastisement an obvious excitement. But at Iona's belly laugh, his pleasure ended abruptly and his manhood drooped and withered. His eyes were wide with shock at being discovered and he mumbled frantically behind his gag, almost choking.

Jemimiah ceased her flagellation in mid-stroke, her arm poised, frozen, arching the air. She swallowed, looked around for something with which to cover her great backside and pendulous breasts which were flopping in Horace's face. She uttered a ladylike, 'Oh dear.'

'Don't mind me,' said Iona, smiling.

Horace groaned behind his gag, struggling quite pointlessly to try and cover himself, his embarrassment.

Jemimah looked contrite. 'I . . . we . . .'

'Please, don't worry about explanations,' stressed Iona, enjoying their discomfort enormously. They were both becoming deepeningly scarlet with each moment that passed. 'I just need you to sign these papers from the Consulate, dear, and then you can continue . . . with my blessing.'

Horace was so flabbergasted by her calmness that, when she'd unbound his right wrist, he took up the scratchy-nibbed pen she proffered as meekly as you please and signed without a murmur.

Jemimah flinched at Iona's nearness, half expecting to be attacked by a wife who *should* be irate, her red, wet mound still pressed down upon Horace's pot belly, her vast breasts with their large red nipples hanging over her pretty black corset.

'There,' said his wife, sweetly, 'all done.' She touched

one of the welts on her husband's unmuscled chest, heard his breath draw in with pleasure-pain at the stinging touch, made a sympathetic *oohing* sound, and was on the point of turning away and leaving the room when an idea suddenly struck.

'Might I borrow the riding crop for just a few moments, milady?'

'I . . . why . . .' Jemimah was uncertain, she didn't fancy being on the receiving end.

'I swear t'will not be used upon your own good self.'

'Well . . .'

Iona made up her mind for her by simply relieving her of the crop and then re-tying Horace's wrist. She smiled at her husband. 'You'll never know how much pleasure this is going to give me, dear. Certainly more than it will give you.'

The crop trailed over his chest, down an arm. She saw his eyes darting apprehensively, saw the gag drawn in and out of his mouth with increased rapidity as his breathing quickened. He was frightened, but was was excited, too, she could tell, because his penis was growing again, starting to stand up.

Jemimah stayed where she was, astride him, hardly daring to move, mesmerised by Iona.

'So you like pain and fat women, do you, Horace? Well you shall have both. I shall chastise you for the repeated wrongs you have done me over the years and Lady Jemimah will ride you. Won't you, m'dear?'

'If you wish it,' said the Amazonian, amiably.

'Do *you* wish it?' said Iona.

'Well, truthfully, I should like to ride a little and tease a lot.'

'Sounds interesting,' laughed Iona. 'I'm intrigued. And how do you like to be whipped, Horace? Not too hard, I suspect, just enough that it stings. Am I right? But, of course, you can't speak with that horrid gag in your mouth, can you, sweety. Can't scream either. So I'll just have to do things my way, trust to instinct. There. Too hard? Not hard enough?'

Horace's body leapt up on the bed, his penis hard, the head disappearing into Jemimah's artfully positioned crotch. Then he fell back again.

She whipped. He reared, sometimes finding Jemimah's sex, sometimes not. His eyes were frantic, his face red and perspiring.

Iona moved about the bed, striking his legs, the soles of his feet, sometimes hard, sometimes so soft that she could hear her husband groan behind his gag with disappointment.

The two women – temporary allies – knew exactly how to manipulate him to the point of frenzy. One denied him pussy, one the pain he so needed, then they gave him both in full measure, Jemimah letting him find her sex and then grinding down upon him, Iona delivering a particularly stinging blow.

Soon Lady Jemimah was lost in her own pleasure and jerked up and down on Horace's little member energetically to bring herself to a climax.

Iona handed her a silk dressing-gown and told her, 'You may go now. I shall see to my husband. Sleep well.'

Jemimah was happy enough to comply, slipped away into the shadows and let herself out quietly.

'Now,' said Iona, drawing out the word meaningfully, 'I have you where I want you. And all to myself.' And she hit him, hard, much harder than previously, making Horace cry out as he bucked, tiny beads of blood breaking the skin on his thigh.

'You should have let me know your preferences earlier, dear. I could have been most accommodating; I can certainly mete out punishment with the enthusiasm required when its your good self on the receiving end.' And she hit him again, to within an inch of his balls.

He went white with terror.

'But I'm not going to hit you any more, Horace, because I know that's what you like. And the last thing I feel inclined to do now is give you any pleasure. Not when you have given me none. And so I'm going to leave you now, dear, unfulfilled, naked, vulnerable, and looking absurd to no small degree. I'm in no mood to give you your fun.'

He was struggling again, looking worried, pleading with her behind his gag.

She was deaf to him, immune. She took up the water jug from the washstand and poured the entire contents over his genitals, watching as he shrunk to insignificance from the shock and chill.

He gasped, looked, for a moment, as if he might expire.

Then Iona walked to the door, turned, and said, 'Goodnight,' and moved out into the corridor, leaving the door wide open so that any who happened along the corridor that night might see Horace in all his glory.

Iona had left that very night, packing the minimum of clothing and boarding the barquentine *Lady Luckington* along with the diplomatic bags.

Chapter Seven

She was never a prisoner. After all, what would have been the point? Where could she have run to? Iona was treated with the same deference as the rest of Tiku's seven wives. At ceremonials she stood amongst them, a pale-skinned redhead in stark contrast to their sultry, ebony haired, black-eyed beauty. Iona envied them their complexions, their light brown skins that coped with the heat so well and never freckled or burnt like her own. She envied them, too, their height (which was on average six inches above her own) and their long legs that went on forever and were showed off to wondrous effect in their short skirts of black cockerel feathers. Iona felt diminutive and insipid and, somehow, inferior. She thanked heavens, therefore, that they all seemed to like her well enough, or at least tolerated her joining their exalted ranks.

Her best friend amongst these women was ultimately the youngest wife whose name soundedly oddly like Mam. Mam was giggly, undisciplined, and frowned upon by the older, more decorous wives. It was Mam who would teach Iona to swim, to dress her hair with the heavenly scented blossoms that sent Tiku wild with desire, and which oils were best to stop her delicate white skin burning in the ever present sun.

The second oldest wife, Moona, was polite but reserved with Iona. Mam said this was because she was important, Tiku's old favourite, and jealous of the new female who was so obviously different. Mam said it was best if Iona let her come round in her own good time, learn to like and lose reserve. Most of their talking was done with hand signals and amusing mimes, though by the time the moon had waxed and waned for the fourth time Iona had learnt a repertoire of some two dozen words. Yes. No. Food. Water. Bed, etc.

Tiku never slept alone, his wives taking it in turns to cuddle up at night on the big bed in the wooden palace. But he lived there alone during the day, counsels and visitations conducted on his shady veranda. The women's quarters – slightly less splendid than his own – were situated in his private pleasure gardens. Each night one of them took the little path to his door, anointed with oil and decorated with orchids and shells. Each day they were left, generally, to their own devices and amusements.

At first Iona had felt it her womanly duty to show some reluctance at this procedure. She went to him because the other wives insisted that she must, that she couldn't insult Tiku by not attending. But she tried not to be too readily submissive, to show some spirit, defiance. Perhaps something in her upbringing made Iona feel that she had to act thus, as if it was expected of her as an Englishwoman.

Her mind had been filled with disturbing memories of their last encounter as she took the step onto his veranda that first time, pushed back the fantastically dyed cloth that hung over his door and entered. She couldn't help but remember how devastatingly weird and, frankly, wonderful had been that coupling up on the ceremonial plateau, high above the village; how he had turned her fearful, shrinking body to a thing of fire, of wantonness. Even before she laid eyes on Tiku awaiting her upon the vast platform of the bed, she had doubts as to her own strength of will.

There were coarse woven mats on the grass covered floor, weapons of war and grotesque masks on the woven lath and grass walls. Spears and knives lay on a heavily carved side-table also. The vast bed was softened with fresh moss and ferns and draped over with an indigo dyed sheet of material not dissimilar to linen. Hanging about it and making a softly draped canopy were more of the garishly dyed lengths of cloth like the one at his door. On them were fearsome faces and large, all-seeing eyes, blue waves and huge red suns. In halved coconut shells wicks burned in seas of scented oil, casting a pale, meagre and softening light over the room. At the rear of the side-table a small stone god, his belly a scooped out receptacle for incense, smoked away insidiously, filling the room with its lulling essences. The smoke stung Iona's eyes and throat a little.

Her cough roused Tiku from his dreamy contemplation of the ceiling and he came upright with easy grace, crossed his legs Hindu fashion and smiled beckoningly at her.

She had prepared a short speech of a moralising nature, full of grievance and indignation. One look from his smouldering, heavily lashed eyes and she forgot every word. One glance over his naked, beautiful body, his manhood already growing in response to her entrance, and Iona faltered in her intentions, knew she was going to be a happy pushover.

She had wanted him again, allowed Tiku to seduce her with effortless ease.

He gestured to the two full goblets fashioned out of smoothly polished, turned wood. Iona fetched them. He took one, signalled for her to drink. She did so with almost mesmerised obedience, the growing girth and length of his manhood, glimpsed out of the corner of her eye, making her breath catch.

It was a huge penis, dark, veined, the head an angry red knob that glistened. If she didn't know better she'd never have believed it could fit inside her. It rose up from a taut sac of plump balls, pulsing, throbbing, dominating. Only a prize bull could have been more awesome.

The drink was the same potent brew which had been given to her on that sunset-lit evening when she had been sacrificed upon the altar of desire. She matched him sip for sip, drained the goblet dry.

Iona had allowed herself to be pulled atop the bed, to be undressed without protest. She wasn't wearing much: a rescued scrap of her camisole tied about her breasts and a skirt of feathers. About her neck and resting down between the valley of her generous breasts, was a string of tiny pink shells given to her by wife number three, Arnk.

Where his hands had touched caressingly, his mouth followed – breasts, neck, thighs, navel. He made her quiver. She groaned, snaked her arms about him. He kissed them up to the armpits, thrillingly, before disentangling himself. He rolled her over, kissed her nape again, played with her russet spill of waving hair, ran his tongue down her spine and cupped a buttock with an elegant brown hand. Iona had groaned louder.

She lay, torso atop the bed, knees on the floor in a languid kneeling position as he explored her, stroked her, ran a finger between her legs and into her, his thumb artfully stimulating her externally. Then he was between her legs and probing with the tip of his manhood instead of the fingers which had taken Iona to a state of wanton pleading. Her rounded white rear wiggled, pushed out against him in an unmistakably willing display.

Tiku pushed into her, fully, hard, groaning himself when he felt he had reached her depths.

Her face, lying sideways upon the deep blue sheet of the bed, Iona gave a delicious little squeal of delight, panted and moaned as he stroked away, exquisitely slow. In, to the hilt. Groan. Out. Quiver. She pushed her buttocks against him, wanting all, more, shivered when he fell upon her neck with hot kisses, filled her ear with warm breath and sexual noises.

'Sweet lord . . .' she breathed, contracting about him in waves of ecstasy. 'Dear, oh dear, oh dear . . .'

He reared, pumped harder, jamming into her fiercely then and with urgency, his teeth nipping her shoulder as he knew true pleasure, pushed and groaned and shuddered himself into her with greedy possession.

So it was every eighth day when Iona went to Tiku's bed. They had glorious sex and he gave her something as a reward: a comb; a particularly beautiful shell lined with Mother-of-Pearl which she might use as a dish; a length of gaudy cloth.

She knew not to be offended by these gifts. He was not paying for services but showing his regard for an individual wife with the presents he gave. The finer the gift the better her standing amongst the other wives. Iona's length of cloth which she frequently wore proudly as a sarong, was a prize indeed and elevated her instantly.

Moona, who was the second oldest wife at nearly thirty, was also the number one wife, though no longer Tiku's supreme favourite because of past misdemeanours. When she saw Iona's new garb, she adopted a stony expression and became even more reserved. Only she, up until then, had ever received so fine a piece of cloth. She felt threatened, she turned cold. Mam noticed this with some anxiety and warned her friend to henceforth be wary of Tiku's erstwhile favourite.

Tiku set about winning and wooing his newest wife after possession had been attained. She amused him. Some of the village chiefs and elders said it wouldn't last. Others said his curiosity might endure a little longer.

One night both Iona and Mam were summoned to the Living God's lodge. It was not surprising. They were the youngest and most sexually enthusiastic of his wives and, obviously, this night he was feeling adventurous.

He was naked when they arrived and already aroused as he sat on his cushioned throne, a collection of amethyst and hardwood figurines on the consul beside him. He was turning them this way and that and studying them carefully, his long tongue moistening his lips, a broad grin making his cheekbones sharply pronounced.

The wives bowed before him, one tall and dark, the other plump and fair, red hair spilling down her back.

'Witness my enthusiasm for the evening's sport,' he laughed, stroking the daunting length of his penis and caressing its globular tip.

'Come,' he bade, crooking a finger, 'see what it is that I require this night. Look.'

They studied the ebony figure he presented on the flat of his considerable palm. It showed a male figure seated, with a female figure hovering in a semi-seated position just above him, a little wooden phallus disappearing into her rear.

'That I should like, thank you, Mam,' he ordered, politely.

She inclined her head, smiling serenely. 'As my husband wishes.' And slipped off her skimpy skirt, anointing her body from the oil vessel upon the consul beside the copulating figures. She circled her breasts then delved immediately at her sex, skirting her clitoris and inserting lubricated fingers into herself.

Tiku, of a mind to be lazy it seemed, did nothing, merely waited, studying her rounded rear, her slim, straight, dark back.

Mam reached through her legs, took him in her hands, wiggled her rear and inserted the fat head of his member at her opening. Then she put her hands on the arms of his chair to brace herself and lowered onto him, taking all of him in with great difficulty. He was huge, as usual, and, although Wahwuese women had big feet denoting a lengthy passage between their sex's opening and the necks of their wombs, even they found accommodating the bull-like Tiku no mean feat.

He sat perfectly still as she raised and lowered, bringing her oiled buttocks down to meet the bush of black hair from which he sprang hard. Occasionally he sighed.

Iona watched, waited, growing moist at the sight of them.

Tiku licked Mam's backbone, then glanced past her to his other wife, pointing to the row of false phalluses on the consul. 'Come select one,' he murmured, voice gravelly with desire as Mam, greatly aroused now, ground down upon him. He slipped a finger into her rear, rotated it. She tightened about him.

Iona selected a phallus of golden satinwood, captivated by its carved smoothness. It wasn't as large as some, certainly not as lengthy as the longest, which was an exact replica of Tiku's engorged member prior to copulation. But it was the thickest.

He smiled at her choice, eyes opaque with lust, gauged. 'Only a man's hand could fill you more so.' He oiled his right hand from the jar and ran it down over Iona's thrusting mound, gliding under, into her folds, finding her wet hot, her legs opening willingly to him, feet planted wide, allowing in two fingers with ease, then three, four. She was tight.

'Let me see you pleasure yourself,' he decided.

She nodded, eager now that he had touched her, set her quickly afire. She wished that he had forced five fingers into her, his whole hand, damn it, so enflamed was she by the sight of Mam so expertly servicing him, his thick hardness sliding out and then ramming into her slippery rear.

Iona sat on the floor facing him, legs wide, attaching the dildo to her heel by means of leather straps and then placing the golden tip of it at her eager sex, her fingers holding back the pink folds of skin.

'Ooh, how lovely you are,' cried Tiku, appreciative of the sight. 'So ripe. So wet. Push it in. Slowly. Don't hurry, Let me watch. Ah, see how you stretch! Your skin is so tight. Is it not uncomfortable?'

'No. It's beautiful. It fills. It opens me, stretching . . . so weighty, so round. It is a great intrusion, both between my legs and in my mind.'

'Withdraw it. I want to see it go in again. Oh look do, Mam. See how the juices ooze from our beloved Iona. How she gapes now that the monstrous thing has been pulled out.'

Mam watched, found it all too much, screamed out with pleasure as spasms racked her body.

Tiku held her tight by the hips, pulling her down atop of him, forcing up into her, ramming at her core, holding her there.

Iona inserted the dildo again, every inch of barbaric possession enthralling Tiku. He jerked frantically into Mam, forcing his legs between her own and making her widen still further to his considerable demands. He came noisily, thrusting and pumping, his eyes never leaving Iona's glistening sex and the great lump of hollowed out wood that invaded her.

Spent, he lowered the vanquished Mam to the floor where she lay, exhausted, his essence seeping from her raw flesh. He went to Iona, laying on the floor before her on his belly, watching intently as she pleasured herself.

She was bright red, her clitoris engorged and prominent, her womanhood a series of flesh folds and crannies that he knew and loved so well, and there, invading, withdrawing, tautly stretching her beloved flesh, wedged between her pale thighs, was the satinwood phallus she had selected.

Her heel moved in and out with great urgency now, driving the instrument deep within her, and her eyes were half closed, glazed with passion.

'It's divine.'

'Is it as good as me?'

'I cannot compare. You are flesh and blood, a superb lover,' she breathed huskily, still remembering to be diplomatic, even in the headiest throes of passion. 'This is but wood, a hard devillish thing that rends me. It could never replace you.'

'But it is good?'

She laughed, head thrown back, the most delicious sensations overtaking her body. 'It is delightful.'

He grinned, extended a finger and reached out, oh-so delicately flickering the nail over her cherry.

She moaned loudly, thrust the dildo harder into herself and held her legs about the ankles to make certain that each stroke had full power, taking her quickly to a climax. She shuddered, making little jerking movements with the phallus until all desire was spent. Then she collapsed exhausted, lying on her back, allowing the instrument to slip from her body.

Still tickling her clitoris, Tiku watched the expulsion intently, noting how she throbbed, her muscles contracting.

The sight made him go rock hard again. He untied the dildo, threw it aside, and lifted her limp legs up and over his shoulders, ramming into her used flesh, his loins slapping against her, his balls dancing softly against her wetness.

She groaned, but hadn't the energy to fight him, lay back and let him have his way, his mouth sucking hungrily and possessively at her hardened nipples.

He wanted to prove that he was better than the dildo, she knew, and, accordingly, she put on a convincing act to keep him happy, but that night a lifeless piece of wood had brought her an exquisite pleasure that Tiku couldn't better.

Mam slept through it all.

Chapter Eight

*I*t was Christmas Day. Jack had worked it out, marked it on his bamboo calender which was a series of notches (months), grooves (weeks), and skewered dots (days).

He ate, he swam, he cut his beard into order with a slither of pearlized shell he'd spent hours honing upon a wet stone. He stalked the pigs (unsuccessfully as usual) and at midday when it was too hot to do anything save seek the shade, he flopped onto his grass mat beneath the deep shadowed porch of his shelter and snored away the time until things cooled.

Almost every day the savages trekked down to the waters edge, to take outrigger canoes to fish. Some days they swam, amazing Jack – who watched them from the trees – by the number of minutes they could stay submerged. The first time he'd watched them he'd been alarmed, thought they were drowning in some mass suicide pact. Now he knew better.

They knew he watched them. They did nothing either to dissuade or encourage him. And with time, Jack longed for their company; the laughter, the arguments, the discussions from which he was excluded stabbing him to the heart. He was desperately lonely.

Once or twice he lay in wait at dawn when they

brought his food, hoping to catch them. But the moment he stirred and tried to make a friendly overture, they were gone, melting into the dense greenery around his ramshackle hut, (a hut which fell down without fail once a month and had never succeeded in being completely waterproof).

One morning past, just as the first weak light of the new day turned his surroundings from blackest black to patchy monochrome, Jack was awoken by giggling and, lying flat on his back, mouth dry from snoring, he came up onto his elbows, blinking groggily.

There before him, staring out from the lush undergrowth were three naked backsides in a rudely irreverant youthful display of high spirits.

'Cheeky young beggars,' yelled Jack as they ran off hooting with laughter, doubtless thinking themselves brave in the extreme for executing such a prank.

'Cheeky young beggars,' he repeated, more softly, chuckling as he relaxed back into his bed.

On Christmas evening, having saved his alcohol-based drinks for days and then downed them in a celebration of the Christian holiday, Jack climbed up to the village of the cannibals, drunk and in the mood for high jinx. He'd been there before, usually waiting until most of the village was off on a fishing expedition so as to minimise the risk of encounter or capture.

It was a small village with modest round huts made of mud, grass and bamboo. There were skulls on poles and pig skins pegged out to dry after scraping. It was a messy place. These cannibals were none too keen on domestic niceties. They cooked at a communal fire, threw their debris into one convenient corner behind the old hut where they stored their meat and went to the toilet behind any bush or in any ditch that wasn't right outside their own front door.

He waited above the village while they cooked their evening meals in the clearing at centre of their village. The sun set, turning all afire. The moment seemed right.

Positioned and ready, plainly visible to them before the backdrop of sunset-lit trees on the steep slope that led up and away from the village, the inebriated Jack let out a cheery, 'Yo there! Merry Christmas and God Save Mad King George!' and waved enthusiastically before about-turning.

He dropped his ragged breeches, bent over and gave them a whiter, far more dazzling display than their children had been able to manage, beaming down at them like a huge, luminous moon gone out of orbit.

The village erupted with bawdy laughter, greatly appreciative of Jack's effrontery and sense of humour. Perhaps he was brave to do it. Unquestionably he was a fool. They chuckled. They decided they quite liked the foolish man of deathly pallor, decided he could live a little longer.

They mimicked him. High, on the content of their chewing nuts, they cavorted about the camp fire, laughing maniacally, exposing their rears and prodding at those of any within reach.

In the cover of the trees, Jack watched with surprise the sudden orgy he had unwittingly incited, growing hard between the legs, his shaft bowing out, rearing before him. He'd have given anything then to have had the nerve to clamber down to the clearing and join in their spontaneous bout of sexual horseplay. He lacked the nerve, still feared them far too much. He watched instead, and rubbed himself longingly, eventually taking his engorged member and giving himself hand relief as he watched.

The heathens fell upon each other, the sight of so many dark rumps and sex mounds enticingly presented, bringing on a mass need to copulate.

Men buried their shafts deep into any available woman. Others, when a woman wasn't readily available, buried themselves into the backside of a male friend. Men who were pleasuring women seemed to take no exception to being buggered at the same time. Indeed, it seemed to give them sublime delight which was further enhanced out of all proportion by the drug that fuzzed their senses.

Jack found the sight intoxicating, pumped hard into his tight circling fingers, wishing, almost – and knowing that it was crazy, not normal to do so – that he could savour such an excess. To take and be taken. That was something he had never tried.

His mind spun back in time to his schooldays, to being away from home, a new boy in an institution of upper-class learning where the older boys were bullies and the younger boys their victimized prey. He'd learnt what it was then to be taken. It was not a fond memory.

One day he'd been trapped by the older boy, Darting Major, and three of his spotty-faced cronies. They'd locked the door to the Latin classroom and circled him like hyenas, their laughter a braying assault upon his ears.

Jack had been backed into a corner, had wanted to cry, felt tears pricking, but fought desperately against the urge, for to show weakness was to bring down more bullying upon one's head.

Four pairs of hands had grabbed him, ripped off his breeches and forced him belly down over an ink-stained desk. They'd held his writhing body still, punching him and bloodying his nose, and forced his legs wide, holding them, fingers digging at his bottom mouth, opening his cheeks.

He'd been an innocent until that moment, hadn't even understood then what they were about to do, going rigid with shock as the first hardened member pushed into him with difficulty. He yelled; they screwed up several sheets of foolscap paper and stuffed it into his mouth to silence him.

Darting Major thrust and pumped, came quickly to a climax, leaving the way slimed and easy for the next boy. They had him in turn, raping him, holding him still for the next, while Jack shook his head in disbelief and sobbed in outrage.

Afterwards they'd threatened him, and he, being so young, hadn't dared to tell anyone.

For the next year the same thing happened with sickening regularity. They trapped him, raped him, drawn to Jack, it seemed, by his blond angelic looks. He was the handsomest boy at the school.

Once, they'd forgotten to lock the Latin room door in their eagerness to rape him and a master had walked in upon them. Jack had thought salvation at hand, had cried out gratefully around the soggy ball of paper in his mouth. But the master had joined in, ordering the bullies to step aside and hold Jack while *he* showed them how it was done. He was big and athletic, played cricket and football, did cross-country running. When he caught Jack at the hips and thrust into him the boy howled, used only to accommodating the slimmer blades of the adolescents. The engorged member of a full-grown man was something else.

The bullies left at the end of that term and Jack avoided the master thereafter whenever possible. Thankfully, the following year the man moved on to another boys' school in Berkshire where he'd secured the post of Deputy Head, and Jack's terror ceased.

His head ached and there was a sour taste on his tongue. He'd never had such a hangover. Whatever that drink was, it was near lethal in large doses. He promised himself he'd stick to moderate rations from then on and went for a swim.

Floating, eyes closed, the late afternoon sun playing on his eyelids, Jack felt better, let his mind wander, began unwillingly to remember.

Henriette. She floated into his mind as clear and alive as if he'd only left her yesterday, the image disquieting him.

Henriette had been married to his elder brother, Algernon. But Henriette had always wanted him, Jack. And she'd pursued him in deadly female fashion, both before and after her wedding. On the death of their father, The Lord Reeve, Algernon had succeeded to the baronial title and The Honourable Jonathan Savage (known as Jack to his family and friends) had felt it best to leave, to set out and make his fortune. At least that's what he told Algernon. In truth he knew he had to get away from the family home or succumb to Henriette's increasingly unsubtle forms of temptation.

Given any opportunity, she flaunted her charms, the high-waisted, low-necked gowns of the period, which some notorious females (including Algie's wife) wore dampened down, the better to show their enticing contours – their nipples, their rounded buttocks, the creases between their legs; all looked good on her; too good. And Jack was only human.

Henriette had employed her tactics mercilessly, and when Algie was away from home and Jack could find no plausible excuse to be likewise, she would waylay him on his way to or from his bedchamber, barely clad in her most alluring slumberwear.

One night she had come to his bedchamber, pulled the bedclothes down and taken Jack's member in her tiny hands.

Her touch had roused him and he'd woken to find her working on him, her fingers circling the highly sensitive head, taking an encompassing grip and sliding her hand down the hard, veined length to cup his balls, stroke his right around to his rectum.

His eyes had opened wide and he'd blinked with shock. 'God, woman, what're you about?'

'Don't be cross, Jack. I *know* you want me really and truly. Don't fight it. Just let me pleasure you . . . us,' she'd purred.

'Get away!' He shoved her by the shoulders.

She clung onto him, two hands around a thick, hard penis. 'No, don't make me, Jack. I love you, I want you. Always have. I only married Algie so's I could be near to you. Here, look, aren't I pretty?' she demanded to know, pulling open her dressing-gown violently to display her slim and naked body to him.

She was pale and slim, her breasts near non-existent.

'Damn you, Henriette!' he growled, in an agony of loathing and longing. 'Get out of here. Nothing would induce me . . .'

'No?' she challenged. *'Nothing*? Can you resist this?' she caught hold of the post at the foot of the bed and hoisted a leg brazenly up onto the mattress, her sex fully revealed, angry red and swollen with longing. She began to play with herself, to dip her index finger deep into herself and roll her eyes theatrically with pleasure. 'Take the place of my finger, Jack, please do.'

He snarled. 'You disgust me. Never. You're a whore. A harlot . . . not worthy of this family.'

'If you will not love me, then let me love you,' cried Henriette, crawling up the bed towards him then and taking his manhood lovingly, longingly into her rosebud mouth. Her lips were tight about him, he hit the back of her throat, began to lose the will to resist as lust took over.

A look of triumph came over her face, she smiled around the considerable girth of his phallus, her teeth running down his skin.

He couldn't bare to look at her, see her gloating face. With a roar of anger he dragged her off, threw her to the floor, over the little stool that stood there to help people up into the high, old bed. He held her there while he spat on his hands, worked them around her anus and thrust himself deep into her.

She screamed, her wantonness giving way to whimpers of mercy as he used her viciously, taught her that final, exacting lesson.

She never sought him out again, was a little frightened of him thereafter. But it made no difference anyhow. Within the week Jack had left home, citing a need to travel and see the world as his excuse.

He'd gone to London, gambled, fooled around, was a member of one of those notorious gangs that were all the rage then, until the novelty had worn off. That hadn't taken long.

They'd thrived in wickedness, savoured every excess, every forbidden, damning experience. The men were rakes, the women high-class whores, and *nothing* was taboo. Sodomy, bestiality, witchcraft and rape; they tried them all, were forever seeking the new experience, the ultimate thrill.

At first, Jack had found it all a diverting amusement, had been led along by the rest. Willing and at the forefront on such escapades, as bold as any, as dissolute. He was game, and he was in demand. The women loved his looks, his body, were eager to make themselves available to the new man.

The men dominated the club, the women taking on a wholly submissive role. They were to be meek, willing and inventive in the pleasing of the men – their lords and masters. They entered into the spirit of the licentious business with gusto; wantons, whores and nymphomaniacs all. Like wild cats they could show their claws on occasion, but ultimately had to submit to whatever flights of fancy their male counterparts cared to invent, forced to submit to all or be barred from the club. Like cats on heat they were compelled to allow all the gang to ravage them even if it left them half dead and licking their wounds.

The turnover of female club members therefore was noticeably swift and steady. The excesses were too much for most in the end, despite the most enormous sexual appetites of some. Being raped in all but name, or buggered night after night, took its toll eventually, leaving them sated, used and bruised. Mostly they retired graciously, going back to their unexciting titled husbands to enjoy a rather empty peace after such a sexual bombardment.

Some nights they'd been tied to a footstool and suffered a delightful sense of helplessness as twenty men in turn had taken them from behind, parting their sex lips with artful fingers and thrusting into their vaginas. Some nights they'd been spreadeagled upon the Tudor four-poster with its crimson hangings and covers, and ravaged by two men at once, one using their pusses the other thrusting into their mouths and coming in a flood that nearly choked them.

Another night they'd gone to the Gothic mansion of one particular gentleman member and frolicked naked in and around his lake by moonlight, the women captured in the water and probed at every orifice by aroused males. They coupled in the water or else waded ashore, the females squealing with delight as they were captured, brought belly down by the ankles and opened to their pursuers to be taken in the wheelbarrow mode, that is to say with their legs held straight either side of their partners torso, standing on their hands amongst the leaves and grass as the man entered them standing, and pumped away.

No sooner would one be finished than another would take his place, sliding into sex-lips still slimy from the man before, sometimes masked and smeared with silt from the lake, the female trying desperately to identify him. Usually they could make an accurate enough guess, having come to know each male by his engorged member – from the non-entities to the gigantic nine and three-quarter inches of Lord de la Vallee. He, surprise surprise, was always in great demand. But he lacked somewhat in finesse, was rather quick and brutish.

Jonathan Savage, on the other hand, at nine inches and with a sensuality and technique that provided the epitome of womanly pleasure, was the ultimate partner as far as most of the females were concerned. They were always on the lookout for Jack. Homed in on him. If they were sex slaves in this upper-class club of debauchery, then it was Jack whom they wanted to master them.

One had knelt before him, bending over backwards to please him, literally, as he, hard, long and moon-kissed, mounted and covered her like a stallion, thrusting into a wet sex and rubbing against a red-budded clitoris that longed for him, loved him, swelled and throbbed with every firm plunge of him.

Another had lain before him in the wet grass, not looking at his horned, devillish mask, but eyes popping at his once again hardening shaft. She grinned, raised her legs, spreading them until her toes conveniently found the rough bark of two silver birch trunks between which she lay.

He had knelt between her legs, staring at her flaring opening, the dark triangle of hair, the glint of moisture escaping from her, caught in the moonlight.

She reached for him, trailing his penis from its base to the angry tip, squeezed it. 'I am your slave, oh master. Do with me as you will.'

She wanted him to take her, desperately. She'd had him before; he was magnificent.

Another reveller nearby, who pumped into the large round rear of a certain notorious duchess, called out to him, goading him, egging him on. 'Go on, Jack. Make her cry out for mercy. Give her *The Bull*.'

The eyes of the woman in the grass registered trepidation and anticipation. 'Oh no, no, surely not?' she cried in mock dismay. 'Not *that*!'

Jack laughed. 'Quiet slave. 'Tis your duty to submit, not question.'

She was quiet, lay there licking her lips, her nipples hardening. She'd never been subjected to *The Bull* before. Was full of dread, and delight too, that it was to be Jack who would put her through such a trial.

A crowd had gathered and through it, almost ceremoniously, came *The Bull*, a penis-like sheath of some twelve inches in length and eight in circumference. It was made of leather. Exquisite workmanship, with ridges and nobbles in rows down its length.

Jack fitted it on ceremoniously and, as the men in the crowd dramatically held down the 'prey' and began fondling her ample breasts and stroking her to a heightened state of readiness, Jack set the knobby end of the phallus to her open and contracting sex and eased into her. Three inches. Then out again.

'Yes, please, again,' she murmured, eyes bright.

He stroked. Four inches. Out. In. Ground it about, his loins rotating.

'Again,' she begged.

He withdrew, then poised at her entrance, plunged in again, six inches, rotating, withdrawing, thrusting again.

'Again?' he asked, sporting a wicked grin, his weight on his arms, his artificially lengthened shaft, in her but an inch and driving her sensitive body mad.

'I beg you, yes, *More*.'

'More? Are you certain now, my beauty?'

'Yes, do it. I love it. Cannot possibly get too much.'

'Really?' His grin turned wolfish and he plunged nine fat inches into her, made her squeal. The length was his, but the girth was greatly enhanced, for his penis was a rather slim and silky blade, a rapier of pleasure. Now it had been turned into a shaft as merciless as any pike staff.

She called out, caught her breath. 'Ah, dearest ravisher, do what y'will.' He thrust again. 'Do it . . . harder . . . deeper. Again . . .'

He complied, giving another inch, rotating inside of her. She cried out, reached a climax. He thrust on, through her throes of passion, carrying her on, taking her higher with another inch, then another, grinding into her finally with a foot of hard, unreal shaft, filling her, rending her, so that those who watched wondered how she could possibly accommodate it. They could see her sex stretched to its very limits by Jack's unholy appliance of lustfulness.

She cried out again, another crisis of pleasure washing over her, throbbed, contracted, throbbed, held prisoner by a dozen hands as Jack took her to a climax a third time and then withdrew, removing the sensation deadening sheath and lay back frenziedly while another willing female slave straddled him, took him all up into her with a sigh and jerked him quickly to a climax.

So it was, whenever the club held a 'meeting'. He'd had all the women at least a dozen times, done everything, to all of them, and had just about everything done to him by females, and males when too drunk or drugged on opium to care.

In the end he found himself growing bored. The new delights that were dreamt up were only variations of the old ones. The novelty wore off.

Then he'd moved to Florence for a while, thinking to digest some culture. Paris, which would have been his obvious choice, to enjoy the frivolous and fashionable, was closed to all English people by the Terror and then the military brilliance of Napoleon Bonaparte, who seemed to be subduing half of Europe with his campaigns.

From Florence he'd gone to Venice, from Venice to Rome, sometimes, it seemed, only one step ahead of the advancing French Army.

He left Italy, took the first ship going anywhere. He didn't much care. He'd landed up in Botany Bay, Australia. Now that had been a novelty for quite a while, the land's rawness appealing to him, the rough and ready people (away from those awful military types in Sydney) fascinated him.

With a freed sheep stealer who'd served his term as a convict labourer at His Majesty's Pleasure in the colony of New South Wales, and two aboriginies who knew the land beyond the city like the backs of their hands, could read the stars and listen to the earth, Jack had set out on a modest expedition.

He hadn't known what to expect. Kangaroos had startled him and frightened the horses they rode, and his black guides cautioned him against doing anything except making a tactical withdrawal if he encountered spiders or snakes. Apparently there were deadly ones. Jack only half believed them, thinking that the aboriginies liked to dramatise things in order that it should appear that they were really worth their wages and food rations. He had no doubts about their sincerity, though, when the fatter of the two got bitten on the backside one day as he squatted to relieve himself and died painfully in just under ten minutes, according to Jack's silver pocket watch. It was a sobering incident. Thereafter, Jack and his convict friend, Arthur, carried out bodily functions, slept and sat with the greatest vigilance. The only time they felt truly safe was on horseback.

Floating like a dead thing atop the water, Jack felt something brush his leg. It wasn't pleasant. In fact it felt like someone had rubbed his skin with a sheet of sandpaper.

He broke free of his thoughts and looked about, saw the dark grey fin breaking the water immediately.

'Christ Almighty!' he breathed, arms and legs instantly in motion as he swam for shore. He didn't dare look back. Was too frightened, didn't want to spare even a moment on an unnecessary action, knew instinctively anyhow, that the great fish was circling in the shallows, coming back after him, alerted by his mad thrashing in the water.

It got him, snapping at his ankle, its hold poor, causing it to open its mouth and take another bite with razor teeth. A better grip.

Jack felt it, knew pain, a cold burning fierce agony that was pain gone beyond the pale, somehow beyond the point where it hurt even. It was very strange.

He struggled against the great weight and strength of the shark, tried to keep swimming, felt the sandy shore between his fingers, clawed at it, screaming.

He was half out of the water, the young Thresher holding tight to his ankle, twisting and smashing its tail into the foaming waters at the shoreline.

Then out of the trees appeared the youngsters from the village, running fast in answer to Jack's unmistakable cry of anguish and terror.

Three in all, they splashed into the shallows, surrounding the man and the sevenfoot shark and proceeded to stab the impressive piscean carnivore with their spike-headed wooden play spears.

Surprised and wounded, it let go of its prey, cavorted in pain-crazed fashion in the water while the children stabbed it continuously, thinking it a hoot of a game, the water turning magenta with blood. Whipping and twisting one final time, a spearhead embedded in its brain, it died and was hauled out by the tail to lie ashore. Then they turned their attention to Jack, took him by the arms and dragged him up onto dry sand. They prodded his leg with their spears, eliciting a groan of agony from him before he passed out.

Chapter Nine

*H*e came to.

They (two women who knelt over him while half the village stood curiously behind, watching him) doused the wound with a treacley, stinking mixture that had alcohol as a base. That was more than he could stand: he fainted again. He came to, groaned. One of the females – a short, plump little thing of an age somewhere between twenty and thirty – was threading a fine bone needle with a length of glistening sinew. The other lifted his head, held a bowl of drink to his lips. It was their home brew. They made him drink, though he was in too much pain to feel any particular desire for such a beverage. Though, as the needle entered his flesh for the first time, he thought he understood their attempt to try cloud his senses.

The pain was more than he thought he could bear. Yet he did. He felt several stabs of molten fire into already agonising, traumatised flesh before he fainted again.

It was dark when he awoke next and instantly the woman was bending over him with a drink. He sipped, wanting the temporary numbing of alcohol, her motives well understood. She smiled, showing teeth that were beginning to discolour, turning brown from habitual chewing of narcotic nuts. He managed a grimace in response.

She held out something. He gaped groggily at it. It was a sharks tooth, triangular and razor tipped. Evidently it had been extracted from the wound at his ankle.

Chapter Ten

No other part of the world had sunsets quite as awesome and beauteous as the South Seas, surely? The salmons, magentas and mauves endlessly captivated Iona. Often she went down to the shore, positioning herself upon some outcrop of volcanic rock to watch the sun set as the fishermen came home in their outrigger canoes, the hulls of their shallow vessels shimmering with an abundance of seafood – fish, crab, lobster and octopus. Others had been diving and showed off good crops of oysters and clams, their Mother-of-Pearl interiors as highly prized by the islanders as the oysters and pearls they nurtured.

Sometimes as she stared out over an empty, deadly blue, shark-infested sea, Iona thought of home, of green lawns and country houses. Sometimes she missed them dreadfully. But not this evening.

Tiku stood behind her, had his arms about her so that she rested back into the now familiar expanse of his broad chest. When she was with him her need to go home diminished.

'You Tiku's woman,' said the man whose arms tightened affectionately around her. His was a low voice indeed, a rasping voice. It sent little shivers through

Iona whenever she heard it. And when he was possessive and demonstrative, as now, she adored him.

'Yes,' she agreed wholeheartedly.

His large hands crossed her midriff, cupped her breasts.

She began to breathe raggedly, to lean back into him invitingly, rub at his manhood with her buttocks. He nuzzled his way beneath her hair, kissed her nape.

Yes, she thought, I am. Nobody had ever made her feel the way this man did – except, maybe, Jack Savage. But it seemed so long ago now since their solitary night together, that it was difficult to remember, to be totally logical.

All she had ever known and been was gone, lost to her, probably for ever. She was, she had learnt from Arnk, the only white woman that they had ever seen, sent to them (and this always made Iona smile) by the Gods to please their chosen one, Tiku. Evidently, then, Cook's expeditionary voyages had by-passed Wahwu, left it uncharted. She seemed destined to live out her days with these people. These days the possibility in no way made her unhappy.

Tiku released her, gave a joyous yell and dived sleekly into the salt water pool below. He broke the glassy surface of the water, swam under the ripples like some dark, predatory salmon.

Iona leapt in feet first, nose pegged between thumb and finger. Having only recently learned how to swim, she still sank better than she swam, didn't find it quite the effortless joy that the natives did. Still, she persevered. Subconsciously she did so for Tiku's sake, feeling that as his chosen one she had to be extra worthy of his adulation, a white woman of some note. But she was far from feeling that then, she felt very insecure at times in her new position. Tiku found such reticence charming. All his other wives were noisy and confident enough. Indeed sometimes they were far more sure of themselves and bossy with him than he cared for. Sometimes they seemed almost to forget that he was a

Living God. Sometimes he had to remind them of the fact. But that wasn't very often; they knew how far they could go in their playfulness with him, knew the mark of propriety over which they stepped at their peril. When and if they did, they knew they might, at the very least, expect a beating.

Once, some time ago, Mam had told Iona in a scandalised whisper, Moona had angered Tiku greatly by taking a new lover. It wasn't the fact that she had done so, for their culture allowed for partnerships to be flexible, extra-marital diversions being a common thing; no, it was the fact that she hadn't paid Tiku the courtesy of asking his permission first. As a Living God he was, he felt, a little bit special and had expected to be treated with more deference. Some said he was jealous. They may have been right. Certainly afterwards Moona never again enjoyed the same amount of power over him as she had. Tiku had cooled towards her and her reign was over in all but name.

She had never forgiven him the scars across her back where the thin switch of young bamboo had welted her flesh in punishment for her lapse in etiquette.

The water was ice clear. It felt funny against Iona's eyeballs as she swam beneath the surface after her lover, who was as agile in water as an otter, and caught him in a playful hug about the waist.

She had been wandering the shoreline with the other wives and their attendants until a short time ago, but once Tiku had appeared upon the scene the others had melted tactfully away. They knew that when Tiku was with Iona he usually wanted to be alone.

He turned in the water, his grinning mouth emitting air bubbles, and kissed her as they surfaced. They went ashore, their feathers waterlogged, their arms linked; climbed over the rocks until they found a sheltered patch of dry sand and fell upon it, bodies instantly entwining. She welcomed his weight upon her, his stiffened shaft within her, and wrapped her legs about his waist, squeezing him in delight, a willing prisoner of love.

His arms went about her waist and shoulders, he came up onto his knees, drew her up with him so that she sat then, arms about his neck, making little cries in his ear, his hands cupping her buttocks, his manhood in her to the hilt, seeming to rend her. His savagery was almost too much, it made her moan against her will, but she let him have his way. She came to a shattering climax in mere moments, so intense were her feelings.

She gasped, he rammed, up, up, filling her, piercing her and then emptying himself into her with a great cry of masculinely possessive joy.

He laid her gently back down into the sand and kissed her all over, and especially at that sore, wet spot, which he'd just ravished.

In no time at all Iona was panting and clutching at his mane of black hair, her legs twitching, her mound afire. She reached out, caught hold of his penis. Even dormant after lovemaking it was a majestic ten inches, the biggest member in the whole of Wahwu. That was an indisputable fact. She had made a surreptitious study of all sets of wedding tackle in the village. It was easy, given the tribal dress.

In their skimpy feathered skirts a woman's genitals and buttocks could be glimpsed quite easily, when they sat, bent over, crossed their legs, or just plain flaunted themselves for the illicit pleasure that came with enticement. Tiku's wives did it a lot. It was a wicked form of amusement, for they were Tiku's and his alone and the other men could never hope to taste the morsels that were flashed naughtily at them. Only Moona had ever taken a lover from the village in preference to her master, Tiku, and she was ostracised for such a disloyal act.

No man compared with Tiku anyhow, and Iona had studied them all. She had a simple method. She watched someone, noting his 'sleeping' state, then opened her legs so that her russet-furred mound stared him in the face. Invariably the man would grow, stand to attention and she would gauge, six, seven inches? and so on. Tiku was the most well endowed male she had ever come across, certainly he was the most exciting and ardent lover. That's not to say she loved him. She didn't.

She encircled him, ran her fingers lightly up and down him, feeling the ridges, the ripples of veins, as he inevitably began to harden again, watched the dusky silken length go iron hard and begin to throb under her touch.

Her lover's head was buried between her legs, his tongue flickering over her bud and then plunging deep within her, to waggle, drive her crazy.

She leant over and took his engorged penis into her mouth, determined not to grimace at the taste of him, her lips tight about him, tongue playing over the tip. He grunted, thrust into her even as she arched against him, pulled at his hair.

He hit the back of her throat. She almost gagged. He was holding her by the hair now, forcing her down onto him, thrusting up into her saliva-filled mouth, her tongue whipping around the silken knob.

His tongue thrust into her, his thumb stroked her sex, while his other hand cupped her buttocks, allowed the odd finger to invade her bottom mouth.

She did the same to him, and a moment later they were both crying out, tipped over the edge once more into ecstasy, Iona wrapping her legs about his head as she tried valiantly to swallow the rush that spurted down her throat.

Chapter Eleven

He inspected his leg, as he did worriedly every morning. And every morning he thanked God for keeping the blood flowing to his toes and not allowing gangrene to set in. He wondered, too, whether the foul smelling paste that his nurses insisted upon plastering it with was more likely to kill than cure.

His leg was a horrible looking mess; a series of raw-edged clefts competently sewn together. Never again, Jack had thought with delirious gallows humour, would anyone compliment him on the elegant turn of his ankle!

His nurses arrived. As usual they were fascinated by his blond hair and beard, which had now grown untidily long, causing Jack to look like some strange medieval hermit or such like, when he didn't secure his locks back into a pigtail.

This morning he was in no mood for them. They annoyed him. He grunted when they playfully ruffled his hair, growled threateningly when one of them pulled his beard experimentally.

They were a curious pair of girls, sisters perhaps. Short, slightly rotund, like all their tribe, they had smeared their dark bodies with mud and ashes, giving themselves a rather ghostly appearance. This body make-up was worn for most of the time, though was frequently washed away by their nautical activities; the cannibals loved swimming and messing about in their outrigger canoes.

The girls fed him, tended his wound, vying as usual to be his special helper. Elbowing each other out of the way was quite normal. Sometimes they got extremely violent. In their tribe the women didn't regard themselves as the weaker sex. Indeed, apart from their heavy breasts adorned with strings of shells, they hardly looked any different from the men at all, having similar stature, musculature and brown-black woolly hair bushing from their heads.

He needed to relieve himself. He hated the procedure which followed and the way it embarrassed him (and them not at all) and underlined his helplessness. At a signal (he'd devised a teeth-gritted grimace that spoke volumes), the girls hauled him up onto his feet and, taking an arm each, helped him to the bushes not too far away. Here they undid his fly, taking ages over the buttons which were totally alien to them, and yanking down his breeches. Like a child he gave free rein to his bladder and bowels, knowing blessed relief and burning shame all at the same time. It was – he had decided, on mulling over this necessary yet abhorrent procedure – the amused way in which one of the girls collected a handful of soft moss and handed it to him solemnly so that he could wipe his backside, that was the ultimate humiliation. Yet submit he must to such ministerings, was grateful, humble, even as he wished he might be swallowed up by some black, bottomless hole of biblical awesomeness.

Finished, his top fly button was done up, his helpers manhandled him back to the shade of his awning. He winced and muttered in pain all the way, collapsing, as if exhausted, down onto his matting.

The girls hovered over him, chattering, eyeing the fly of his breeches. One nudged the other. They giggled. Jack, feeling oddly vulnerable, raised his eyebrow. He came up onto his elbows, hating being flat-out all of a sudden.

He wasn't mistaken. They were up to something. 'What're you girls thinking? Why're you looking at me like that?'

They didn't understand him, of course, and the edge of concern to his voice amused them greatly. They dissolved into girlish, conspiratorial laughter, one undoing that fly button again while the other came and sat back on her heels at his shoulder, taking Jack's head onto her lap and rubbing her pendulous brown breasts either side of his head.

Authoritatively she turned his head, so that he nuzzled the globular abundance of flesh.

The other girl had his trousers down and had taken hold of his manhood, was squeezing it, smoothing her cheek upon it and running the tip of her tongue up and down it.

He dug his nails into the palms of his hands, cried out in husky delight, then pain the next moment as his body jerked, the wound protesting violently.

The one who had been cushioning his head between her breasts wriggled around so that her body was now straddling his shoulders, her red loincloth lifted enticingly to show off her dark sex for Jack's delectation. It stared him full in the face, only inches from his eyeballs. He blinked, looked dumbfounded. She put her hands behind his head, lifted him towards that hungry spot, her tongue jutting between her teeth and flickering snake-like so that he was left in no doubt as to what she wanted him to do.

Meanwhile, her companion straddled his hips, took him fully and with practised ease, an appreciative noise issuing from her as she pushed down and glided up.

They were blatantly using him. He knew it but was divinely happy in such servitude, put his all into the task, and if he wasn't smothered in the process, he wrily calculated, they'd all end up happy.

For several minutes he forgot all about his pain.

Chapter Twelve

*I*n the black shadows of the night Moona stood motionless, watching her husband and his favourite wife, her teeth gnashing, her black eyes narrowing to slits of hatred.

They were in the Living God's lodge, the white woman dancing for him, laughing, her hips rotating, full breasts wobbling beneath necklaces of pearls and coral.

Moona didn't want him, but she didn't want anyone else to have him either. She was by no means logical, didn't worry about such a thing. She was wealthy, beautiful (some still said the most beautiful woman in Wahwu) and so she felt that contrariness was quite acceptable. She would act as she pleased and none, save the Mighty Tiku himself, could dare to object.

She glared through the darkness, thinking that Iona, as a European, didn't manage the dance, the Ootalana, at all well. She could have done it with so much more allure, had the kind of sinewy grace that Iona could never hope to acquire.

The white woman swayed, bent backwards, knees bent, her red hair sweeping the floor. And all at once Tiku was up and out of his chair, was snatching her to him and kissing her with such ferocity that Moona gasped, feeling something like a stab to the heart.

The Living God lifted his wife and impaled her upon his stiffened shaft of flesh, holding her captive in his arms, she wrapping her legs about him, running hands through his raven hair, nuzzling at his neck and ears.

Moona fled the scene, red hot with temper, going to the hut of her lover, Amandu, and snatching down the bamboo switch from its wall hook. Amandu came in shortly afterwards with a basket of prawns and two meaty looking fish. He, along with some two dozen other villagers, had been out all day fishing.

He dropped his fare into the hands of an efficient servant who then melted away to the kitchen at the rear of the dwelling, and eyed his lady love. He didn't need to be told that she was in a vile mood.

She struck her palm, her skirted thigh, any piece of furniture that came within range. She prodded Amandu in the chest, and looked sour. 'Where have you been?'

'Fishing. You know that.'

'I did not take you for my lover so that you would be absent all day long in that boat of yours.'

He frowned. 'I don't go out every day.'

'When I need you, I want you here.'

He didn't have the energy to argue, the rowing having depleted his reserves of energy. He nodded. 'Very well. I shall try to be more thoughtful in future.'

'That's not good enough. Say you're sorry. In fact I want you to get down on your knees and tell me you're sorry,' she raged.

'You are a bossy woman, Moona. I should not be much of a man if I let you treat me in such a way. I'll not kneel,' he hissed.

She struck him, eyes fixed with his, determined to win any battle of wills. A welt flared across his chest. He snatched for the bamboo switch but wasn't quick enough. He came at her. She hit him repeatedly, to stop his advance, ordered him again, 'Down,' rained blows upon his naked shoulders and head until he was forced to comply, crying out placatingly, 'Very well, I kneel. I kneel. And I beg your pardon.'

But she wasn't about to be humoured now, as she towered over him, eyes afire, her black hair a veil that oft times hid her convulsed features.

'On your back,' she ordered, a bare heel pressed into the middle of his chest lending weight to the command.

The coconut matting scratched his bare flesh. He scowled up at her, half annoyed, half enjoying her fire and need to dominate, saw it as a game. Moona liked to order people about, liked to inflict pain, even on those she professed to love. He'd been in several situations similar to this and hadn't been slow to note that they'd increased considerably since Tiku's taking of a new favourite. She vented her temper on everyone else and especially him. But he didn't mind so very much, found such bouts of violence and passion alarmingly enjoyable.

He lay still, obedient looking, his near naked body brown and beautiful, his eyes watching her every move, wary, excited.

Statuesque, trembling with anger and sexual aggression, Moon straddled him, flicked aside the black feathers of his skirt and exposed the curled, dormant member that twitched under her exacting gaze.

'Harden for me.'

He found it difficult to do so under such circumstances. Felt threatened rather than aroused by the sight of her towering over him.

She squatted, lowering and bending until her breasts were brushing his muscular chest, trailed them in light caressing movements across his body, and her sex lingered over his flaccid manhood, warm, immediately sending shock waves of lust coursing through his body, radiating out from his loins.

Amandu tried to touch her woman's parts, could see the tip of her peeping from between russet lips, moistening the hardening, veined underside of his shaft. He wanted to put a finger to it, watch it respond to his touch. But Moona slapped his wrist, bit his shoulder and, when he shouted out in objection, thrashed his thigh with the bamboo switch.

He jerked, his pelvis thrusting, penis rigid and as hard as bone and she grabbed him none too gently, driving down upon him, crying out as he pierced her so exquisitely. Kneeling either side of his slim thighs, his shaft deep within her, his balls pressing against her meatily, she bounded up and down upon Amandu, her breasts swaying before his eyes, hard nippled, ripe and dusky. He tried to reach out, to caress, but she hit the hand away, wanted to use him and torment him while she did so, keeping complete control over the situation.

She jerked, she gasped, her bouncing becoming frantic and then she called out, her climax upon her.

Amandu wanted to hold her tight, to pump up into her with all his might and savour an intensity of feeling akin to her own. But as soon as the waves of pleasure had died within her Moona climbed off him coldly and disappeared into her bedchamber without so much as a word or a look, as if he didn't exist; was nothing.

Huge and hard with longing, he came up onto his feet, groaning, calling for a servant.

A girl arrived instantly, knelt placidly over a footstool as directed and widened her knees for her master. He put his silken member at her sex-lips and ran the glistening tip up and down, entering her with a finger, then thrusting his member deep within her. Pumping, forcing her wider with his hands, his balls dangling down over her sex and tickling it. She ran a hand down beneath her belly, stroked herself and cupped his balls, soon squealing with delight and breathily calling out, 'Oh thank you, my Master, for honouring me in this way, for using this poor unworthy body, for bringing me such pleasure . . .'

He did not hear her, wasn't listening, his climax upon him, he withdrew his member and shot his essence all over her buttocks and into her invitingly tight bottom-mouth, his loins jerking and shuddering.

* * *

The baby meant that she could never go home. Never. She resented that. Then, in time, she came to terms with it. This was her home now, for ever. There was no alternative. Even if a ship did come in the future she would have to forego rescue, would have to stay with her child, a heathen sprung from her own loins. She would never be accepted by her family once they knew all that had befallen her. They couldn't live with her shame, wouldn't be able to forgive her. Instinctively she knew how her father would have reacted: he'd rather she'd died, whether horribly and martyred or not, than quietly accept what had occurred. She knew her father well. A man of high morals and principles, a very stuffy English gentleman, the man who had given her in marriage to Mr Horace Stanley. Somehow *that* said it all.

She'd been queasy. Tiku had been pleased, though not, strangely, with himself. Iona was perplexed until she pieced together his words, realised that as far as he was concerned sex and babies didn't go together. What they did – his never-ending dalliances between her legs – was for pleasure. As far as he was concerned it had nothing to do with what might happen nine months later – birth. Iona tried to explain. He pooh-hooed her suggestion as nonsense, said that babies came from the Gods, *everyone* knew that. She gave up, amused.

He carried her to the high plateau where the great waterfall emptied, after a hundred foot fall, into a crystal pool. It was far above the village; way beyond the altar at which offerings were placed for Tiku, and where the Living God himself prayed to mightier deities still.

It was the custom for the lover or husband of the pregnant woman to take her to the birthing place, to endure the hard climb as a means of sharing the woman's pain, somehow experience something of her labour. Iona thought cynically that a man had undoubtedly thought that one up, for no female would have had the audacity to compare the pain that consumed her now as in any way similar to the bearable exertion of a mere climb. And she was angry with Tiku, too, for being so gentle, so understanding, so bloody patient. He'd done this to her, got her in this state; God help him if he ever came near her again, to repeatedly cause her such agony. She'd kill herself first. No. She revised that decision. She'd kill *him*, the cause!

'We here,' he said huskily, as ever, a man of few words. Before them, shrouded in the densest of vegetation, was the pool, the noise of the waterfall emptying into it, blocking out all else. Through the trees the sun touched the scene, bathed the dark, deep water. From its edge the midwife came to greet them, bowing low and smiling winningly at Tiku, her manner full of deference.

'Oh Great One, this place is blessed by your presence.'

He inclined his head vaguely in acknowledgement and set Iona gently down on her feet. Instantly, the midwife took charge of her, her arm about the back of the woman, steadying and supporting. Her voice was reasuring: 'You are safe with me, Little One. There is nothing of birth which is any longer a mystery to me.'

Iona wanted desperately to believe her.

Tiku patted her on the head, infuriating her. 'Be strong and brave for me, woman. I shall wait with eagerness for your return.' Then, knowing he had no place there, that in this instance the midwife was even more powerful than himself, he bowed and turned, heading back down the well-trodden path, and was soon obscured by vegetation.

She took Iona by the hands and led her into the water. It was pleasantly warm from the sun's concentrated rays. The women submerged themselves to the necks, still holding hands, relaxing.

Iona floated, the pain lessened by the water that bathed her, and in a surprisingly short while there he was, her son, mouth instinctively closed against the waters of the pool as he surfaced in the midwife's capable hands. He was plump, whole and the colour of coffee with cream. The midwife laid him upon Iona's now flaccid belly, orchestrated the final stage and cooed approvingly as Iona touched the baby's wet black head, sobbing with joy.

Tiku had his son.

When the midwife decided that Iona's body had healed sufficiently and she had recovered enough strength, Iona started back down the treacherous side of the mountain.

She paused often, to feed the baby, then herself, surprised at how eagerly he suckled and caused her belly to ache in response. She kept looking at him curiously, trying to make up her mind whether he'd be handsome or ugly. She couldn't decide. He capitvated her though. She looked him over repeatedly, from his tiniest toe to his incredibly delicate ears, endlessly marvelling. Certainly in her heart she knew she could never reject him. No matter what.

Sitting cross-legged with the baby in her arms suckling at her breast, she had been so deep in thought she hadn't noticed that he'd fallen asleep, replete, a trickle of milk running from the corner of his mouth.

She smiled, rearranged her cotton top and came leisurely to her feet. She was in no hurry, knew she would reach the village before dark, in time for the evening meal. The meal was bound to turn into something of a celebration, for Tiku would be proud of her.

She looked out to sea, inhaling deeply of the salt-tinged air, eyes on the brash blue waves. It looked so dark, so deep, so cold; she hated it. It separated her from that other world where she still felt she belonged, even as she acknowledged the fact that she no longer did, could. And as a feeling akin to bitterness assailed her, something else entered her field of vision, instantly wiping her mind clear of such emotions.

A ship!

A real ship, large and packed with sail. She wasn't imagining it. But it was miles away, no more than an inch sized blob in the vast panorama spreading out below her. It seemed set on a course to skirt the island, give it a wide berth, not tacking for Wahwu.

She wondered why it was there, where it was going, but something in her told her it would be best if it came no closer. She waited until it had sailed out of sight around the headland, making for northern waters, and began walking again, her baby sleeping contentedly in her arms, a soft burp escaping its puckered mouth.

Chapter Thirteen

Jack paddled the outrigger, his passengers: Mia and Sanga, his women friends, and Mowi, their adolescent brother.

In the two years since the shark attack Jack Savage had gone completely native, continuing to live alone in his rather squalid camp near the beach, but joining in frequently with village life.

Ever limping, he hunted with them almost every other day and was turning into quite an accomplished diver and underwater harvester. But today he wasn't in the outrigger and heading for open sea to fish. He was going to witness a punishment, his brown tanned face grave, pale eyes troubled.

He knew what to expect. Once before in the past two years someone from the village had been caught stealing. First offenders were shown cannibal mercy, had their right hand cut off and offered to the victim as symbolic compensation. Second offenders were rare. But they had one today. A fool, Jack had decided, for what else would you call someone who chanced death in order to illegally acquire the possessions of others? And death was the obligatory punishment for a second offence. The man had been caught red-handed with the fresh batch of pearls recently dived for by a neighbour.

The theft made no sense, especially as the islanders attached no value to something as easily attainable as pearls. Jack assumed that the man had a compulsion that he just couldn't overcome, no matter what the risk.

The thief sat trussed and quiet in the lead canoe, no doubt thinking fearfully, perhaps regretfully, on what was to follow. One man paddled steadily to a chilling communal chant; another acted as warder over the condemned man, brandishing a saw-edged club.

They headed forever outwards, past the dark band of coral which scraped the bottoms of their shallow boats at low tide, past the high breakers, out to where the sea was cold, startlingly blue and indecipherably deep.

Then every canoe – and there were some thirty or more, each carrying three or four villagers – emptied its cooking pot cargo. Mia was no exception. Her leftovers of roasted wild pig, trotters still intact, were discharged into the pristine sea, clouding it. Her face was gleeful, Jack observed. The cannibals were greatly appreciative of all forms of punishment, found them highly entertaining.

Fish heads, tails and vertebra; offal, lights and jugs of stinking old blood; all were emptied, tainting the sea and souring the air.

Jack's nose twitched in a sharply handsome face.

Gone native he truly had, deciding that – once it was established that they weren't likely to eat him – he'd make the best of things, integrate as well as he could. Some of the things they did were still deeply distasteful to him. Sometimes he found it very hard indeed to like these people. But they were company for him, companionship, especially after he had learnt a few basic words and could converse, after a fashion.

Nowadays he dressed as they did, in red pigskin loincloth and precious little else, his trousers having rotted away to embarrassing inadequancy many moons ago. His blond beard he hacked occasionally, usually after he'd glimpsed himself in a pool somewhere and noted uncomfortably, that he looked disquietingly biblical, like some Old Testament prophet. But his hair just grew and grew, tied back most often in a bleached, ill-kept pony tail, or sometimes, rarely, flying around his face in a crazy mass.

He was leaner, browner, harder; undoubtedly fitter, too, after the regime imposed by nature and circumstance. The islanders made no concessions now. They no longer fed him, having deemed their debt to him paid. In exchange for their continued tolerance and sometimes friendship, he was expected to pull his weight and fend for himself. He did, was learning all the time. His achievements were few at first and he was often ridiculed by the cruelly humoured islanders, but when his leg had finally healed and he'd forced himself into pained exercise and activity, he reached certain goals. He caught his first pig, fought his first fight (confounding his adversary by using fists like some Whitechapel pugalist), and speared his first fish. There were no congratulations. Cannibals did not believe in praise. The only thing they dished out happily was scorn when he did things wrong. Jack loathed their scorn far more than he needed compliments. He became a very determined and aggressive man.

An awed murmur rose up from the water-borne islanders, rousing Jack. His head turned in the same direction as all the rest. A shiver ran down his spine as they chanted low, almost worshipfully, to the distant fins of some dozen or more sharks who had smelt food, blood, and were coming in search of their supper. Jack swallowed hard over the lump in his throat, didn't want to watch and yet felt compelled, as fascinated as all the rest, self-disgust smothered.

The condemned man began howling the moment his gag was removed, his dark face – moon-like within its frame of dark curls, noticeably pale with fear – contorting with the most awful, devouring emotion. He was dragged up onto his feet in the wildly rocking boat, his bonds severed in the same instance that he was unceremoniously pushed over the side.

Supposedly, the villagers were giving him one last chance. But Jack knew it was no chance at all, that the thief's frantic swim towards shore with the sharks closing in was solely to amuse them. No man had ever out-swam the sharks, not from this far out.

Jack's innards knotted. He knew what the man was going through, the hell, the terror, every moment a lifetime. Jack had been there, had been pursued and caught, could still remember vividly that icily chilling moment when the teeth mashed through his leg, relaxed and bit again. But no one was going to rescue the thief.

The sharks glided under or around the canoes, heading ashore after the thrashing, frantic thing in the water which attracted their undivided attention.

'Poor bloody sod!' swore Jack, watching the dark fins cutting water, eating the yards to the swimmer oh-so effortlessly.

They caught him before he reached the coral reef, tore into him as a ravening school, tossing him in the air, slamming their tails. They bit him. He screamed just once. They played with him for a moment only and then each took a bite, another bite, and the thief was no more. The bloody water boiled for a minute or so while the deadly fish fought each other over the scraps, then they dispersed, their black, torpedo-like shapes gliding back under the canoes and out to sea.

'God Almighty!' Jack said, sickly.

When he rowed back ashore in silence and the girls and their brother had jumped, laughing, into the sand as if they'd been on some sort of excursion, Jack stayed alone by his canoe, waving them away moodily, telling them to go home. They went, mimicking his sourness to each other and giggling. Jack's moods were not new to them. They knew he'd snap out of it sooner rather than later. He looked now as he did that day he'd first witnessed them butchering turtles on the white sands as the females came ashore to scratch a hole and lay their eggs: unhappy and full of distaste. But they couldn't understand why. They turned on the path at the tree line, called out once and waved, but either he didn't hear or wouldn't acknowledge them.

The sun began to set on another day. Still he lingered, fiddling with his lobster pots, his fish spear, his paddle which had developed a split in the shaft.

He didn't like them. It was all he could think of. Their cruelty disgusted him. But even more so his own behaviour on this day disturbed him. He'd behaved no better, had watched, in thrall, his fascination akin to their own. He was just as much a barbarian. He reminded himself of the mobs who gathered at public hangings back in England. He'd always thought those people ghouls for enjoying the holiday atmosphere surrounding such events in Bristol City. They'd watched almost lasciviously as pirates and the like swung from gallows on the quays in the docks; he'd felt elation at the gruesome death of the native. He was as base as they. He blamed it on the island. It was this place which had turned him from a gentleman into such an abominable creature. It was the place and its people.

Inside his head there was a desperate cry: *God, let me go home. Please.*

He'd never felt so desperate, so unhappy. Tears actually pricked at his eyeballs. And then, through his hazy vision, out to sea, Jack saw the ship, distant but definitely a ship, sailing from east to west as large in his line of vision as a good old English penny.

Laughing crazily with joy, Jack jumped to his feet, cried out, 'Thank you God, thank you.'

He was saved. He could go home. He'd learn to become a gentleman once more and put all this behind him.

'Thank you God!' he shouted again, almost choking on a sob.

He watched intently, fearfully, but the ship was growing bigger, heading straight for him, for the island. Within the next hour it would have dropped anchor and sent the jolly boat ashore to investigate, and then he would welcome his rescuers, perhaps speak English once more to someone who understood him.

He knew a wonderful lightness within himself, seemed to breathe it in and become more buoyant with every breath. His eyes stayed glued upon the silhouette of the ship against a fiery sky.

He started off up the beach, having made up his mind to go tell the natives he was leaving, looking back every couple of yards to assure himself that the ship kept to her course. She did. He could not know that it would choose his beach on which to come ashore, but something in him felt it *had* to be so. Fate had brought the ship . . . for him. It wouldn't go beyond the headlands to east and west; it would come to him, here, on the northern shore, the most hospitable piece of coastline. Elsewhere there were jagged promontories, coral reefs, whirl-pools. It *had* to come here. This was the only suitable place; fate had seen to that. Elation was making Jack a shade fanciful.

He stopped at his camp, adorned himself with necklaces of pearls and shells, looked around to see if there was anything else he wished to take. There wasn't. A tumbledown abode, some wooden bowls, grass mats and a post-type calendar were his only possessions.

Then he worried that they might not recognise him as a European, might take him for an albino islander and shoot him down on the spot. For certainly, they would be armed. All landing parties were since that fiasco with Cook on Honolulu in the Sandwich Islands. Then he chided himself for being an alarmist, for anticipating all manner of mishap when there was likely to be none, and he set off on a well-worn path that arched up and across through the dense tree belt – his hunting grounds – to the cannibal village.

Chapter Fourteen

A little procession followed the limping Jack down the village track to the beach. It was darker, the sky redder still and sporting dramatically dark storm clouds to the west. The ship loomed large and black, masts and sails, hull and rigging clearly outlined.

Jack's blond eyebrows knit.

Something wasn't quite right here.

Everyone else stopped in confusion, queries flying at the white man from all quarters.

'What wrong?' asked one of the natives.

Jack could only shrug. 'I'm not sure.'

'They your friends?'

'I'm not so certain. Hold back. Wait,' he cautioned.

'Why?'

'They bad?' asked another.

He couldn't think for all the chattering, frowned in consternation at the vessel which was dropping anchor even then some half a mile out.

Think, Jack, think, he told himself. What's worrying you? Something. Something wasn't right. The hull? Yes. The shape wasn't European. It bore no resemblance to any Man-o'-War or barque that Jack had ever seen. And the sails, too, weren't as they should be. This was all beginning to feel like a bad dream, with everyday things distorted and suddenly alien.

Then the ship shifted slightly at anchor, went about, and Jack saw, understood his unconscious disquiet. The sun caught the hull, the sails, uncovered the mystery.

It was a junk, Chinese right down to the green dragon emblazoned on its fan-like sails which were then being lowered. Upon a smaller sail, characters from the Chinese alphabet stood out bold and black.

It was an oriental pirate ship, Jack just knew. The insular Chinese weren't great seamen and rarely strayed far from their eastern seaboard, preferring to keep as close as possible to their coasts. Only pirates would be likely to venture this far into foreign waters, looking for ships to prey upon and islands to rest at while they collected fresh game and water.

Fear gripped Jack but he didn't dare falter now. Lives depended on it. He had to be decisive and quick.

'They're not my people,' he told the gathering, gravely, relying on his expression to say much which his poor grasp of their language failed to convey.

Instantly he had their undivided and worried attention.

'Yes, they bad,' he added. 'Much bad. We should hide. Wait for them to go away.'

There was consternation at such an idea. *Hide*? 'No, no,' they chanted, indignantly. 'We no hide. Never!'

'They kill us all,' argued Jack, taking hold of Mia and Sanga's upper arms and forcibly pulling them along with him, up the beach. 'Chop heads. Many head. It their way.'

'We chop their heads first,' argued Ping, their elected leader-cum-petty king. He was determined to show some bravado, truly not believing that any man from across the sea could be stronger than he, certainly not if he was anything like the strange one called Jack. He'd never rated Jack much, felt that anyone so pale and therefore probably thin blooded was no match for a physically perfect islander. True, Jack was taller than all of them by several inches, but what was height compared to superior strength? Ping had no doubt who should assume control in this present situation, who should lead and give the orders and he resented Jack trying to orchestrate things.

'I say we fight. *We fight*,' he said with finality, his face determined.

'Then you're a bloody fool,' snarled Jack, leaving him to his fate. It was up to the others what they did. They were uncertain, looked between Ping and Jack in a quandary, hesitating. About half followed him, half stayed on the beach with Ping, spears at the ready, clubs tied at waists.

Jack could hear the pirates rowing in past the band of coral that ran parallel to the beach, even as he anxiously hurried his followers away.

The yells, the cries, the pistol shots, went on long into the descending darkness. Jack and his followers – hiding near the village, they anticipated reluctantly having to try and defend it, wincing at each noise and wondering how the battle was going.

Before dawn broke they had got to the stage where they could stand it no longer, they had to go see, go help if they could. Ping and his party had been hasty and foolish in their actions but Jack's council had reached the conclusion that they just couldn't be left to their fate.

Armed to the teeth with every weapon from the village, the men and women crept down through the trees, leaving the old to care for the very young.

The scene that met their eyes as they got their first glimpse through the palm trunks at the treeline, brought Jack up short and had everyone else halting deferentially in his wake, eyes popping with horror, anger.

They were too late. The pirates were rowing back to their junk, their craft black blobs on a midnight sea where every wave had been moontouched in silver. But not half so many rowed out as had come ashore.

The Chinese were every bit as barbaric as the cannibals. They'd committed just about every atrocity against their vanquished foes save cannibalism.

Jack and the rest went towards the carnage with slow reluctance. In Jack's mind was a picture from long ago; a picture of cannibals killing and eating the seamen from the *Lady Luckington* who had struggled ashore after the vessel went to the bottom. For sheer vileness this was just as bad.

The few women who had fought alongside Ping (and most had been prudently wary and declined) had been raped, their breasts hacked off, their heads, too, in some cases. The men had been buggered, genitalia sliced off, hacked limbless and decapitated, their heads lying all about the beach, some were stoved and their brain matter splattered. The white sands, grey in the moonlight, were darkly patched with absorbed pools of blood.

With Ping and the choicest warriors of the island dead, those who remained were very worried. He'd been a natural leader. Now they didn't know what to do. They talked and talked non-stop through the next several hours, coming up with one strategy after another, agreeing on nothing. Jack thought it good that so many ideas were being put forward, but hoped that some decisions would soon be made. Time was limited. He knew that the moment the lookouts came running in with the news of the pirates' return, that panic would break out, especially if the men were unsure of their roles.

He looked to Tig across the council fire, hoping the man – a natural successor to Ping in his eyes – would take up the kingly mantle. But Tig wasn't sure, he had self-doubt. He knew himself to be a fearless warrior in the right circumstances, but accepted, too, his own failings as a thinker, a sage, a strategist. Planning was something he'd never been able to apply himself to, found it a real chore for which he had no real natural talent.

Jack began to worry greatly. This situation couldn't be allowed to continue. He cleared his throat, spoke earnestly, with almost an air of timidity, as if he hardly dared address them, knowing he had no real right to do so.

'If I might suggest something . . .'

All heads swivelled in his direction. They were eager to hear anything, no matter that it might come from the Ghostly One. They were desperate.

'Well, as I see it we must protect our village. But we do not want the pirates to get this far before we try to repel them. Our walls are not strong enough. We must destroy their strength before they reach us.'

'Yes, we all see this,' agreed Tig, looking to the others to back him up. They all nodded, in response. 'But how, Jack. How we do this?'

'Well . . .' Jack's mind had been ticking over feverishly during their earlier discussions, and he had something in mind. 'We need time to prepare, more time than we probably have. Some of you – those of you who can jungle creep unseen – will have to delay them. Ambush them on the trail here, pick off the tailenders, that type of thing. Let's give them a taste of what to expect and worry them a little. Let them know we won't be pushovers.

'And while some of you are doing that, the rest of us can ready the village. Everyone must help. Together we can beat them.'

Hope blazed in their eyes, enthusiasm was fired. It was one of the islanders' traits that if *told* they could do something, oft times they could, even the most difficult of tasks.

'Now listen carefully.' They drew in physically about Jack, intent, purposeful, brown faces and tight curls dusty grey with ashes. 'We will need a carpenter; children to collect stones.' Big stones, Jack had been about to say. As big as football bladders, but remembered they had no knowledge of that most English of games, and showed the desired size with hand gestures instead.

'Why?' they all wanted to know.

'We're going to have a spot of medieval warfare,' said Jack, excitedly, enjoying their mystification just a little.

'Med . . . Med evil? What is this thing, Jack, this *evil* thing you would mix us up in?'

'Something I was taught as a boy, my friends. Something that might just save us. Now, let's get to it. You must be firm with your people, tell them what you want and demand that it be done *now*. Fires must be lit, water boiled, weapons must be honed, wood for building must be found, and quick. We have little time.'

'Quick everyone. Do as Jack says,' said Tig, on his feet already and racking his brains to try and remember where he'd last seen the old carpenter.

Chapter Fifteen

*B*y the time the twenty-five or so pirates caught their first glimpse of the village they were greatly irritated. They'd lost three men on the way through the jungle, heard their cries and saw them drop; one with his head clubbed in, another with his throat slit, the third with a spear thrust squarely between the shoulder-blades. Yet they saw no one and began to conclude that these natives wouldn't be quite the pushover conquest they had envisaged.

And when they came within range of the village fortress batteries, they didn't know what had hit them, were taken utterly by surprise.

Even without the aid of gunpowder the little cannibal garrison was devastating in its bombardment, waiting only until the 'pasty yellow ones' appeared in the clearing on the lower slope before unleashing the first of their untried weapons.

The carpenter had been very busy, was enraptured by the trebuchet that had been created from palm trunks, vine bindings, a wicker-type shallow basket more often used for collecting seafood, and Jack's know-how. He'd done the drawings – hurried sketches on the village's hard packed dirt street, scraped with a sharp stick – and explained with much pantomiming how it would work.

Thank God for all those tedious history lessons, thought Jack, and thank 'me' for learning something without even knowing it!

The first giant slinging from the trebuchet was wide. Quickly the villagers brought it about, first a little, then a bit more, as Jack directed. Another rock was brought, football-like, and placed, just so, in the basket. The great catapult was drawn back taut, set free, flung forward with a loud whistle and projected its missile. It whooshed, smashed into the pirates who – finding their approach observed – had decided to charge their enemies with much waving of swords and yelling.

One fell instantly, headless, the blow taking his body back several feet. Two more were knocked over by their dead, mangled accomplices and took some time to come groggily to their feet, bringing up the rear of the attacking party with cautious reluctance.

A few more large stones were catapulted, a few more adjustments made to angle and range. Another two men were killed; one seriously injured and screaming with pain on the ground.

After the large stones came the small clusters that could knock out, even kill, and certainly hurt like blazes. The baskets were filled to brimming with pebbles, sharp pieces of broken crockery and (the cannibals loved this gruesome touch) some hands, feet and jointed torsos from the Chinese pirates who had died on the beach. There were screams of horror and outrage as well as pain when this particular cargo reached its destination.

Running for cover and cowering behind fronds of lush undergrowth and the odd scattered boulder, the pirates shouted to each other in their fiendish tongue, produced firearms and began loading. Jack observed this and cautioned his men behind the palisade of upright palm trunks:

'They have pistols. Listen to me, believe me. This will

sound stupid to you, but their weapons will fire deadly shot, shot you cannot see.'

The gathering of men and women looked at him with knitted brows, uncomprehending.

How could he explain? He racked his brains, and said, 'Think of your blowpipes. When the dart flies from the shaft, do you see it?'

They shook their heads. No, they never saw the dart until it was stuck into the intended victim, its wagging tail protruding.

'Well pistols are like that. They fire the shot so fast – far faster than any blast of breath from a blowpipe – that you will not see it. And it hits with such force that it can kill. If a pistol is aimed at you, duck, hide, put something solid between yourself and it. This wall, for instance, will stop their shot.'

They listened, and nodded, there were murmurs of understanding, acquiescence, but Jack wondered if they truly understood, or indeed believed him.

Thereafter, they warily peeped out, darted back behind the wall for cover, mimicking Jack's actions. The first few loud reports from the pistols made them scream out loud, unable to hide their terror, then, when no one fell either dead or wounded, they calmed, began to respond once more to their leader's orders.

Having found their advance temporarily unchallenged, the pirates came at the walls in a rush, showing off their gymnastic prowess as one leapt up onto the shoulders of another, was balanced expertly and moved towards the summit of the wall. He could just get his hands to the top, grip, launch himself up. His athleticism took the cannibals and Jack by surprise, but they quickly regained their wits, managing to finish him off with spears before he could fire. The next pirate came quick on his heels. Jack took up the pistol from the dead man's fingers, aimed and fired. The Chinaman fell dead, a neat hole through his temple. The cannibals cheered, kicked the corpse, showed curiosity over the wound. One of them must have forgotten to keep out of the pistol sights for a shot rang out and he clutched his arm, squealing with surprise more than anything else. Luckily it was only a flesh wound.

Meanwhile, the women were bringing the vessels of boiling water to the wall. The men helped to lift them up and over, mindful of staying out of sight of the pistols, especially now that they'd seen just how lethal such a weapon could be in Jack's hand, seen a comrade wounded too. They poured out the contents with merciless accuracy, scalding those below. The screams were horrible. The cannibals smiled with pleasure. The men fell off their partners' shoulders, demented with pain, their bodies flaring in hideous patches. Blindly they bumped into each other. The cannibals emptied three more pots down upon them, steaming, boiling, wickedly effective.

Their foes were vanquished, running amok, unable to find any release from the pain. The islanders spilled out of the compound, set about the 'pasty yellow ones' in an orgy of gleeful violence and finished them off. Having been part-boiled alive like lobsters, death, when it came, was a blessing.

There was jubilation. Jack was hoisted up aloft by four stout warriors and paraded around the village, the old and young and the warriors of both sexes singing his praises. Jack was their hero. Jack was wonderful. He beamed, tried to be modest, giving the credit to the warlords of a medieval world who had employed similar basic but oh-so effective tactics to defend their keeps and castles in Olde England. They didn't understand that. They weren't interested. Jack had saved them. Jack had showed himself to be one of them. He was the man of the hour.

That night there was a council of the leaders, the bravest warriors. The men sat about their fire, chewing narcotic nuts and coming to conclusions. Around them on poles were the heads of their vanquished foes. They'd decided upon their new leader; it was to be Jack.

Doped by the fare on offer and drunk, too, after several celebratory dishes of their home brew, still he had sense enough to refuse, to put forward his own choice. Tig. Tig declined humbly, singing Jack's praises most eloquently. Not only had be masterminded the repulse of the invaders, but he had showed himself to be fearless. He was all they could want in a leader, surely? And he, Tig, would happily follow him to the death.

There was a hearty cheer of agreement, Sanga wrapped her arms around Jack's neck, kissed his nape, his ear. Mia brought him food, more brew. On a high, he consumed all that was set before him, even allowed himself to be led to the throne, occupied on occasions such as these by Ping until his fatal débâcle of yesterday. How quickly he'd been forgotten!

They draped the red, green, yellow and black gaily beaded cloak of office about his shoulders and set gifts before him: fruit, coconuts, small baskets of pearls and a large earthenware jar full of those strange and dangerously powerful nuts. He was encouraged to chew another, to work it until soft in his mouth like gum, and feel the true benefits. Jack, not wanting to spoil the party or offend, graciously complied.

At his feet young femals rubbed their breasts against his bare legs trying to entice him, mindful of the prestige of coupling with such a man. Sanga kicked away the nearest with a rush of vehemently vile words, laid her hand possessively, blatantly, at Jack's groin.

His senses seemingly heightened by the drug, he hardened immediately, moved a lazy hand, greasy from the roasted meat he'd been gnawing, to her nearest breast. It was large, firm, hard-nippled; goose bumps of delight ran up her arms as he fondled her. Yes, everyone grudgingly liked Jack; the men admired him, the women desired him. They watched this sexual foreplay with some interest (henceforth everything that Jack did would have an inflated sense of importance attached to it because he was Chief), feeling themselves hardening or moistening, visually stimulated. They paired up, littered the ground with their copulating bodies. The old and young were abed. Everyone (probably without exception) had sex that night, at least once. It was an orgy, a mass celebration.

Jack chewed on, absently hoping that the narcotic nuts juices didn't stain his teeth, while Sanga straddled him, lifted his loincloth and sat on him, taking all of his engorged penis into her with a groan of longing. She jerked up and down on him, almost until the tip of him slid out of her wetness, then lowered herself, grinding into his groin to make certain she had all of him.

He didn't last long; just long enough for Sanga. Then he growled, thrust up into her, up and up, holding her tight about the waist, forcing her down. Her head lolled ecstatically, she quivered, was spent, melted away into the drunken, drugged mists which surrounded him.

There was more drink, more food. Meat, fruit, berries.

A young female placed an orchid behind Jack's ear, rearranged his blond locks in the process, and gave a tinkling laugh.

A female's rear stared him in the face, a wet, pink mound so welcoming that he was instantly on his knees, a finger tracing the route that only a moment later his once more erect penis was to thrust into hungrily. He cupped her breasts, pumped mindlessly, to the hilt, over and over, his eyes on the other bodies, the other legs wide spread and cradling rampantly thrusting males, their penises driving in, stabbing. He pinched the woman's nipples, bit her shoulder, came with a shudder and emptied himself into her.

Breathlessly he reclined on the floor, taking the cup offered to him and gulped down its contents. He had barely finished before another female was upon him, fondling him, kissing his exhausted flesh and taking him into her mouth. He lay back and let her have her way.

Tig rolled over next to him, a woman rising and

falling upon him with much moaning and arching of her plump little frame. Gasping a little with mounting pleasure, he offered Jack his congratulations again, adding: 'Truly you are one of us now, Jack. You have dreamed our dreams, drank our brew, eaten with us the flesh of our enemies. Truly you are the Coconut King, a worthy leader.'

Jack's mind was a fog, almost impenetrable by then. Still, something got through and struck him as awful. He looked through a psychedelic maze towards the cooking fire, the joints of meat roasting there and something in him exploded with a revolted realisation. Somewhere in his mind he felt horror, but it was overshadowed by everything else – by sensation, delight, mindlessness.

Tonight he'd become one of them. The thought made his stomach churn and knot, as if it wished to throw out such an abomination. But he found he couldn't care, not as much as he knew he should, not then. He was too enraptured, too much a slave of his own body and its weaknessness, vices, too much possessed by the madness all around him.

The girl sucked, lips drawing him to the back of her throat, pulling, pulling until he stiffened, arched, cried out. She gulped, swallowed greedily, pleased with herself for bringing the Coconut King so much obvious pleasure.

He floated off then into troubled unconsciousness.

When Jack finally awoke the next day in Ping's former lodge, he felt desperately ill. He took up the water pitcher, eyes red and blinking rapidly, and drank the vessel dry. Then he called for another. Mia came in immediately, saw to his request with a knowing grin. He grunted, tried not to think, but it was no good. It was in his head. He remembered all too clearly what he had done, what he had eaten. The fact that it had been a sin committed unknowingly did nothing to ease his mind. He put his fingers to the back of his throat and tried to vomit but it didn't work. He went to the latrine beyond the village instead, decided that he would squat there and use his bowels until he felt certain the abomination had passed through him. Only then did he guess that he'd feel only remotely better.

A cheery Tig came to keep him company. This was quite a normal practice. A great deal of talk amongst the males of the village was done whilst they performed the most basic of bodily functions.

'You look ill, Our King. Too many nuts?'

Jack shook his head, came right out with the truth, believing that to be forthright was best in this instance. 'It is the eating of human flesh, Tig: I cannot. Never again. Do you understand? If this disqualifies me as your leader, I shall understand, but I *cannot* . . . I feel that it is – ' he strove to be diplomatic as well as honest ' – wrong, goes against everything I was taught as a young man across the sea.'

Tig looked mildly amused, not in the least offended. 'Yes, I think I understand. Maybe there are things that your people eat, way off across the waters, which we here would dislike. It does not matter. If you no eat, that is fine. It was just honour paid, the best cuts given to you. If you like, Friend Jack, I speak to council, have law passed forbidding them from ever again offering you such fare?'

'Thank you. That is gracious of you.' The agreement made Jack feel a little better.

'No trouble. Now, what would Jack like to do on first day as leader? Have you plans? Orders?'

Jack was doubtful. 'Not today, Tig, have mercy! I want only to drink water, purge this tainted body and recover from all the excitement and excess of yesterday.'

Tig looked woeful. 'Jack, that very dull. But so be it. Might some of your warriors paddle out to the ship . . . explore?'

Jack shrugged his shoulders, couldn't quite get used to this being in charge business. 'Sure. Why not. But take care; they may have left a lookout on board.'

'No problem, friend.'

Overwhelmed by the number of islanders that swarmed aboard that afternoon, the old Chinese guard – who'd been the least able-bodied of the ship's company – was quickly hacked to pieces.

The cannibals went below, rummaging carelessly through the booty stashed in the hold of the junk. They were untidy explorers, taking a fancy to the oddest things (copper pans, mirrors and a European gentleman's wig) and throwing what they didn't fancy destructively overboard. The gold coins they thought pretty but useless and consigned them to the deep. The ticking clock on the satinwood desk in the main cabin frightened them. They smashed it with their war clubs. And the fine pieces of ladies jewellery they hung about their necks, fingers fumbling with delicate clasps.

That evening when Jack – recovered somewhat and breaking out of his fit of the horrors – took the trail back to his camp to collect his belongings, because henceforth he would reside in the headman's lodge in the village, he saw the flotsam from the junk, the bobbing barrels of salted meat and gunpowder, the unravelled bolts of cloths shimmering crimson and gold in the shallows. And when he looked out further to the oriental craft riding at anchor, he could see smoke wafting up from its hold. The junk was on fire.

He hurried down to the beach, reached the water's edge just as Mia and Sanga waded breathlessly ashore through the foam.

His eyebrows knit in consternation. 'The ship's afire. Do you two know anything about it?'

In answer to his suspicious stare they acted all wide-eyed innocence. 'Afire? The ship? No! We not know. It not us. We were bathing. That truth.'

Jack found his eyebrow giving a sceptical quirk, tried hard to believe them, but couldn't quite manage it. Still, it didn't matter now. The ship was belching smoke and sparks like some infernal monster, the yellow-green sky of late afternoon besmirched with black clouds and smuts. There was a groan, a creak, she began to go nose-heavy.

The flanking girls each took an arm of Jack's whilst they watched the ship gurgle and sink out beyond the coral reef and, while Jack was absorbed by the sight, they exchanged knowing smiles around his tanned torso.

It was as if each could accurately read the other's mind. They nodded imperceptibly and wound their arms about him, of a collective mind to take his interest away from the lost ship.

They pulled him down into the wet sand, the tide lapping about their entwining bodies, rolling with a now laughing Jack as bolts of crimson fabric from the Chinese junk tangled about them, hugging him, kissing him in the European fashion he'd taught them, Mia circling her legs about his tapering waist and locking her ankles as he entered her with his silken length.

Sanga called out to the warrior, Tig, who strode the beach, resplendent in a grey wig complete with queue and black silk ribbon, mimicking the rather upright, faintly foppish posturing he'd seen Jack unconsciously employ occasionally in his movements.

Sanga liked the look of him suddenly, wished to copulate, told him so. 'Ho there, Tig, your Joy Bringer pleases my eye. Shall we join?'

He strode up, looking interested in a no-nonsense kind of way. 'Yes. I'm happy to. Where shall it be. On the sand . . .?'

'No. In the water. Like Jack and Mia.'

Tig threw away the wig which kept slipping into his eyes, ran into the foam after the squealing Sanga, one hand around his stout member to work it to swift stiffness.

He pounced upon her, made her shriek with laughter, fell into the breakers, arms wrapping about her, his hand cupping her mound, guiding his throbbing flesh to the spot. 'The octopus ravages, invades his captive *everywhere*,' laughed Tig, demoniacally, pushing into her and rolling around in the buoyant waters, on top one moment then holding his breath the next as he flapped his legs to keep control. She squirmed in his arms, playing the part of ravaged maiden in the hands of some sea monster with enthusiasm.

He caught her afresh, arms tight around her waist, filled her from the rear, jerking his loins.

She cried out, contracting about him, choking on a mouthful of water.

Tig carried her ashore, dropped her there in the dry, warm sand. He thrust into her again and she climaxed almost immediately, then lay there languidly, smiling contentedly, the sun caressing her.

Still hard, Tig entered the water again, making for the thrashing, intertwined forms of Jack and Mia. They were a mass of limbs and tangled silk, lying in the shallows, the inrushing tide lifting and dropping them.

Tig fell upon them, rolling about, hands everywhere, his unsatisfied member prodding.

At one point Jack rolled, jerking into Mia and playfully fighting off Tig, his rear uppermost, his shaft deep in the girl, Tig saw his chance, fell upon the blond Adonis's back and slipped a finger into him.

'Cut that out!' Jack shouted above the noise of the surf, unable to turn and cuff the young man, because Mia was holding him so close, so tight.

Tig ignored him, inched the tip of his penis into his friend, entered him.

Jack felt that he should be outraged, might well have remembered his unhappy and humiliating schoolboy experiences at the hands of Darting Major. He felt neither. What Tig was doing was, to him, just overexuberant horseplay. He and the other young men of the island did it often, especially when they'd been devouring the narcotic nuts. By penetrating Jack, Tig was, it could be said, only underlining the fact that the white man had been fully accepted amongst them.

With the three of them thrashing about, writhing and jerking, it was an untidy copulation, with much laughing and shouting. Sated, they doused themselves thoroughly in the gentle breakers, than waded ashore to flop down beside a dozing Sanga to join her for a nap.

Chapter Sixteen

It was Tiku's feast day, a celebration of the birth of the Living God. All the villagers brought gifts and food for the early evening feast. By mid-afternoon the scented garden before his dwelling was full of people, full of offerings.

Tiku appeared with his wives and their children in his wake. He was splendid in a shell and bead tunic of pearly lustre, his shoulders draped about with his flowing black feathered cloak. He had been born thirty-eight monsoon seasons ago. He was in his prime; magnificent.

On his left side was his favourite, Iona, and her wobbly legged infant, Ran, who held her hand tightly and walked with the precariousness of a normal eighteen-month-old.

Tiku had started out desiring her, perceiving her as a rare oddity, perhaps. Certainly the islanders had never seen anything like her – so red, so white. But he had come to love her, too, passionately, deeply. Observers gossiped as to the reasons for her prolonged shining as the brightest star, and all cited her quick smile and rather mushy regard for her child and those of her fellow wives. Also she was *very* English. They found her quaint, odd behaviour highly amusing and not a little endearing.

A great mat of grasses had been unrolled before Tiku's abode, the feast placed in the centre. The Living God and his wives took their places and everyone else bundled in about them, wanting to be as close as possible to those most important, sitting cross legged.

They ate as the gifts were presented, male and female attendants vying to serve the wines, juices and cordials. It was deemed an honour to do so. The food was luscious: roasted bantam, grilled fish on giant leaves, dressed crab, lobster and prawn dripping with rich, chilled sauce; fruit and nuts filling the scooped out inners of pineapple; dainty sweetmeats, honey dripping. The islanders feasted without restraint. If, over the years, they grew progressively plumper they didn't mind at all, seeing fatness as a testament to good living, a thing of prestige. If you or your wife were fat it meant you were doing well, were a good provider. Consequently, very few inhabitants of Wahwu were sveltlike, not even the very young.

If the feast was lush, the gifts were sumptuous.

From the village elders came amulets and cloak brooches fashioned in silver with semi-precious stones. Wahwu's silversmith was more often employed in the making of farming implements, his forge an infernal hovel where the fire was kept constantly stoked. The ore came from the near mountains: iron, silver, sometimes small quantities of tin.

From his wives there was a new throne, a grand affair in glowing hardwood. It was oversized, as befitted a living god; dark, heavily carved, its backboard fashioned into two fretted fighting cocks. Tiku beamed a smile of thanks to each of his women in turn, ran appreciative palms over the smooth workmanship on the arms.

Seated then in his new chair and looking down upon them all with great bearing, Tiku received the rest of his gifts: the flower garlands (rare orchids which had been searched for for days in the jungle); pottery ware for his household; cloth for his clothes.

Iona and Mam sat at his feet, nodding approvingly as the rich pile of offerings mounted. Such presents spoke eloquently of the people's love for their divine leader.

Finally, a speech was made by the most ancient of the elders, a wrinkled old skeleton of a man who was reputed to have seen one hundred and seventeen monsoon seasons. Longevity was quite common on Wahwu. His eulogy had Tiku beaming vaingloriously and even, Iona noted with a suppressed smile, nodding in agreement with some of the old man's words. The Living God was like a child really, needing praise, lapping it up. Such transparency only endeared him the more to Iona. It made others sneer though.

Moona watched him with something like contempt, though prudently she masked her feelings to a greater extent. Beside her sat her paramour, Amandu, a sleekly handsome young man of no more than twenty years, who showed her dog-like devotion. Once Tiku had been like that also – besotted, loving. Now it was as if she no longer existed, was wife only in name. Rarely these days did he waste words upon her or she on him. Where once there had been fiery passion and power for her in being his number one, now there was something like dislike, distaste, hatred even. She enjoyed her young lover, didn't want Tiku back, but she missed the rest – the passing of her glory days. She had liked having power, queening it. When the elder finished his speech with a joke, only she – and her lover, out of allegiance – did not laugh, remaining sour-faced, whispering with their heads together.

Mam nudged Iona and nodded in their direction. 'Her tongue drips acid. But on who, I wonder?'

'Some hapless soul,' said Iona, momentarily intercepting that malevolent, slanting gaze.

As the evening progressed the tales became more colourful, their content more suspect, Iona thought, surmising that in many cases the drink was doing the talking. There were stories of giant lizards in far off archipelagos that made St George and the Dragon sound positively tame; and there were stories of the Living God who had ruled them before Tiku – his father, Rantavitiku, after whom Tiku and Iona's son were loosely named. Iona listened to these tales with interest, not for the first time either, the exploits of Tiku's sire fascinating her with each new and different recounting. Each orator brought something to the telling, seeing events from a different perspective, having different memories.

The stories all centred around Rantavitiku's expedition beyond the volcano to the land of mountains. This was a place where few save the very old had ever ventured.

Beyond the volcano they had seen birds they didn't know existed; ugly, odd little animals with curled tails and four legs which snorted in the undergrowth, gored if given the chance; and people, other people, a tribe quite different from themselves.

Rantavitiku, being a moderate, peace-loving man of liberal persuasions, had tried to parley with them. But these people – ugly, squat red devils, was the unanimous consensus of opinion – were hostile, hadn't given him a chance to try and be friendly. There was a brief skirmish, each side lost some dozen men and Rantavitiku decided prudently that it was time to head for home. His people were farmers, easy going for the most part. They'd stopped warring amongst themselves generations before. They were disinclined to start a war with some far off, obviously primitive tribe.

Unfortunately, on the homeward journey, with the men wary and nervous, Rantavitiku was accidentally hit by the poisoned dart from one of his own men's indiscriminately fired blowpipes. It was a dead Living God who was brought home in mournful procession to be buried on the terrace near his temple altar. Thereafter, it was decreed that no man should ever set foot in the land beyond the volcano, lest he be sent into exile.

The young men especially listened to these tales almost wistfully. They'd never tasted battle. Sometimes they longed for it to such an extent that they even contemplated self-imposed exile, a life of wandering, looking for the mysterious tribe of red devils.

Iona listened engrossed, leaning in to Tiku's muscular leg, while he lovingly stroked her hair, ran a tantalising finger that was more like a promise than reality, over her sensitive nape. Tonight she would walk the path to his lodge, give herself up wholeheartedly to a night of delight.

The elder came to the end of the tale reverently:

'And Tiku it was, of all Rantavitiku's many people, who was chosen to be the anointed one, our beloved leader. We thank all the gods for keeping him safe unto his thirty-eighth summer. We pray they continue to do so.'

Everyone said in unison: 'Let it be so. Bless Tiku our Living God. Keep him well and safe to guide us with wisdom.'

He raised a hand, gave a magnanimous, very regal wave, inclined his head in acknowledgement. He drank in their adulation, basked in the glory of the moment. Never had he felt so powerful, so strong, so content.

Everyone raised their cups; pottery, iron and silver filled with the liquid toast.

'Tiku! Tiku!'

Iona had the cup to her lips and was about to sip heartily as an unmistakeable show of allegiance, when Mam snatched it away frantically, warning shrilly:

'Don't! Poison!'

Tiku, whose eyes were popping, his jaw set threateningly at the sight of his favourite being so treated, digested Mam's words slowly, gaped. The crowd were quicker, were gasping with disbelief and shock before he'd thought to bellow, 'Poison? What's this you say, Wife? Poison? Explain.'

Mam trembled as she spoke in her usual small voice employed in addressing his person. 'Truly I believe so,

Lord Tiku, saw them – Moona and Amandu – heads together, whispering, saw him put something in Iona's beaker when he poured her wine.'

Everyone turned to stare at the accused pair. She was as defiant and cool as ever. He looked frightened.

Chapter Seventeen

There was a scuffle as Amandu made to escape through the crowd. Dozens of hands grabbed out to apprehend him. He struggled. Moona stayed still, only her eyes blazing with emotion. She was haughty and defiant, even smiled as the enraged Tiku advanced upon her. That infuriated him. He struck her, a hard slap to her cheek, the great ring on his finger catching the side of her nose, gashing it. She cried out then, more in angry indignation at being chastised in public than in pain.

'Do you deny Mam's accusation, woman?'

She threw back her head, laughed acidly. 'Do I look like a poisoner?'

Yes, she did. But Tiku refrained from snapping out the retort. She would not make him lose his dignity. His gaze shifted malevolently to Amandu. There was still a touch of jealousy in him whenever he looked at the man she had passed him over for, a pretty man who was little more than a boy. That rankled. Always would. He crooked a finger, drew it towards him with deliberate slowness. 'Bring him here. And, Mam, bring the beaker.'

There was a buzz of speculation amongst the gathered throng, a place magically cleared amongst the coconuts, pineapples and chicken carcasses. Berries were squashed under toes. Amandu was brought into the cleared circle before Tiku's chair. His eyes were on the beaker Mam brought forward. He struggled all the harder and there were knowing nods from the observers.

There were four people in the circle now.

'Drink,' Tiku ordered, himself holding the brimming beaker to Amandu's lips.

The young man kept them tight shut, shook his head from side to side. His eyes were bright with fear and panic. All at once he started sobbing, his plea choked out amongst tears. 'Please, don't make me. It was her . . .' his eyes went to Moona, 'She made me do it. How could I not?'

'You should have refused,' spat Tiku. 'Should have feared me far more than you did her. You have made a grave mistake. Now drink. I *command* it.'

'No!' screamed Amandu, jerking his head about, struggling wildly.

It took four men to subdue him, keep his head still. Then Tiku raised the beaker once more.

'Wait,' shouted Moona, not so haughty now as she saw her lover facing death. She had loved him, his youth somehow rejuvenating her for a while until bitterness reaffirmed its grip. She didn't want to see him die. 'Let me drink it.'

She was being uncharacteristically brave and stupid. And in vain.

Tiku shook his head, smiled maliciously. 'Oh no, I have something else in mind for *you*.' That said, he gripped Amandu's nose between thumb and forefinger and squeezed until the boy was forced to open his mouth for air. Then, mercilessly, he poured the liquid down his throat. Amandu spluttered, coughed. His mouth overflowed, the tainted wine dribbling at the corners.

The same procedure was followed over and over again until all the liquid was gone: his nose was held, the beaker thrust at lips which gasped open for air, the wine ran down his throat, he choked. When the beaker was emptied Tiku ordered the men who restrained Amandu to let him go. The boy immediately fell to his knees, began to groan. The crowd observed with serious, cold faces. Moona began to cry, struggled trying to get to her lover, to give comfort. Tiku wouldn't allow it.

Iona watched and, perhaps not totally irrationally in that instance, she felt a twinge of pity for her old rival. Tiku was playing the vengeful god to the hilt, was totally without compassion. Because of what had almost been perpetrated against herself, he was acting ruthlessly, cruelly, and enjoying it. She disliked what she saw in him then.

It took Amandu – writhing on the grass matting amongst the leftovers of the feast – several agonised minutes to die.

No one touched him. No one said a word. The scene would haunt Iona for a long time afterwards. But worse was immiment.

The climb up the mountain trail was exhausting and trecherous in the dark. Tiku was carried in his ceremonial chair. Torchbearers flanked the grave column of people.

Tiku wore his ceremonial robes and a black carved mask through which only his eyes, cold and dark, could be seen. Led before him, so that he might observe her distress with ease, was the bound Moona, a rope halter about her neck.

At the rear of the column the villagers followed, chanting.

Up and up they went, legs aching in protest, seemingly forever.

The first crimson rays of dawn were riddling the muted blue-green sky by the time they finally arrived at the place, touching everything with an infernal paintbrush; flesh, clothes, undergrowth and overhanging jungle . . . all blood red. It was ominously prophetic.

Soaring up above them was the summit of Wahwu's volcano, but they didn't have to make that final, exhausting climb through the black rock. Iona groaned with relief, for her lungs were at bursting point.

This was a place seldom visited by any villager, yet it was far from neglected. The undergrowth was cut back and a vast area cleared. Around a dark fissure a wooden parapet had been built, was kept in good repair.

The crowd kept back from the abyss warily despite the railings and waited and watched for Tiku to orchestrate things. No one knew quite what to expect, could only guess. No one had ever before so angered a god, certainly not in the living memory of any who were present. Yet this place had always been there to serve such an eventuality.

There was a stone platform behind the parapet and Tiku now climbed up onto it, towering a foot at least over the tallest man.

'Wives, come stand with me,' he ordered, indicating the space behind the platform.

Sheepishly they complied, wrinkling their noses as a cloud of sulphurous gas belched up out of the fissure. It was a gaping crack in the Earth's surface caused by the subterranean upheavals of ancient volcanic eruptions. Far, far below, glowing in the blackness where the torchlight couldn't penetrate, an underground river of lava flowed, red, yellow and white hot at its centre.

Moona cried quietly, throat sore where she'd fallen on the trail and been dragged by her neck rope. Exhausted and consumed of grief for her lover, her mind all but destroyed by the sight of his slow and painful death, she didn't care what happened to her, was far beyond caring. She was out of her body almost and beyond this place and any punishment Tiku cared to mete out.

His eyes rested on her, black, dead, merciless. 'Bring her forth.'

Instantly it was done.

As if drugged, the motionless Moona stood before him, her gaze blank. He snarled at her passivity, would much preferred to have heard her scream her hate or beg him for mercy. Her silence riled him, he found it disquieting.

He snatched her to him, making the assembly gasp, and shook her, tearing frenziedly at her clothes until she swayed, half collapsing in his arms, in a state of tattered nakedness.

He clamped an arm about her waist and, snatching aside his feathered robes, thrust his ever-ready penis deep into her limp, unprepared body, taking her speedily, cruelly, before everyone.

She moaned unconsciously, bent backwards deliriously with no control over her own body, her muscles seemingly turned to jelly.

Noiselessly, hardly showing any emotion, Tiku came, jerking into her and then flung her from him.

Iona clung to Mam, hiding her face against her friend's shoulder, disturbed by the hatred in her lover, suddenly afraid of him.

He roared out to the males who hovered near, members of his council, elders and such like, 'You, you, you . . .' he pointed, 'will all take her. All. Use her in the dust at my feet. Come, I command it.'

Of the seven selected in all, six did as bid, hating it and consumed by self-disgust, yet terrified of Tiku, of declining. Only one couldn't oblige, despite the shouted threats from the Living God. Just couldn't get himself to harden enough to penetrate Moona's flesh, was repelled by the ravished body from which the juices of so many men dripped. Tiku ordered him away in disgust.

And when they were finished, as if she weighed no more than an infant, Tiku lifted up Moona with ease, hands at her knees and small of her back, hoisting her up and over his head. She uttered a tiny sound, feebly made as if to flail her dangling arms and legs, then ceased as if she had lost all strength, sensed the futility.

'So die all who would anger their God,' cried Tiku.

Iona blurted. 'No!' before she could stop herself, then shook her head.

And Moona was thrown into the abyss, gobbled up by the darkness. For the briefest of moments, her body – from which no cry or scream ever came – flared in the unimaginable heat and then she was lost in the fiery stream.

The crowd murmured, gasped, cried out in shock, surprised despite themselves, and Tiku turned slowly to his group of wives. His face as he removed his mask and focused his gaze fully on Iona, was livid. She, more than anyone else, to his mind, had no right to say 'no', to try to countermand his will, no matter how ineffectually. He was displeased with her and she would know it later and regret it.

Iona cast down her eyes, concerned that he might see plainly the dislike flashing in them, and knew that never again would she be able, without reserve, to say that she loved the man . . . or liked him, even.

Chapter Eighteen

He'd lain so long upon his belly by the pool, bathed by the sun and with the silence of his companion to lull him, that Jack was almost asleep, the spear in his hand slackly held and virtually on the point of being dropped.

Suddenly Tig spoke, wiping Jack's sleep away, bringing him back to consciousness with a start.

'Huh! What?'

'I said, Old Friend, would you like my sister, Mara, as your woman?'

Jack blinked, looked across the pool drowsily to the place on the opposite bank where the women congregated lazily, talking of whatever women talked about and occasionally laughing that certain, worldly laugh that excluded men. Mara was amongst them – young, pleasing, with curly brown hair, a robust figure, good teeth.

Jack's mouth moved expressively as he gave the suggestion some thought. He knew what was behind it: Tig was still feeling grateful, indebted to him.

The day before they'd been out wandering, watching the sky, the birds, talking of this and that, male things – the changing seasons, the plentifulness of game and fish. They'd been above the village, surveying it, their talk had been idle and lazy, their thoughts free to wander.

Seated with their backs to the trunk of a great mahogany tree they'd enjoyed each other's company much as they did this day too; easily, comfortably, like only true friends can. They felt no need to talk unless they wanted to, no overt need for politeness and etiquette.

The wily old pig, his tusks formidably curled and pointed to dagger sharpness, had taken them both by surprise, dashing into their clearing, charging straight at Tig. They were unarmed, not even on their feet. Tig could never have escaped.

In a split second Jack snatched up the coconut beside him, and upon which he'd been leaning an elbow only a second before, and smashed it down on the pig's head, who'd reached them, head down, in for the kill. The beast was stopped in its tracks, somersaulted past Tig who was scrambling frantically to his feet, squealed and staggered groggily, trying to regain its feet again to charge anew.

Tig had leapt forward, taken up the same coconut and brained the animal one more time, killing him, his belaboured breath ceasing quite abruptly.

Then Tig clapped his arms about Jack, kissed him as he'd seen Jack kiss his women, and said wondrously, 'You saved my life.'

Jack had spluttered disgustedly, wiped his mouth with the back of his hand. 'Not on the mouth, Tig! On the cheeks. Only *women* on the mouth.'

'Sorry. I forget. No big deal. You taste fresh.'

That was yesterday. Now today Tig was still going on about it, trying to show his gratitude.

A fat fish wiggled its way through the shallows below them. Tig stabbed at it with his spear, missed.

'No, I don't want Mara. I have too many women already.'

'Women like you, Jack.'

He sighed. 'I know.'

'Mara like you, want you. She said so.'

'I'm flattered. And, please, tell her so. But she should look for someone more her own age. I'm much older. Too old. Mia, Sanga and the rest are plenty enough trouble, thank you.'

'She will be disappointed.'

'She'll get over it.'

Tig had another go at the elusive fish, got it with a yell of triumph.

Jack lay his head back down on his folded arms and began to daydream.

Women. He didn't want them. There were too many for him to cope with already. And they were very demanding. They exhausted him. Sometimes – and he truly did think this – he wished he needn't bed anyone for a while, stay celibate for a whole month, say. It would be bliss.

He had too many women. And they were all the wrong women. His mind drifted on to thoughts of the right one, to Iona Stanley. He remembered the first time he had ever set eyes upon her.

He'd come up on deck to take the air aboard The *Lady Luckington*, lounging in the doorway from the companionway, and there she'd been, at the rails, staring out to sea. She hadn't seen him. She was so angry, she wasn't aware of anything else.

She'd struggled with her wedding ring, cursed it, pulled and pulled, then exclaimed with satisfaction when it slipped violently off.

Jack had wondered whether he should do the gentlemanly thing and withdraw. But he'd resisted, was too intrigued.

She was dressed in a serviceable woollen dress of an unflattering greyish-green colour and wore a hooded cloak of dusk pink velvet over the top. The hood had been blown back by the wind. The folds of the cloak flapped about her. Her damp hair plastered her face. She shouted something that was swallowed up by the wind, for the weather had been turning bad even then, and she had hurled the ring out towards the unfriendly sea.

A blast of rain-sodden wind brought it straight back. It hit her mid-torso and fell to the deck. She turned on it in raging disbelief, screaming at the inanimate object, jumping up and down on it in dainty shoes that couldn't have so much as buckled the sturdy gold thing out of shape.

There was so much hate in her, such wildness in her eyes, that Jack felt himself shrink back into the passageway instinctively. She was a very unhappy, very angry woman and it showed in her face. Its features were out of control, quite ugly in their contortions. She repulsed and fascinated all at once.

She'd stooped, taken up the ring, hurled it out into the wind with such force the second time that she'd actually wrenched her shoulder and grabbed it in sudden pain.

Jack, sensing that she would have hated to know herself observed in that instance, had stepped back inside, descended the stairs and entered his cabin. He stopped short on finding Miss Harker waiting nervously for him inside.

'Ma'am?'

'Sir, I . . .' she went bright red, wrung her hands. 'I've come, sir, to appraise you of a delicate matter and ask for your cooperation. You see, it is my charge, Miss Cosgrove. She has developed the most unseemly crush on you, Mister Savage, and I fear, with even the slightest encouragement, it could get dangerously out of hand. I'm asking, sir, that you do the gentlemanly thing and ignore any childish advances she might make upon your person.'

Amused, Jack nodded understandingly.

She fanned herself and looked most uncomfortable, her breasts heaving behind the prim confines of her starched bodice, her breathing laboured.

He knew what ailed her; Miss Cosgrove wasn't the only one with a crush. He took advantage, sensing that

that was what she wanted from him and the real purpose for her visit to his cabin.

'My dear Miss Harker, you look faint. Let me assist you. Please. Don't struggle. You need air,' soothed Jack, quickly unbuttoning her bodice. 'Better? A glass of water perhaps?'

'I . . .' overwrought, she could find no words, only gasped when his fingers inadvertently touched her bulging breasts where they rose over the top of her corsets.

'Or perhaps a kiss?' queried Jack, getting straight down to business. His earlier encounter with Mrs Stanley had fired him strangely. Suddenly he needed a woman. Miss Harker had therefore appeared at an opportune moment.

His mouth swooped before Miss Harker could protest, and the pitch of the ship threw them together, bumping them into the cabin door. He pinned her there. She struggled but little, was soon groaning and pressing against him.

He dropped his mouth to her breasts, freeing the large dark nipples and pulling at them lustily with his artful teeth and lips, his hands going to her skirts, fumbling, hoisting, nudging her legs apart.

Beneath her prim cotton petticoats she was naked and already hot and moist. He gentled her, caressing and only lightly touching until she thrust her eager mound against his hand. Then he slipped a finger into her, let her feel the hard length of his penis pressing through her skirts, like an iron bar that reached up bruisingly to her navel.

He unbuttoned the fly flap on his breeches and set his silken-headed member at her tight vagina. He took it steadily, sensing that she might be a virgin, pushed into her slowly, inch by inch, felt her tighten fearfully about him, a novice indeed. He eased back, then pushed again, a hand moving down to open the folds of her womanhood the wider, make his passage the easier, flicker over her clitoris and give her a degree of pleasure that would blot any discomfort from her mind.

Then he went fully into her, making her cry out with shock and delight, thrust up into her, lifting her toes almost from the boards with the force of his possession, in her to the hilt, long and thick. He felt beneath her skirts, caught her rounded buttocks in his hands and held her fast while he took her, Miss Harker instinctively wrapped her legs about him, smothering him with grateful kisses.

She trilled, 'My dear Mister Savage, your conduct isn't at all gentlemanly. Not at all. But *please* don't stop.'

He closed his eyes, gloried in the act, all the while thinking of another, a wind-lashed virago, loving one body while longing for another.

Thus it was that the headstrong Iona had usurped Henriette in his affections, his obsession new but just as strong, just as hopeless.

It was Iona's night to share Tiku's bed. She didn't go. One of his servants came to remind her, request her presence at the Living God's lodge. She declined. Minutes later an armed guard, made up of four strong and excessively beweaponed males, came to escort her: Tiku demanded her presence. It was an order. Oozing recalcitrance, she went. And she paid for her effrontery, paid but didn't give in, was still hissing and spitting like a she-cat when her master dismissed her less than an hour later.

He'd bound her wrists, tied her to a ceiling beam carved like intertwined kimono dragons and bared his teeth in a grin of cruel satisfaction as she hung there, only her toes touched the floor. Then he'd ripped the clothes from her in a frenzy of anger and taken a thin switch to her belly and thighs, striking Iona half a dozen stinging strokes. Still she wouldn't cease her glaring, her unwavering stares of contempt.

He snapped completely, cut her down and fell upon her as she crumpled to the floor, snatching aside his loincloth and entering her with a painful stab that made them both cry out in dismay; raping her.

The pattern for their future relationship was set.

Sometimes he was brutal, sometimes just cold. And Iona responded accordingly; either spitting and snarling and being thoroughly uncooperative, infuriating him; or else giving in passively and closing her mind to him completely.

He tried punishing her by shunning her publicly, favouring another wife – any wife – and leaving Iona out in the cold socially. When that had no effect, he tried buying her affection back with more and more lavish gifts: strings of pearls so long that Iona could encircle her neck twenty times with a single loop of perfectly matched size, colour and lustre; and figures copulating in coral, which were meant to excite her visually into wanting him. Iona put them away in a cupboard and never looked at them again.

Nothing he did could make her feelings change.

One evening he summoned Iona to his lodge, ordered her to serve him wine and fruit while his handmaidens oiled and massaged him all over, from his big toes to his thick, corded neck.

She seethed, hovering in the background, wine jug at the ready, face set with grim determination. When he growled, 'More!' she obeyed with a composed face, pouring the drink with a mocking solemnity.

'I wish only to serve, Oh Great One,' she said sweetly.

He glowered. 'Your tone displeases me. Bathe my feet.'

She bit her tongue against a retort and brought a bowl of scented water forward, infuriated at being ordered to such a menial task, especially before his haughty handmaidens. He was humiliating her deliberately, trying to humble her. Well, if he thought *that* the way to win her back he was sadly mistaken.

She washed between his toes with studied conscientiousness, while another girl oiled his balls and penis and proceeded to give him leisurely hand relief.

His breathing deepened. His eyes, hard and black, stayed on Iona. She wouldn't catch his eye, kept her gaze on his feet. At length she dried them, perfumed them and took the bowl of dirty water away, saying, 'I am done.'

He watched her disappear with a frown, watched her return and commanded, 'Come, take over here,' pointing at his huge, rigid member and waving the rest of the women away. 'Shoo . . .'

Alone with him, Iona knelt by the side of his couch and took his mighty shaft between her hands, working them up and down somewhat mechanically and deliberately without finesse.

He growled, caught hold of her flaming hair and yanked her head up so that she was forced to look at him. 'Woman, you anger me!'

'Why? Have I not obeyed your every command?'

'You obey, yet you take no delight in your tasks.'

She hissed, nails digging into him oh-so slightly, 'How can that which is commanded be carried out with delight?'

'Your tongue is sharp, woman. Curb it, lest you would know my wrath.'

She jumped up abruptly, as if she would have the audacity to leave without seeking his permission. 'No man is *my* master!'

He jumped up too, caught her hair again, snatched her back.

A tingle of fear ran down her spine at his lethal look. His black eyes bore into her, he took up the switch that was more often used to ward off irritating flies and mosquitoes, and began thrashing Iona, tearing off her clothes as he did so, her necklace clattering broken to the floor, her little feathered skirt literally disintegrating beneath his brutal and frenzied attack.

The grass-like fibres of the switch bit into her shoulders and back, breasts and belly, stinging excruciatingly, making her deep pink nipples harden and her knees quake.

'Don't, Tiku. Don't!' she pleaded, half frightened, half incensed, trying to strike him back, retaliate. One haphazardly aimed blow found its mark and the Living God's nose trickled blood.

'Why you . . .!' He was beside himself then, and delivered a stunning blow to the side of her head, knocking Iona to the floor.

She blinked, saw stars. Then she saw Tiku reach up and snatch the ceremonial dildo from the wall above his couch, his face demonic, his fingers brutal as they prised Iona apart at the knees. She cried out, slapped him, tried to clutch at the wooden phallus that was trying determinedly to invade her, and repel it.

The Living God snarled his fingers in the curls surrounding her mound, delved there trying to force her open.

She fought him, scratched his face. 'Hurt me with that thing and I'll *never* forgive you. Never. Y'damned heathen!'

With an oath he found her opening, thrust into Iona, but it wasn't the agonising battery she had expected.

He was devious, oh-so devious. He plunged in so far, a very carefully calculated distance, then withdrew and repeated, apparently wanting to frighten her more than to savage her.

Her relief was such that all the fight went out of her. She lay like a quivering heap on the floor and began to cry.

His brows puckered, his eyes turned inky and tender. He removed the false phallus and inserted his own warm flesh with the utmost care, slipping into her already used and lubricated passage and filling her to the hilt, then moving ever so gently.

'My dearest one, my only one, why do you treat me like this? Why must we fight?'

She sobbed, 'Because we must, because . . .'

He frowned, his next thrust harder, making her gasp,

stretching her to the limit, the flesh at her opening taut enough to tear if he was brutal enough.

She saw the switch lying redundant on the ground and reached out a hand for it, her fingers groping blindly. She found it, and when Tiku was at the height of his passionate assault, clutching at her hips and forced her to arch up and accept him the fuller, Iona hit him on the buttocks with all her might, again and again.

He cried out, like an enraged bull, not shrinking away as she'd anticipated, but rearing up madly and ramming into her so that she squealed in pain, felt him hitting at her very core and could do naught to escape him, no matter how she fought.

He came with a barbaric cry of triumph and pumped into her, his buttocks clenching in spasms as he emptied himself into her, spurting and spurting, until she could feel it running from her, wetting her buttocks and the coconut matting beneath them.

She lay where he left her, vanquished, trembling, her opening trembling, seeping his fluids, her bud red and sore but unfulfilled.

He laughed at her as he wiped his limp member dry and poured himself wine.

She should have liked to jump up and slap him but she hadn't the strength.

' – *Now* who is the master here?' he probed.

She narrowed her eyes with fresh defiance. 'How can you claim mastery of a body that hasn't succumbed to you?'

His black brows knit. He gulped down the wine, poured a hefty measure over her mound so that Iona gasped with shock, and dived at her most intimate spot head first, his hands keeping her knees widespread.

His tongue and lips were full of artistry, delving, nibbling, circling her clitoris. Iona held out as long as she could but there came a time – and it wasn't long in coming – when she caught hold of the black maned head and held him to her, loving his tongue, his artfully chiselled nose and his deft fingers that kept her lips apart and her womanhood so expertly exposed to his ministerings.

Each thrust he made into her sent her wild, so that she called out against her will, 'Oh damn you, damn you,' convulsed with pleasure and went stiff beneath him, her knees poised wide, her braceleted ankles together.

She came, shuddering and squealing, calling his name, speaking of love, of a sort. 'Tiku, I love your tongue, your spit . . .' Then collapsed into an exhausted heap, curled up her legs and looked sleepy and quite childlike.

Tiku lounged on his couch, his hair smelling of her sex, was eating fruit, composing himself and attempting to look his desirable best. She was going to beg his pardon, he sensed, was sick and tired of being cold-shouldered and humiliated. He was going to forgive her magnanimously and reinstate Iona as his favourite. He looked forward to the moment with no small amount of relish.

At length she roused herself languidly and came first up onto her knees and then gained her feet, stretching seductively, breasts rising, hips thrusting. When she parted her dishevelled mane of flaming hair it was to disclose a smirking smile.

He raised an eyebrow quizzically, then shrugged his shoulders in a dismissal of interest at the reason, saying with the conceit borne of the life-long adoration of the islanders, 'And now you will acknowledge me as your master, yes? There is a place at my side once more if you are ready.'

Haughtily she looked down her nose, full of dignity and bearing despite her nakedness and replied simply, 'No.'

Breath rushed noisily from his nostrils and his mouth thinned to nothingness. He should have had her whipped but he couldn't bring himself to mark that delicate, pale skin of hers. And he was tired, too, wanted to rest now. Exasperated, he jerked his head towards the door. 'Get out then. You are dismissed.'

Head held high, she left, musing as she wandered back through the garden to the women's quarters, that she had won yet another skirmish in their on-going battle.

She'd been summoned there that night to be humiliated and so forth, but she had ended up being pleasured by her 'master' who was oh-so obvious in his desire to please and win her back fully to him. But she wasn't yet ready.

Tiku would learn, after some frustration in attempting to prove it otherwise. He couldn't best her, would never cow her no matter what he did to her. She'd rather face the same fate as Moona than be a meek love-slave to some spoilt child of a Living God; an obedient female without voice or will.

Chapter Nineteen

Ran could smile like an angel, but sometimes Iona thought he had the very devil in him.

This evening he'd gone missing. The wives were in their quarters, the younger children safe abed in the nursery. But Ran wasn't with them. Iona realised this with exasperation when she went to wish him and his younger sister, Tula, goodnight. She started to search, first the ante rooms and meeting places, then the gardens.

She was far too lenient with him, she decided. Too easy going. Well, not tonight. Just wait until she found him. He'd get a good spanking, English style.

Tula was nearly two years old, as dusky as her brother and a darling, as far as her mother was concerned. Her children were everything to her now, the most important people in her life, for ever since the deaths of Moona and Amandu, her relationship with Tiku had been less than perfect.

Where once theirs had been a romance of fire and surprising tenderness, now there was little save domination – male lording it over female. Still, she showed spirit, never let him entirely get the better of her. He still loved her better than any other woman, that was the thing, but he couldn't quite forgive her that outburst on the night of Moona's execution, her unmistakable look of distaste. He'd done it for her. She should have understood that, backed him up and forgiven him his excess of pleasure in the deed. He loved her but he couldn't get that out of his head.

She had understood to some extent even on that sad and sorry night. But there was something else – a look of glee in his eyes as he'd consigned Moona to the fires of the fissure – that she could never forget. So still, in a way, they loved each other, but it was no longer perfect. It likely never would be again.

And there was something else. Tiku had a new woman, a young wife. That hurt Iona more than she'd thought possible. With the other wives – Arnk, Mam and his 'political' trio – she had always felt an odd closeness, had never resented their sharing his bed. Perhaps it was, simply, that they hadn't, too often, that she had been the Chosen One, had felt able to show magnanimity towards them.

She scoured the garden, called softly to every bush where her wayward son might be hiding. Once she thought she heard him giggling, headed in that direction, and she had come up to the walls of Tiku's house before she knew it, could hear him talking softly. She bristled at the velvet voice. She knew the tone, knew that he was wooing his new love with honeyed words and ardent kisses. Just as he'd done with her years before. She seethed with jealousy, was disgusted to find herself snorting down her nostrils like a madwoman.

So she called softly still for her son but there was an edge to her voice now, a clear undertone of anger. She wanted to be gone from that place, quick, away from all the unhappiness it caused. She didn't want to think of him with another woman. Hated it. She loved him in a fashion, certainly loved having sex with him. As a lover he had ever been demonstrative. But he hadn't summoned her to his bed now for many days, whether out of disinterest or spite, she couldn't say.

'Ran? Ran! If you don't appear right now I shall see to it you eat nothing but chicken liver for a week!' she hissed. He hated chicken liver and the threat had the desired effect. There was a scraping above on wooden roof slats, then he was peering over the edge and grinning.

She swore in English, which was one of those traits that amused the villagers so greatly. 'Bloody monster! Come down this instance. If you're caught Tiku'll have you thrashed. That's for sure.'

'Catch me, then, Mother, catch me,' laughed Ran, dangling then by his fingertips from the overhang.

She drew in her breath, fearful lest he should fall, and hurried up onto the veranda, her arms reaching up to take him firmly around the waist. 'All right, you can let go.'

He did. Fell into her arms and immediately put his arms around her neck and covered her eyes and nose with wet little kisses. He was quite devious and she was wholly gullible under such circumstances. She forgot all about spanking him, simply set him on his feet and propelled him towards the women's quarters with a slap on the backside.

'Go. I shall be there directly to kiss you goodnight. No god will be able to save you if you're not under the covers by then.'

He was gone, laughing still, strong and quick in his sprint.

She turned, query in her eyes, trying to fathom how he'd managed to climb up onto Tiku's roof, spotted the anciently thickened and gnarled vine that grew up the veranda post and assumed that to be the route of ascent. Then her eyes flitted down over the window, drawn by the light.

They were disgusting, their antics making her feel physically sick, angry, jealous. Once she had cavorted with him so brazenly, wantonly, without inhibitions. Once she had lain under the powerful lamps, exposed to the glare, his eyes, his body. Once it had been she who had knelt so trustingly upon the brightly woven carpet whilst Tiku rammed lustily at her rear, penis slipping into her, thrusting. But now now; not lately. Iona hated it.

'Bastard,' she snarled under her breath, so that hardly any sound was forthcoming. 'Bloody bastard.'

She hadn't retraced her steps far towards the women's quarters when she heard a female scream. It was slightly muffled, odd. 'Bastard!' she said again, thinking that the pair of them were trying some outlandish sexual position. 'Filthy bloody dogs.'

Then the scream came again. It stopped Iona in her tracks. Now it didn't sound in the least bit playful. It was a cry of fear; tears choked it.

Its none of my business, Iona thought. Yet her feet were taking her back to Tiku's house. She had nothing against Lula personally, couldn't blame her for being Tiku's new wife. Indeed the girl had been chosen for him totally without prior consultation. It was just assumed that she would be eternally honoured and grateful should he deign to accept her.

Iona peered warily, not knowing what to expect. Violence wasn't something she associated with Tiku, not when it came to lovemaking. But she couldn't think what else might have happened.

Lula lay sprawled on the floor, a prone, lifeless Tiku collapsed on top of her, his rear pointing at Iona, his shaft still embedded in Lula.

Lula lifted her face from beneath the weight of his strong brown arm and screamed out again, feebly this time as if she despaired of getting a response.

Iona rushed around to the door, clattered in. 'Its all right. I'll help. Don't worry.'

It took a considerable effort to ease Tiku off the spreadeagled girl. Then Iona threw her a coverlet from the bed, told her to cover herself. That done, she issued orders imperiously, her stern manner getting through to the shocked girl. 'Go get help . . . his physician. Tell the other wives.'

Lula fled tearfully, doubtless expecting to be punished later for causing this misfortune to befall the Living God.

Iona turned him over as gently as she could, reached out and dragged an indigo sheet from the bed, covered his modesty. He was alive, but his breathing was poor. Even unconscious, his fingers went to his chest, clutched there.

'Oh, hurry, someone,' cried Iona, feeling panic beginning to rise.

He was overweight, progressively so of late, like most of the other islanders his age, a heavy, yet still handsome man. His weight had always somehow added to his stature in more than just inches, making him something more than a mere man, adding to his godly persona. Now it just made him look vulnerable, flabby and out of condition.

'Sweet love, never mind. Lie still. You'll be all right. You'll be all right. I promise.'

His eyes flickered open. He groaned. Blue-tinged lips parted. 'I heard you,' he rasped.

'Don't speak. Here is the physician.' She squeezed his hand encouragingly.

He managed something that might have been a smile. 'I heard you. You still love Tiku. Tell me.' He dared her to deny it.

She couldn't. 'Of course I do. I can't deny. Now, no more.' She put her fingers to his lips, 'shushed' him gently as the physician dropped to his knees, examined the Living God with nervously trembling fingers.

Iona rose, knew that she could do nothing else then, that she had no place at Tiku's sickbed. The dignity of the Living God had to be maintained: none but his physician and elders might attend him. Still, that didn't stop Tiku's eyes following her to the door, pleading.

'I'll visit you later,' she promised, making herself sound full of an optimism she was far from feeling.

* * *

It was dawn when the elders came. They looked grave. The wives knew the news was bad, rose to thier feet and stood, elbow to elbow in solidarity, to face the spokesman.

'Chosen Ones of our beloved Tiku, bewail the news of his demise. Prepare for widowhood and the sadness of mourning.'

They were hushed, stunned. Then Lula began to cry noisily, more out of fear and pity for herself than for her dead husband. She expected to die, thought the disaster entirely her fault.

'Foremost at the end, before his brother spirits took him, was the matter of his heir, a Living God to follow on.' The wives tried temporarily to put grief aside, to listen and concentrate. This was important . . . to all of them. 'Tiku felt that certain of his older sons were too headstrong, too wild to take on such a lifelong commitment. Or too young and lacking in experience. To rule, one must have the love and respect of the people and the knowledge and understanding expected of one so elevated. His decision was not made lightly, or in haste. He told us, his Council, that he had been thinking of his successor for a long time, had reached his conclusions many seasons ago.' He paused, he announced with pomp and clarity:

'Our new Great One, and soon to be anointed leader, is the beloved wife of Tiku, Iona of the red hair.'

Iona couldn't digest that. She just stared at everyone staring back at her. Whatever had Tiku been thinking of? It was a joke, a bad one, she thought suddenly, trying to be rational. But no, Tiku would never have joked about such a thing, he took . . . had taken, she corrected, his godly status very seriously.

Iona felt the first waves of dismay wash over her, shook her head, said 'No' once, twice, stunned into stupidity.

The elders' spokesman matched her positive nod for negative shake of the head and told her, 'Tiku chose you in the fullness of his wisdom, felt in his heart that you were best equipped to lead us. The elders are content with the choice. There is no dissent. You *are* Iona the Living God.'

As he said it all about her fell to their knees, bowed their heads. The wives – her friends – transferred their devotion without question or qualm. In their eyes she had been miraculously changed into a deity, a goddess, *Wham! Just like that.*

Chapter Twenty

Her red eyelids, swollen by tears, had been smudged black, her already pale face dusted with grey ashes. Glaring out of the death mask face, lips reddened with berry juice she mouthed the well-learnt words of the funeral oration. As the Living God it was she, Iona, who must preside over the ceremony, stand erect and daunting upon the terrace overlooking the village and consign her husband to a grave beside his father, Rantavitiku.

She wore white. Everyone wore white. It was the custom at funerals. The garments were simple, full length and shroud-like.

She spoke; they chanted in response. Again and again her eyes kept going back to the deep hole awaiting the embalmed body of their former god. For many days he had lain in state in his lodge so that the villagers could pay their respects, bring offerings for Tiku to take with him to the next world. His viscera had been removed, cremated and placed in a hardwood casket, his body treated with vinegars and spices so that it didn't stink offensively. Now that heady smell permeated the air all about Iona, made her feel sick. She didn't know how she managed it, but somehow she got through to the end of the ceremony.

Iona gave flowers, a very English type of tribute perhaps, but somehow very apt. They had a special meaning for her and Tiku. They were rare white-green cymbidium orchids, their central lips rippled raspberry, their five waxen petals set at perfect intervals like the points of a star. Iona had worn head wreaths made of them during her first years on Wahwu, dancing exotically for her new husband. The dance was called the Ootalana. It had taken months for Patu to teach it to her, with all its nuances, and seductive moves. Whenever she had danced it for Tiku they had finished up making love. And while she'd danced she'd chanted her own little ditty, which amused Tiku greatly. 'I'm dancing the outlandish Ootalana in a land I call Outlandia.' Somehow it went well to the music of primitive pipes and drums played by the musicians outside on the veranda, and when she'd translated it into Wahwuese, Tiku had chuckled at its appealing silliness despite himself.

Six wreaths were handed down into the hole and laid about Tiku, bathing him in their scentless beauty. Then the men covered the body with palm leaves, covered his treated, rather unreal face. His wives wept softly, distressed, as they felt him being taken from them, clung to each other.

Only Iona remained apart, her status denying her such comradely comfort. It was she who must give the next command, thus removing him from them all for ever. It was the hardest thing anyone could have asked of her.

Her voice caught, struggled over the lump of misery in her throat. 'Go, Tiku, go, join the old ones gone before you, sit on the back of the turtle god and embark on your great voyage of adventure. Go. I take your place, I am the Living God, Iona.'

The men climbed out of the grave, began filling it in, with clam shells used as spades.

Lula darted forward, her grief now reaching hysterical proportions. She knelt sobbing at the very edge of the grave, calling to the dead body crazily, begging for forgiveness. Then, before any had time to think, let alone stop her, she had produced a curved, bladed knife and plunged it into her own breast.

'Oh no! Why?' cried Iona, rushing forward.

Lula keeled over, fell into the grave atop her dead husband. She groaned a little, her white gown staining red rapidly, blood trickling from the corner of her mouth.

'Now . . . I am at . . . peace,' she said weakly.

'Foolish girl,' Iona lamented, reaching out a hand to her. 'There was no need, no blame.'

'In my heart there was much,' came the whisper of a reply. Then Lula died.

Surprised into indecision, the elders looked to Iona.

'Bury them together.'

They were slightly scandalised.

'Bury her with him,' Iona insisted. 'There could be no finer offering to our dead god, nor no more fetching a companion for him in the after life.'

They digested, mulled, nodded. She was correct. But of course she was; she was their Living God. Tiku had chosen well. Her wisdom was unorthodox but it was sound.

Chapter Twenty-One

The burial of Tiku and Lula took up only the first hour after sunset. Following close on its heels and allowing Iona no time to grieve her loss or to try and come to terms with her shock over Lula's sudden death, was the Ceremony of Selection. She knew what was expected of her, looked forward to the necessary rituals involved with a clinical kind of trepidation. She didn't care for the proceedings but she knew her position demanded it of her.

Within a circle of handmaidens Iona was relieved of her white funeral gown and dressed instead in the voluminous black cockerel-feathered cloak of the Living God. Her hair was brushed into a gleaming fiery mantle which lay dramatically highlighted against such sombre garb; her face covered by a black wooden mask grotesquely carved and over-painted yellow and green in serpentine dots. A gossamer-fine black veil was then attached to this facial disguise, muting the fire of her hair. Only her black lidded eyes and red mouth showed, the latter set grimly determined and unsmiling.

She took her place upon the impressive, throne-like chair, her handmaidens flanking her. They had served Tiku well since his anointing some seventeen years before. Now it was time for them to step down. There was a new god, and custom decreed (this particular point had been written down in the annuls of Wahwu three centuries before, when the island had had its last goddess) that a goddess's attendants should be male.

They came before her, seductively slowly, a long column of eligible males put forward by their hopeful families as possible soul and helpmates for the new Living God. Great prestige was attached to such a position.

Iona looked each over critically, assessing their finer points: a bridge of nose, a strong jaw, a tight pair of buttocks. Despite herself and her very recent sadness, she found she suddenly had the wickedly funny thought, whatever would Horace have said to this? She grinned. The elders saw and nudged each other, thinking that they knew the reason why, scanning the line-up to try to deduce which male had elicited such a response. But they were wrong.

Her would-be suitors were unaware of anything save, perhaps, their own embarrassment at being paraded thus, and had been instructed to keep their gaze modestly lowered in the presence of one so divine.

Iona nodded, her eye caught by a striking boy of quite unordinary good looks. He was tall, like all the Wahwuese from these shores, black eyed, strong nosed, sound toothed. Dressed only in a black loincloth, he also hinted at an appealingly neat pair of buttocks. Iona thought him worthy of further consideration at a later date.

An officiating elder tapped him on the shoulder and immediately a grateful, pleased smile transformed the worried, nervous features of the youth.

The boy stepped up to Iona's throne, took the hand she extended, kissed the palm, the back, then laid it gently in her lap, his head dropping to plant a kiss on her thigh. It was customary, and Iona had been expecting it. Even so a thrill ran up her limb, centred in her belly and faded lusciously. He *definitely* had promise.

When the final male had come before her, seeking her approval, Iona had already chosen six attendants, who now stood ever-ready and pleased at their good fortune. They were beautiful, dusky, young and, in two cases, virginal.

At the house of the Living God the lamps burned low, the scented oil filling the air with its pungent spiciness. No hint of Tiku remained, not even in the reception room where he had lain in state until that afternoon. Iona was thankful for that.

She reclined on the couch, sighed. Her boys came in, laden. Some had food, others wine and spring water. One of them carried a jar of aromatic oil, he set wordlessly about massaging the tension out of Iona's neck and shoulders. She sighed again, more deeply.

She ate – fruit and a little chicken – and drank wine from a horn beaker which one dusky male kept continually brimming.

They washed her tired feet with scented water and manipulated the toes in a massage which was pure bliss. One of them sang to her, an island melody centuries old. She relaxed deeper onto her couch, her masseuse propped behind her, affording her the comfy cushion of his body. She yawned. He let his hands slip within the loose folds of her robe, circled there with oiled palms. Another brushed her hair, ran it over his own chest, caressing pectorals, a thrill running through him. She smiled lazily at him, her sea eyes almost closing with languor. A hand ran up her leg, starting at the ankle, gliding up, smooth palmed, warm, light. She had felt too tired to be bothered with any of this initiation nonsense, and yet she was being stirred despite herself.

So be it, she thought, I'll let them do as they like, so long as it pleases me. After all, that's what they're here for, their assigned roles. And if I don't like, I can say so, send them away . . . with a click of the fingers, she smiled. Just like that!

One of them smiled in answer to her own. She could

have drowned in that liquid, black gaze. Her legs relaxed, fell open at the knees. His hand ran up, finding her. Her breath caught.

The hands at her breasts fondled firmer, tweaking nipples. One of the inexperienced boys pushed eagerly in, bent his head to those now exposed peaks of pale, abundant flesh. The other stood on the sidelines, watching nervously, perhaps trying to learn something. Iona held her beaker out to him, encouraging. Instantly he jumped into action, eager to obey, to please. She drank, emptied the beaker thirstily, almost recklessly quick, handed it to him again as hands and fingers caressed her everywhere, stimulated her into wanting, longing, despite herself, her grief. She shook her head as he made to fill it once more. 'No,' she said, breathily, 'I'm no longer thirsty. You may go to the kitchen with the others, find your supper. You and you may remain.'

The two innocents she decided to tutor personally and alone some other time. Tonight she wanted sex, quick and hard.

Her gaze fell on the young man at her feet who so expertly set her flesh afire, and his companion into whom she reclined languidly. Grinning over her shoulder gamely, the latter took the lobe of her ear between his lips and nibbled then sucked. She could feel his manhood hard against her buttocks, could see the other youth swelling and poking out at a comical angle in his black loincloth. She wanted them both madly. *Together*, she decided.

She stared imperiously at the boy kneeling before her, gave him an order that was also a challenge, a goad:

'Make me forget. Ease my grief.'

He nodded, eyes bright with determination, took up the jar of coconut oil placed conveniently nearby and dripped three exquisite drops onto Iona's exposed bud of passion. She twitched a little at each delicate caress of dripping oil, caught her breath as he drew two fingers down her silken petals, followed them with his tongue, darted into her teasingly, then out again, then plunged in deep and waggled.

Pleased, she gasped, 'You show promise. Continue.'

He did, full of devoted eagerness, his erection bowing out of his loincloth.

'Disrobe. I would gaze upon you.'

His loincloth dropped away. He was large, as were all the Wahwuese when it came to their sexual tackle; dark, long and of considerable girth. A vein throbbed down the silken length of it. The balls hung full. She reached out, cupped them, making him grunt with flaming longing, feeling each quite clearly between thumb and forefinger, drawing a caressing finger over each before abandoning them. For a moment he looked bereft, groaned in frustration.

'Get back to your business,' she reminded him.

He did, very professionally, working on Iona with his tongue until she went rigid and gave a little cry of delight.

She smiled at him, patted him on the head, poured herself more wine. 'Still I remember,' she moaned, relaxing back with maudlin spirits into the welcoming arms of her masseuse.

He sucked her ear, poured more oil over her breasts and belly, worked his fingers over her; smoothing, kneading, circling her belly, her waist, then her buttocks where his engorged erection throbbed and reared, wanting her, yet not daring to without the Living God's verbal permission.

Oiled fingers found her anus, circled it, stroked it, while the other boy licked her clean at the front like a fastidious cat. A thumb wiggled at her rear, wet and glossy with oil, inching into her. She tightened her muscles playfully around it, then let him in fully.

The other boy busied himself, lying soft, feather-filled cushions on the floor, then lay back into them, his eyes constantly on Iona, filled with longing, imploring, his erection throbbing, the tip moist and pearled.

She laughed low, squirmed free of the finger that

subtley pleased her and dropped gracefully down to the floor, straddling the dusky, glistening body that rippled with muscle.

Behind her the masseuse growled with frustration and with jealousy of his fellow *pleaser*. Bereft at her leaving, he quickly followed, clinging to her, kissing her spinal column, her buttocks, nipping with his teeth.

She felt the tip of the boy's manhood at her core, smiled down at him maganimously and lowered onto him, taking him in with studied slowness, inch by inch, thick, warm, to the hilt, and breathed, 'Very nice,' in her prim English voice.

He sighed gratefully, clutched at her hips, reared up the harder into her, withdrew only a fraction and reared again.

She laughed, withdrew to the tip of him, then lowered hard. It was he who cried out. With ritualistic slowness she repeated the action, watching his ecstatic face, feeling his hands reach up, cup her breasts, clasp, unclasp, fingers hooked around her nipples.

Behind her the other boy chanted in age old adoration of the Living God, caressed the length of her back and buttocks with his body, his rigid manhood trailing her torturously with its oh-so sensitive head, down the crease of her splendid buttocks and back again. His tongue coursed up her spine, across her shoulder, to her neck and ear, slithering and persistent.

She turned her head, a demonic spark in her eyes, bit the tip of that soft pink flesh so hard that she drew blood, saw anger flare in the boy's black eyes, then she ordered him, 'Do it. Take me. Follow the path of thy thumb. Now!'

She watched, neck craned as he oiled her anus and himself, the flesh making voluptuous squelching noises as he handled it impatiently. Then he put his engorged member at her tight entrance, held Iona by the hips and jerked violently into her, still full of anger and spitting out blood.

He pumped, forcing himself into her to the hilt, hard,

harder. She cried out, thrusting her bottom further into the air and enticing him on to greater boldness, while the boy beneath her thrust up into her from below, jerking away frantically, reaching up for the pale, rose-tipped breasts that filled his vision.

Momentarily, taking her weight on one hand Iona reached down, down to where all their bodies merged and felt the two shafts forcing themselves into her, one above the other, her flesh stretched taut by such an excess. Upon her face came the most radiant smile, her eyes glazed almost as if she were in a trance. The pleasure was extreme. But it was perhaps *too* acute, could not last long. She was too full, too tight, just too overwhelmed. When the boy beneath her strained up, chest muscles rippling, and thrust his tongue into her mouth, Iona gave a scream of unbearable delight and felt her rigid body go through the sublime waves of ecstasy.

They gloried in her prolonged twitches of pleasure, the feel of her muslces contracting about them, quickly following her to a climax, penises thrusting, slithering, ramming into her meatily. They grabbed for her greedily, like two dogs over a bitch, her willing slaves showing wilfulness now as they thrust on mindlessly, holding her still, imprisoned, hands on hips, breasts, thighs, to make her open to them wider still. Two men in her to the core, crying out their passion, their adoration of the Living God who did them such honour.

She *did* forget Tiku and her grief for a while.

A floor to ceiling curtain of gossamer-fine material screened Iona at her toilette, but she knew the two 'novices' could see her well enough, sat nervously upon the couch in the main sitting area of the room where she had instructed Oami to seat them.

Oami helped her, a secretive little smile on her face as she arranged her mistress's hair, slim and pretty, a giggle never far from the surface. She was Iona's most devoted servant, always there, always helpful, totally loyal.

Now she stood behind the Living God, red hair worked lovingly in her hands, speaking when spoken to or otherwise seeming to be in some happy sort of daze. Every now and again she turned her head slightly and surreptitiously observed the boys on the couch, then giggled.

Iona smirked, and said softly, so that only Oami could hear, 'Difficult to say which emotion has more of a upper hand, isn't it – fear or excitement.'

'Fear, I think.'

Iona chuckled. 'Poor things.'

The boys had been instructed to strip completely, being allowed to wear only their arm bracelets and talisman necklaces. They were young, beautiful and totally overwhelmed by Iona's special interest in them.

They sat upright and unrelaxed, hands cupped modestly and protectively about their genitalia, toes wriggling with discomfort and nervousness in amongst the coconut matting on the floor.

Iona stained her mouth and nipples with russet berry juice and perfumed herself liberally. She had already anointed herself with fragrant oils and could feel the lips of her sex gliding against each other and faintly exciting her. She contracted her pelvic muslces and felt it the stronger.

'I am ready, I think. Oami, you shall serve the wine and stay in close attendance.'

The girl nodded solemnly, giving Iona's hair one final stroke with the comb and caressing her neck.

In the lamplight the Living God appeared before them, so white, so red, so majestic, that the boys quaked, rose, bowing, hands still shyly cupping their private parts.

Her head held high, she gave them a condescending smile and went to the great bed with its gaudy hangings, sinking into the feather-filled mattress.

'You,' ordered Oami, crooking a finger at the one

with soft brown eyes and feathers woven into his hair, 'go forth.'

He looked for all the world as if he was going to his execution, trembled at the sight of Iona lying atop the bed, her hair spread all about her, her pale body languidly reclining, weight on one arm, a hip thrust up.

Oami handed them the wine and pulled the curtains about the mighty bed so that they had privacy, staring superiorly and without comfort at the black eyed boy who remained, almost succumbing to his anxiety; he looked on the point of collapse through sheer terror.

'Drink,' coaxed Iona, knowing that the special brew would relax the first boy quickly enough. It was the same devious mixture that she had been given so long ago to make Tiku's possession of her the easier.

Trembling and pale, he drank, swallowing noisily in the hush that enveloped them. Light seeped in, but for the most part they were in deep shadow, the red, black and green hangings tinting the shadows strangely.

Iona drank also, though only wine. And when they'd finished and Iona handed the cups through the curtain, Oami was there instantly to retrieve them.

'Now,' said Iona, softly, 'come closer. What is your name?'

'I am Nonijawa, Oh Great One,' said the boy, voice quivering.

'You tremble, Nonijawa. There is no need, you know. You have nothing to fear from me,' said Iona, soothingly, running a hand down his thigh.

He tensed at the touch, quivered, trying to stop his eyes from going yet again to her triangle of red hair, the slight mound there, the hint of a crease amongst the curls. That and her touch were making him harden against his will. He didn't want to because he didn't yet know if it was proper or even permissable to do so without the Living God's express persmission. He was in an agony of desire and fear, stuttered, 'I am not . . . worthy.'

She laughed softly, a tinkling sound. 'What foolishness. I am but a woman. See here,' she took his hand and ran it over her belly. 'Feel.'

His penis reared again and she took it into her hand, reassuring him then with her actions that his manly display of arousal was wholly welcomed.

She lay on her back, a seductive smile upon her face, and opened her legs. Her lips parted a fraction and the pink tongue of her clitoris peeped forth, glistening.

He couldn't help but stare, devoured her visually, his penis rigid between Iona's expert little fingers.

'I have heard,' she said, 'that you have not been with a woman before. Do I need to show you what to do? Or would you like to explore the possibilities for yourself?'

'I . . . I should like to explore. But I fear I would make a fool of myself in so doing.'

'Not at all. I shall enjoy it, Nonijawa. I have known an accomplished lover who knew every way to please a woman. An innocent will be a refreshing change. I shall just lie here and perhaps offer the odd word of encouragement.'

'*And* correction,' pleaded the boy. 'I do not wish to do wrong.'

She only laughed and opened her legs a lot wider.

The brew was beginning to relax him, she could tell. She was very relaxed, felt a sensual pleasure in the warmth of the night and the oil and perfume on her body. 'Possess me as you will, Nonijawa. Would you like the legs raised? Thus.' She drew them up, ankles together, knees raised, let them flop open relaxedly, her sex gaping in peaks and folds, her other passage puckered tight.

He looked at her a long time, absorbing her mysteries, noting the intricacies, the juices already seeping, the bud that thrust forward flushed red and so inviting. At length he found the courage to trace a finger down it, around it, heard his mistress murmur, withdrew it wet and gleaming, pushed it in again, felt her contract playfully around it.

He scrambled between her legs. She didn't have the

heart to stall him as he put the head of his penis at her entrance, watched it disappear into her with a shout of joy, and then buried himself, to the base, holding that position, his buttocks tightly clenched, pelvis thrust out to its fullest extent, glorying in the feel, the compressed feel of her, the composed beauty of Iona's unusual face. He grabbed for her breasts and squeezed hard, overcome almost immediately by his climax. He jerked, he twitched. Within moments he was spent. His look was ecstatic.

'Oh thank you, thank you,' he cried, so grateful, collapsing.

'Think nothing of it,' smiled Iona, clapping her hands. I certainly didn't, her mind added wrily.

Oami appeared carrying the sponge stick, inserted it carefully where the inept boy had plunged so joyously only moments before and cleansed her mistress of all trace of him.

'You may go now,' Iona dismissed, voice devoid of emotion.

Silently, he slipped from the bed.

'The other has already drank the special brew and is now ready, Oh Great One, if you still wish him in your bed?'

Iona nodded, 'Send him to me. The last boy could only wet my appetite. I need someone to quench it.'

Oami stroked her mistress's mound as she dripped fresh oil onto the clitoris, and watched Iona's bud respond to the pleasant sensation. 'If the boy bring no relief, there is always Oami.'

'I know, dearest girl. And shall bear it in mind,' Iona said, momentarily caressing the girl's dark head.

It wouldn't be the first time that Oami had brought that special joy to her mistress. The years of conflict with Tiku had meant that Iona was invariably denied satisfaction in his bed. Oami had taken it upon herself to do those little 'services' for her beloved mistress. And after the initial surprise expressed by Iona that first time when the servant girl had touched her where, previously, only a man's hands, tongue or penis had tresspassed, Iona had found it highly agreeable, the love of an adept female as acceptable any day as the ofttimes selfish antics of the men in her life. Oami's love and devotion were without complication. She wished only to serve, asked nothing in return; being near to Iona seemed to be enough.

The next boy approached the bed, pulled back the curtains with an authoritative 'swish' and stood proudly before her, dark, braceleted, feathered and already aroused, his penis wagging skywards, red-headed and thick, blue veins marbling its underside. His nerves were all gone now; the doctored drink had done its job.

Iona's eyebrows raised at his new air of assurance. She admired it much as her eyes admired him, his slim and lengthy penis, his strong legs, his finely chiselled face. She remembered why she had chosen him now. He'd reminded her of her father's groom on the family estate in Norfolk. They had the same angular features and high, wide foreheads. A handsome face. Strong. Not pretty. The groom had been Irish, called Brian, and when he'd spoken he'd had the most heart-melting brogue. He'd captivated Iona, young girl that she'd been then, but, perhaps luckily, he'd left their neighbourhood long before her secret infatuation had a chance to get out of hand, absconding in the middle of the night after two moppets from the nearest village insisted that he was the father of their expected children.

The boy had that same look about him, black haired, dark eyed. The only difference was in their colour. The Irish man had been pale and Gaelic, the Wahwuese was dusky and quite exotic . . .

He climbed up onto the bed without waiting to be asked, a spark in his eyes. Iona couldn't fathom it, thought, perhaps, it might be defiance or mischief.

She reclined amongst her cushions once more, smiling welcomingly and looking highly desirable.

'And your name?'

'My given name is Unlun, Oh Great One.'

'Then welcome, Unlun. Do you find me pleasing to the eye?'

'Who could not, Oh Great One?'

'Then do what you will,' she told him, the mastery in his voice sending a thrill of anticipation through her.

The spark in his eyes was further ignited and he smiled broadly, flipping Iona over as if she were but a feather and delivering two sharp slaps to her buttocks.

'Good lord!' she gasped, taken completely by surprise.

'Should I stop?' he asked.

She couldn't see his face. His voice held a note of challenge and so she set aside her caution. 'No . . . no . . .' Her voice wavered.

He caught her hank of red hair and wound it around his hand, yanking her head up from the pillow and kissing the lips of her profiled head almost savagely. He bit her shoulder.

She twisted around, eyes blazing. 'What the hell do you think . . .'

He clamped his mouth over hers, silencing her, his kiss so deep that she lost her reason, was left gasping, her arms snaked about him, her mound thrusting up at him invitingly, her legs splayed.

But he pushed her off abruptly, so ardent, so accomplished in his technique that Iona began to doubt his 'innocence'.

'Are you *sure* you've not been with a woman before?'

'I am sure, Oh Great One. I do as you say. "What I will", that's all.'

'You are so . . . intuitive then.'

'That bad?'

'Heavens, no,' she laughed. 'Knowing what a woman likes is no bad thing. But remember to keep your aggresion under control, Unlun. Spanking is all well and good, for a little pain can most definitely sharpen the senses. But never forget that you are dealing with the Living God. She cannot be subjected to anyone's will, save at her own choosing. Spank me if you wish but ultimately know that I am the master here. Do you understand me?'

'I believe so. I can do this,' he said softly, darting a finger deeply into her, 'As long as I remember that you are the Living God. I can do this, too,' he continued, rather cold-bloodedly, inserting a thumb into Iona's bottom-mouth, 'just so long as I remember who I am, who you am. Yes? I can dare anything in the name of pleasure?'

'Well, no . . .'

'But I do,' said Unlun, taking her mound in two hands and all but wrenching it apart to expose her soft, defenceless folds to his gaze, his fingers, his tongue.

He lunged at her head first, burying himself there, forcing her legs wide, wider, a finger disappearing into Iona as his head and the flickering tongue extended from it, assaulted her clitoris.

He reared up, ramming at her then with his engorged member, forcing all straight in, stabbing until she lost her senses completely, gave herself over to his administerings.

He thrust violently, measuredly, his right hand delivering the odd ecstatic slap to her outer thigh, her hands pinned above her head. She came, crying out, throbbing around the fat shaft of him, but still he pumped on, harder.

A hand around her wrists, the other pinched her bottom, then darted up quickly to clamp over her mouth and stifle Iona's protest. Her eyes blazed furiously. She began to fight him, to try and push him off, determined to give him a good talking to.

But he was stronger, determined and quite single-minded. He held her pinned bodily to the soft bed then, chest to chest, belly to belly, so tight and deep within her as he thrust that Iona once again felt her loins turning molten, a series of deliciously intense spasms shattering her.

He thrust on, making her sore, grinding against her, forcing her legs up and so wide that her knees were touching her shoulders, then he rammed, gaining speed, teeth set in a grimly determined line of sparkling white, his black eyes blazing with lust, with power at Iona's grimacing features.

He yelled, he bit, he thrust a thumb up her anus and waggled it, touching at the very core of her as he pumped himself to that suppressed moment of pure pleasure that was all the keener for having been withheld for so long.

He snaked his arms around her shoulders and waist, collapsed, buttocks twitching as he emptied himself into Iona, groaning.

She was glad of the calm, allowed him his few moments of joy in his successful possession, could feel him in her still, the base of him fast against her sex, though he was now softening by slow degrees. Then she tapped him on the shoulder, roused him from his pleasant stupor.

He opened his eyes, lifted his head from her breast and grinned insolently.

'Thank you, Unlun. You may go now,' she said matter-of-factly, calling out for Oami and moving so that she expelled his flesh in the same instance.

'I am dismissed?'

'Yes.'

'But . . . Aren't you pleased, Oh Great One? Was it not wonderful for you also?'

'Your technique is refreshing,' Iona told him, wriggling free of his sated bulk and donning a diaphanous gown.

Oami arrived with the sponge stick, lifted the gown and set to work between Iona's widespread thighs.

'You will make me your favourite though, won't you?' he queried, perturbed, so sure of himself and so full of conceit that her lack of praise offended him.

She shook her head. 'I shall have no favourites. I want no jealousy or fighting amongst my boys.'

'Even after I performed so well? I am better than any of them. You have to admit it. Unlun knows how to give a woman pleasure, has made the study of copulation his main interest in life.'

'Do not question me, boy. Go. Oami, see him out,' said Iona, sternly, exasperated.

Oami returned, shaking her head. 'He too wilful, that one. Trouble, I think.'

'You're probably right, Oami. Whatever, I don't want him, wish him to be sent back to his family. See to it.'

Iona sat alone drinking wine, the servants hovering about the bed, changing the sheets. No, she didn't want Unlun, for all his good looks and prowess. He was too dominant, too conceited, too cruel in his handling. She felt used, had lost control of the situation with him. And that was something she was loath to do with any male she felt she couldn't trust. It wouldn't happen again.

Chapter Twenty-Two

*I*n the first years of Jack's reign as Coconut King seven children were knowingly fathered by him on different women from the squat people's tribe.

His children were growing taller than the average squat person, their skin a shade lighter in some cases, their hair brown and curly but not as dark as their mothers' and, in one case, one of his sons Tootan, was golden-brown-haired and exotically different.

Jack loved all his children in an absent, easy way, much as he had fleetingly loved their mothers. He didn't go looking for love. It came to him – eagerly. And his women were as casual as he, tiring of him as quickly and often as he did of them. It was the squat people's way. They were not overly affectionate, tender or faithful by nature. That suited Jack, for he felt unable to commit himself to any of them for very long.

Tig's younger sister had been persistent. She was a virgin still, but soon to be married. She wanted Jack to have the honour of deflowering her. It was the chief's prerogative. So she followed him around constantly, trying desperately to entice him. For several weeks he was impervious, kindly laughing off her attempts at seduction. Yet in the end her persistence paid.

She was petite and muscular but terribly gauche and unpracticed in the art of allure. She'd tried smiling beckoningly, wiggling her hips, bending over so that her fetching backside and fuzz of pubic hair stared him in the face.

Jack only grinned, shook his head and took off in the opposite direction. He needed another conquest like he needed a hole in the head.

One day, in a fury, Tig's sister, Mara, had begun to despair, stamping off down the sun-dried beach, kicking sand furiously as she went. Suddenly she'd let out a howl of pain, hopped about on one foot and collapsed into the sand.

Jack had heard the cry, knew it to be genuine, and swiftly returned, squatting over her, brows knitting. 'Mara, what is it?'

Tears were streaming down her face. She clutched her writhing leg, displaying the sole of her foot and the sharp spines of a small crustaceous sea creature embedded therein.

'Lie still,' he ordered, taking her foot firmly in his hand and examining it. He removed the painful spines with infinite care, but still she cried out, eyes and nose streaming, face contorted.

'Done,' he said finally, going down to the water's edge and removing his loincloth. He wetted it and came back up the beach to where Mara lay in the soft dry sand beyond the tide mark, his body golden tanned, his dormant manhood catching Mara's attention and taking her mind off her pain.

She'd seen him naked before, of course, for King Jack often indulged in group sex with his comrades and their wives and concubines, which was observed by all and sundry. But she'd never been so close to *it* before. It was paler than the rest of him, beautifully long and thick, hung down his leg, surrounded by golden hair.

He gently bathed her foot with his wet loincloth, then almost jumped out of his skin when her frantic little hand fastened none too gently around him, and gave a violent squeeze.

'I want you, Oh King, give myself to you. Here. Now. *Please*,' she begged, still sniffling.

Jack's lips tightened with exasperation and he forcibly removed her fingers from his shaft, prising them off one by one. 'No,' he was deliberately harsh.

'But . . . but . . . It is honour. Custom. Is it so very much to ask? Am I *so* ugly?'

He shook his head soothingly, though, indeed, in that instance Mara was as ugly as sin, with her face messed with tears and snot, her eyes beginning to puff. 'No, no, you're pretty enough,' he insisted. 'It's just that I feel your husband-to-be should be the first. That is the custom in my land.'

'You are far from home though,' said Mara, low and persuasive.

'How can you think of coupling when your foot gives you so much pain?' said Jack, trying a different line of argument.

'Joy with Jack will take my mind off pain in foot.'

His brows knit. She was just like her brother – wiley and persistent. He discarded the lioncloth. 'Very well, I surrender to your lust, fair Mara.'

'You mean . . . you *will*?' cried Mara, overjoyed, falling upon the kneeling Jack, her arms going about his neck and almost strangling him.

He wrestled free, held her at arm's length, chuckling, 'There are conditions, however.'

'Yes?'

'It will only be the once. I take your maidenhead, then you be a good and devoted wife to your husband.'

'Yes, yes, I agree.'

'And you do as King Jack instructs,' he insisted, determined that if they were going to do it, they were going to do it right, especially it being her first time. Jack decided that he owed it to her husband to teach her the basics.

'Yes, I am very happy to learn.'

'First off then, Mara, stop being so downright eager. You're almost falling over yourself to give it to me. Don't give a man what he wants straight away. Make him wait, make him want. Tease him.'

Her brows knit thoughtfully. She nodded.

Jack lay back in the sand beside her and rested his head on his elbow, watching her. Something was going on behind her eyes, he perceived.

She smiled, as if decided upon a course of action, and proceeded, very leisurely, to divest herself of her skimpy red pigskin skirt, lying beside him then as naked as he. She ran a finger around the heavy globes of her breasts, the dark nipples hardening, then did the same to Jack.

His flesh thrilled and he smiled encouragingly. 'Very good.'

Her palm ran flat and smooth down over her belly, an upraised hip, crossed over to Jack and glided upon from the knee, over the golden down of hair on his thighs, to his belly, then down again.

She ran her fingres clumsily over his shaft, Jack covering the little hand with his own and guiding it, showing it what to do, what he liked. She learned quick. She teased the head, ran her fingers down and around, feeling him growing hard right around to his anus, felt him quiver a little at the contact there, did it again.

'Enough,' bade Jack, not wishing to get carried away in his own pleasure too soon.

He eased Mara back into the sand, kissed her on the shoulder, the throat, then her gasping, full mouth. Western-style kisses were new to her and she cried out in delight as Jack's tongue found hers, played with it.

Her hands were all over him again, oh-so eager to please. He gave in to her enthusiasm, left her mouth and let his lips trail down over her breasts and belly instead, seeing goose bumps of pleasure prickle her skin.

She was pulling on his penis now like a thing

demented, quite out of control with longing for that hard, thick shaft that was now grown to its full, impressive size.

He eased the lips of her sex apart with his fingers, held them wide while he darted over her with his tongue.

Mara screamed then with unimaginable pleasure.

She was an island girl like all the rest, given to energetic horseplay with the boys and numerous self-indulgent bouts of masturbation, but none of that compared to the artful movements of Jack's tongue. He was wonderful. Her belly ached and she grew wetter by the second, her hands tangling in his golden hair, caressing his head.

He slipped a finger carefully into her, worked it about, deciding that she was ready.

She must have sensed it, for she cried out, 'Will the boar mount the sow?'

'If you wish, Mara. Or perhaps you would like to ride me, to control the act that will make you a woman?'

She nodded eagerly, hopefully. 'If King Jack will allow . . .'

'King Jack is more than happy,' he laughed, rolling onto his back, his great penis pointing skywards, as hard and smooth as marble.

Mara straddled him, took the throbbing member between her little hands, eased the tip into her.

'Now remember,' warned jack, 'take it slow,' his hands caressing her quivering, wide poised thighs.

She smiled down at him, felt the hot red head of his thick stem pushing into her, finding resistance. But it was only momentary. Then he was through, had entered her, piercing her and she tightened a little around Jack with the shock.

He held her firm at the hips, not allowing her to take him in further, coaxing 'There, all right? Do you feel me? Is it good? Do you want more?'

She nodded emphatically, squealed, 'Yes, oh yes. All! All!' tried to screw down upon him eagerly, to take the biggest shaft on the island as her trophy, for Jack, being of a different race than her people possessed a larger penis than any.

'Slowly,' he cautioned, feeling her tightness about him and luxuriating in it, 'slowly.'

She lowered herself inch by inch, until she had all of him, was impaled, stretched, her sex wetting his pubic hair.

He cupped her buttocks, explored her, holding her captive about him, a child-woman only just capable of taking all of him.

He raised his head, took a nipple into his mouth and Mara rose again, to the tip of him, then plunged, a little too violently, making her call out and groan in pleasure-pain.

Her eyes were opaque, her loins trembling where he rent her, filling her, thrusting up now, his movements as wild as hers, his hands on her buttocks and stroking her other orifice, driving Mara to a frenzy.

She jerked to a climax with much yelping and hollering for joy and Jack held her firm, pumped up into her – so tight, so tiny – that his senses rioted and he exploded inside of her, spurting in waves until he was drained, left empty and smugly satisfied with his method of intiation.

It was a job well done.

At the head of his fearless band of explorers, Jack climbed up through the dense vegetation on the steep mountainside, the crude blade of his machete clearing an untidy path.

The men sang war songs and such like as they went, the tunes somehow aiding their fleetness of foot. And behind, carrying the provisions and the essentials for their bivouac, came the women and children. They were weary, irritable and impatient to stop for the night.

Amongst the women were Mia and Sanga. The former had given Jack two sons, Jojo and Raf, the latter a daughter, Alaba.

There had been years when he'd hoped that another ship might come. It was possible, after all; if it had happened once it could happen again for there was undeniably some sort of pattern to the tides. But he knew the chances were very slim.

For a time the novelty of being a king had kept him amused. But that too had paled. Cynically he would think with mounting despondence, King of what? King of the Cannibals. It was no great deal, certainly didn't have the prestige that, say, King of England or Czar of Russia had.

When his illusions and delusions finally vanished Jack found that he was very bored. He'd sampled everything that his little corner of island had to offer. That's when he'd decided upon an expedition to inspect all his domain – a kind of medieval Royal Progress – prompted by tales from his more adventurous and mature warriors.

Once, not so long ago (and they swore this was true in the face of Jack's scoffing scepticism) strange black spirits with long bodies not unlike Jack's had come to their lands. Fearful of such macabre beings, they had repulsed the threat, seen them off. No others had come in their place, due (so the warriors had decided after great deliberation) to their many subsequent sacrifices of blood from stillborn babies.

Jack didn't believe in spirits or ghosts, but he did believe that his men had seen people from another tribe. Perhaps they were visitors from another island quite near. A taller, more elegant race, maybe Polynesians. His imagination fired, he'd decided that he was going to find out.

And so here they were. Many months later and after an exhaustive trek across, and more often up and down, some of the sheerest mountained, heavily vegetated country he had ever seen.

Sometimes he had questioned his own wisdom in ever undertaking such an adventure, especially when the women and children showed the effects of prolonged fatigue. But now, as he clamboured, breathing heavily with exertion, the last few yards to the summit of this latest mountain, he felt a strange optimism, felt this had all been for a purpose, as yet undivined. And he could smell the sea.

He was up, over.

Jack paused in wonder. Before him stretched the mile wide crater of a benign volcano, its central layers of treacherous ash belching forth whistling grey plumes of stinking, gaseous smoke. They hadn't been climbing a mountain at all.

Jack shook his head, spoke to himself. 'Well, well, well,' in a voice full of surprise.

Tig came up beside him. 'Where we be, friend?'

'On the far side of the island, I believe. Look, there's the sea.' And he pointed as he spoke. The evening haze shimmered and shifted, showed them a distant and diffused orange sun setting over the unmistakable curve of the watery horizon.

Tomorrow they would start to try and circumvent the volcano and find out what lay beyond.

Chapter Twenty-Three

After a breakfast of cold leftovers, they were off.

It was around midday when they stumbled into the tall black ones, the legendary people they had come in search of.

It was difficult to say who were more surprised.

Tall people and squat people entered the clearing in the trees above the village at precisely the same time. Both groups were chattering, off guard. They never heard the others approaching. There followed a moment of stupefaction while they stared at each other agog, disliking what they saw: strange faces, strange hair, odd stature. Then they took up their spears and knives, axes and clubs, backed off and brandished their weapons threateningly, facing each other like two opposing walls.

This wasn't the way Jack had envisaged things happening at all. Bloodshed looked likely. He swore in consternation at the thought:

'Bloody hell!'

Odd expressions crossed the faces of the tall black ones with their flowing blue-black locks and cockerel feather apparel. They eyed the pale one with renewed curiosity, more than his colouring holding their attention now.

One of them parroted the phrase, a questioning note in his voice, 'Bloody hell?'

'Yes, bloody hell,' snapped Jack. This was all getting stupid, surreal.

'Bloody hell *and* damn and blast?' elaborated the tall, dusky one, eyebrow cocked.

Amazed, Jack felt a laugh bursting from him. 'Well bugger me! Yes, if you like, damn and blast, too.'

The tall one pursed his lips, nodded as if he'd reached a decision. 'You follow,' he said in Wahwuese.

Jack didn't understand his words. His language was quite different from the squat people's. Though confused by events, still he thought he understood the man's gesturing of spear, pointing the way, felt too that it was safe – for the moment – to comply.

He turned to his people. 'I think they want us to go with them.'

They looked dubious. Even Tig. 'I no like,' he said.

'I think we'll be safe enough. We've still got our weapons, remember. Come on now, show spirit, look fearless. We came here to find them . . . and succeeded. Don't spoil it all now by making hostile overtures.'

They listened. Reluctantly they agreed.

Squat warrior leaders flanked by the taller Wahwuese men descended a well-worn path to the village. People came out to see them, wary, fascinated, excited. The women and children were offered small drinking bowls full of fresh cool water. Female took from female, sheepishly, but grateful.

'You wait,' instructed the tall man again, while his band of warriors tightened in about the group of most worrisome looking visitors, containing them. If these strange little people with their ash encrusted curly hair decided to fight, the men of Wahwu thought – hoped – they would have their measure, be able to best them. Certainly they would put up a good fight.

Jack accepted the water handed him with gracious

thanks. They didn't understand but he felt that they understood his politeness.

They waited while the tall one ran up to the top of the village where the largest house of all stood, looking neat and important, its matted grass walls and wooden slatted roof sound and well maintained, its enclosing garden immaculate.

They waited some more.

They began to get impatient, twitchy. Eyes turned to Jack questioningly, and then, just when he was about to admit to himself that he had been a fool for ever getting them into this mess, the tall one returned, cloaked now in a mantle of raven black feathers, and gestured for them to follow him.

By then the sun was going down, the volcanic stone terraces and the great staircase that swept up to the large man-made plateau, bathed in a wonderful hue of salmon and rose pink.

Jack, at the head of his people, looked up and up, his neck cricking, his eyes focusing on the distant figure seated up there, masked and cloaked and veiled so bleakly, so forbodingly.

He began to climb.

Iona watched them coming, curiosity overwhelming. She turned to one of her boys, one who had also been in the party that morning which had stumbled upon the outsiders. In Wahwuese, she asked, 'Which one spoke in my old tongue from across the seas?'

'The taller man at their head. Their leader, I believe.'

She leant forward in her chair, watched the ascending figure intently. What a strange fellow. What a messy oddity! She almost giggled. Stopped herself.

He was not so dark, nor as short as the people he lead, but apart from that there were few things to distinguish him. Like everyone else he had covered his hair in mud and ashes, smeared it willy-nilly over his brown body also.

Iona was amused rather than impressed.

When he'd reached the head of the steps, standing some ten feet from her, her boy gestured for him, and those who came up close behind him supportively, to bow.

They remained stubbornly erect.

Behind her mask Iona arched a brow. 'Bow,' she intoned in English, her word meant exclusively for the odd one.

The line of his mouth set the firmer even while he felt a thrill of surprise at hearing his old language again, although distant and muffled by a mask. A touch prideful, he told her, 'The Coconut King bows to no one.'

'Oh?' she questioned mockingly, amused. 'Even a king must bow to the Living God.'

'Living God, is it?' he scoffed. 'I see only a mortal, a being no more divine than I. I come as an equal . . . as a friend if you'll permit.'

While he'd been speaking Iona had risen, something in his voice drawing her. She stared at him while a terrible excitement burst within her. She hardly heard what he had said, just remembered that voice, knew it . . . knew him.

Her heart beat so alarmingly that she clutched her chest, breath catching as, incredulously, she choked out the question:

'Jack?'

His head flew up then; he was surprised to say the least, and she caught the full gaze of his glinting blue-grey eyes, felt she recognised the sharply handsome features beneath the mud and ashes.

Her boys advanced upon him threateningly with knives drawn, thinking Iona stricken, seeing him as the inadvertent culprit. They would have finished him off there and then if she hadn't had the presence of mind, even in those unreal moments, to scream at them, 'No, no! Take him to my house. He is my guest. *Everyone* is my guest.'

Jack could only gape after the masked figure as he or

she climbed into the ceremonial chair, frowning in complete bewilderment. The person had called him Jack. Jack . . . as if he or she knew him. But in God's name, how?

Chapter Twenty-Four

In a state of trance Iona lit the lamps herself, not wishing to summon her servant Oami and suffer her questioning glances. She changed her clothes three times, finding everything suddenly unsuitable, then decided almost defiantly that he should see her in *normal* garb: her skirt of feathers, her gaudy strip of breast binding and her necklaces of pearls and shells. She was European no longer, felt that it would have been absurd to try to conform to those silly old standards. Besides (and at this thought she blushed deeply) Jack had seen her quite naked all those years ago. She was in her thirties now, but she knew her body was still . . . well . . . She pondered, trying to be objective and honest on this point. She came to the conclusion that she was as acceptable an example of womanhood as she had ever been. Plumper perhaps, but that was the norm with her people, highly acceptable.

Why am I worrying? she wondered proudly. But she knew why, deep in her head: Jack was the one man she had loved above all others. More than Tiku, more than her boys. Certainly more than her boys, she acknowledged honestly. They were pure indulgent amusement; handsome servants of whom she was fond. But Jack she had missed, mourned, cried for. Jack had stayed in her memory.

And now he was back. Once again the realisation hit her like a hammer blow, wonderful, frightening.

Still in a state of shock herself, Iona never appreciated how devastating her sudden appearance would be on Jack. She entered her reception room, instructed her boys – who were serving him wine and prawn dip and eyeing him somewhat suspiciously – to leave her alone with her guest, and only then let her eyes fall to Jack.

Sitting stiffly on a couch as if he was about to take tea in a stranger's drawing-room, his mouth had fallen open the moment the door from her dressing-room swung to. His eyes widened, shone brighter with wonder by the second. He meant to exclaim, 'God!' but his throat had dried up. He choked instead, had to gulp down wine between gasps, while Iona slapped him between the shoulder-blades.

Anxiously she enquired, 'Jack, are you all right? Oh dear, what shall . . .'

'I'm all right. Almost,' he reassured, gasps of breathlessness subsiding.

'Thank God,' she cried, close to tears. What a sublime irony it would have been if she'd found him again only to have him collapse with a seizure and die!

He stared at her, head shaking. 'Iona Stanley. God in Heaven . . . Iona Stanley. I thought you were dead.'

'I thought *you* were dead.'

They both laughed unaturally, hysterically, then fell onto each other, hugging tightly, hurting each other, so firm was their possessive grip. Rather noisily they cried in each others' hair, he lovingly recapturing the feel of her burnished silk locks, she wrinkling her nose at the earthy smell of him. Once he'd been so fastidious; now he'd gone wild. She clutched him all the more frantically, sobbed his name over and over again, so thorough in her joy that the tears just wouldn't stop.

It was many minutes before they quietened, calmed.

Even then they clung to each other, kept saying the other's name in wonder. After a time she pulled away, looked him in the eye and asked:

'Are you married?' Perhaps the time wasn't quite appropriate, maybe she was tactless, but she had to know.

'No, I'm not.'

'Nor I,' she said, sighing at the beauty of their situation; everything was perfect.

They both smiled a quirky, amused smile and then they kissed. The warmth of his lips, the pressure at once gentle and desperate, was the stuff of her dreams, her memories. Her fingers raked his hair, caressed his neck and she found herself moaning low with love, tenderness and sheer wonder. It was, without doubt surely, the most wonderful day of her life? This was joy . . . elation.

He clutched at her, reacquainting himself with her breasts, which immediately hardened to roseate peaks, with her rounded belly, her thrusting mound which strained against his exceptional hardness.

Jack dragged her to the floor, his mouth seemingly locked with hers, rolling with her amongst the coarse coconut matting, finding her with a frantic finger, then nudging at her with his engorged penis.

They'd both dreamt of such a moment so many times that they needed no preliminaries, she ripe and oozing her juices, he so hard he ached, so sensitive suddenly as he drove deeply into her, that he cried out as if wounded.

Ecstatic, she cried out his name. 'Jaaack . . . I can't believe this. I've missed you . . . wanted you for so long.'

She hugged him tightly, as if fearing she'd wake from this wonderful dream at any moment, and felt him slip through her taut flesh, as she wound her legs about him, kissing him, covering his darkly tanned and muddy face, raking his encrusted, spiky hair.

He rolled again, caught her by the hips and forced

her up and down upon him, hard, harder, until her eyes turned opaque and she cried out blissfully.

They rolled again, hitting a small table by the couch. It rocked, toppled, spilling a platter of fruit and berries all about them. The fruit was crushed beneath and between them.

Jack licked her breasts, buried his face between the pendulous mounds and pulled her down close atop of him, as if he wanted to expire thus, suffocated by her abundant womanliness.

He moved again, frenzied now, sitting up cross-legged, Iona taking his lengthy shaft fully into her, her legs closing around him.

'Ah, the feel of you,' gasped Jack, overtaken now by their mutual delight, her nipples pressed hard against him, making his senses riot. 'So warm, so tight. So very very lovely. I've dreamt of your petals a thousand times, of your little hands, your prim expression that vanishes when I fill you, possess you, show you the woman you truly are. So lovely . . . so . . . ah, oh God . . .!' He screamed out as if in agony, bringing Oami running to peer worriedly through a crack in the door, thinking that some dark deed had been done.

She watched the entwined bodies, so close they merged, were a mass of heaving arms, legs and torsos. Iona was arching, grasping at his hair, little animal noises coming from her, his shaft piercing up into her, thick, hard, thrusting and flooding with a fast flowing torrent of come.

Oami admired the splayed buttocks of her mistress and the huge member so soundly lodged within Iona, watched as they collapsed in a languid mass upon the floor, gasping for breath and laughing. She discreetly stole away.

As invariably happened at the sight of her mistress's exposed sex, Oami felt a wave of longing sweep up through her, ran to her curtained-off sleeping cubicle and searched with urgency beneath her bed.

She pulled forth her personal dildo and quickly fastened it by the straps to her heel, Japanese fashion. It was an imposing phallus, made especially for her by a master craftsman from the village, out of a hollowed cylinder of beaten silver. Its tip was bulbous and some eight inches in circumference, its stalk a series of intricately hammered Repoussé patterns that raised the surface in bobbles, all finished as smooth as silk.

Sometimes Oami filled it with hot water prior to use so that it took on a human kind of warmth, but she was too impatient today, opened her darkly-curled sex-lips and set the end at her wet opening, dropping her knees to the floor as she sat, in a loosely cross-legged fashion, so that she was agape and fully accommodating, then she pushed with her heel, watched the truncated object slowly disappear within herself, until her heel was jammed against her vulva. Then she withdrew, leaving just the tip within herself, and pushed in again. This time it was easier, the passage lubricating nicely. Oami held on to her ankle and forced the phallus into herself with greater speed and force, the fingers of her other hand clamping about her clitoris and pulling, pushing, rubbing deliciously.

She thought of Iona, of the pink sex with its russet curls, of inserting the cleansing sponge stick amongst its folds, deep within, and she contracted about the hefty shaft that rent her, calling out softly, her mistress's name on her lips.

Continually Iona watched Jack, as if she feared he would just disappear into thin air at any moment. Still she couldn't believe that he was alive, with her, that there was a very good chance for romance to blossom, for total happiness. Her eyebrow raised, therefore, with unconscious query as she intercepted a look that passed between him and the fretful Mia. She'd noted the female's close proximity to Jack earlier yet had refrained politely from questioning it. Now she couldn't stop herself asking, 'The women is . . .?'

'Mia, mother of my daughter, Alaba.'

'Oh.' It came out a little blunter than intended, the speaker quite evidently taken by surprise. 'I thought you said you weren't married?'

'I'm not. The squat people don't bother too much about such ceremonial nonsense, they're more spontaneous, and sometimes not so inclined towards lifelong commitment. The woman beside her, her sister, Sanga, has borne me two sons also. And there are other women, other children. It is our way.'

Iona sniffed superiorly. 'It sounds a might casual and promiscuous to me.'

His eyebrows raised, almost amused at such haughtiness. 'Evidently your moral code is much stricter now, Iona, than on our previous encounter all those years ago.'

She blushed, his cynicism making her uncomfortable, a little ashamed.

'And who,' he continued, adding deliberately to her discomfort, 'are these two children who sit so familiarly at your feet and the male attendants who give me such hostile stares. Perhaps *you'd* like to explain?'

'I . . . well, they're my children. Obviously,' she said, an irritated edge to her voice now.

'And are *you* married?'

'You know I'm not. I told you. I'm a widow.'

He digested that thoughtfully but said nothing.

Iona waited, tortured by the embarrassment of her thoughts. If he asked her how her husband had died she would die rather than tell him! Cut out her tongue rather than say Tiku had died like a stallion mounted at the rear of *another wife*.

'And the young men?' he persisted.

'They are my attendants, just as you said, a necessity for a Living God.'

He smirked. 'Really?'

'Yes, *really*,' she hissed.

'They're not your lovers?'

Iona smiled deviously then, disinclined to accommodate him with straightforward answers, even if she partly understood his need for such intimate questions. 'They have a duty to keep the Living God happy and content. It's a time honoured tradition.'

He laughed, put a hand about her shoulders and pulled her forcefully close, whispering in her ear, 'It's a tradition I hope you'll dispense with forthwith.'

'Why?' His breath upon her ear sent delicious thrills through her, the steady rise and fall of his mud-daubed chest mesmerising.

'A woman only needs one man in her life . . . if he's the right man.'

She laughed then, his conceit self-mocking and quite unreal, intended solely to amuse, even as it captivated her.

'And are you the man for me, Jack?'

'Could be,' he said musingly, eyebrows quirking as supposedly he gave the idea some thought. 'Could very well be.'

They let the subject drop then good-naturedly and concentrated on setting a cordial example to their respective peoples, twice having to mediate when fighting broke out between those from north and south. Luckily the flare-ups were quickly over with, no real harm done, no one killed and weapons only reached for threateningly but never actually drawn.

Iona watched Jack's women and appraised them calculatingly. Years of being a sublime leader had conditioned her to getting her own way – to getting what she wanted. She wanted Jack. She felt almost certain that she had him, but she didn't like the thought of those women being around, available.

At length, after spending many moments deep in thought, Iona stood up, raised her hands in a gesture requesting silence. Jack watched curiously, sipping his wine.

'People of Wahwu I would address you all.' She turned to Jack. 'Please relay my message.' Then she turned back to the crowd before her. 'Tall people, short people from beyond the mountains, it is a fact that you both share this island, and that at last you have come together as the gods ordained.'

Jack repeated word for word, amused by her grand style.

'I, the Living God, Iona, wish you to become one people, to live together. To this end I decree that unattached males and females from both tribes should henceforth make a concerted effort to select a mate from the other . . .'

Jack balked inwardly, thinking that she attempted to go too far too soon, but kept translating, furious, too, that she should take it upon herself to make such a major decision without consulting him first . . . privately. This had needed discussion, thought, tact. Instead it was being railroaded quite ruthlessly.

She kept smiling serenely, triumphantly, even while eligible bachelors and blossoming maidens looked about at what was being offered them and gave vent to cries of rebellion and expressions of unwavering distaste. Marry a stranger, and one so very odd? Never!

'You may not care for such a suggestion now. You see strangers, people with different outlooks and customs, but this *must* change. It has to. Otherwise the squat people might as well return to their own lands, live a life of isolation once more . . .'

Jack relayed her words, trying to digest them as he did so. Now that he'd got over his initial surprise, he quite liked her idea.

She continued, the words coming easier now, with greater enthusiasm as the idea blossomed, burgeoned, gave vent to all manner of imagined possibilities. 'Mixed we would become stronger, future children neither too tall nor too short. We need no longer be hostile, could exchange knowledge, spread about the island, tame it, build roads . . .

'But I would not ask anything of others which I felt unable to ask of my own. And so I propose that when they become of a suitable age, my son, Ran and your king's daughter, Alaba, shall be paired. A living symbol of the joining of our two tribes.'

From their positions at the feet of the mighty ones the children concerned poked their tongues out at each other, but were otherwise unconcerned, even disinterested. Time went tortuously slow when you were a child, and maturity seemed a comfortably long way off still. They had nothing to be concerned about . . . yet.

Jack was in shock, repeating like a robot.

'Also I wish my boys, who have served me well, to now do my bidding one last time and take as partners the principal unattached women from King Jack's court – his former mistresses and companions. They shall be an example to us all of harmonious living. And I'm sure that they won't let us down, will realise the importance placed upon their unions being successful.'

Jack translated still, despite the growing look of dismay on his face, his voice faltering even though he made a valiant attempt at self-control. The bitch! The devious, scheming, clever bitch! Her brilliance impressed him, her unmitigated gall filled him with fury.

He finished. There was uproar. At any moment a pitched battle might erupt. He raised his hand, pleading for quiet, had to shout. 'Such measures seem too harsh, I know, and have come as a shock. But, please, sleep the night on them, think on them. The Living God's method of putting such things before you all may have been unsubtle, to say the least,' said Jack scathingly, 'but what she proposes is logical, the only sensible way for our peoples to progress. Please, as your king, I ask you: don't fight. Think. You are wise, I know, and will pick the correct path.'

Then he turned his shrivelling gaze fully on Iona and hissed, 'I wish to speak to you alone. *Now*. Do not decline or I shall drag you off, despite the offense it'll cause your elders.'

She smiled sweetly, a trill of laughter punctuating her words. 'Of course I'll come with you, Jack. Willingly. Whatever could have made you think otherwise?'

Chapter Twenty-Five

The way to her lodge was not easy. Her boys blocked her path, snarling at Jack and pleading with her not to forsake them, not to resign them to such a dreadful fate. They loved her, adored her. Surely she couldn't be so heartless as to set them aside? Coolly, Iona told them that her decision was final, that one day they would thank her for giving them back a normal way of life. Being constantly at the beck and call of one woman was not good, not natural. But they wanted nothing else, they insisted. She stamped her foot in exasperation. Jack threateningly told them to clear off, gripped Iona about her upper arm and dragged her homewards purposefully.

The moment the door closed she was pushed back against it, pinned there, his fingers bruising her upper arms. Eyes blazed, the looks transmitted hostile, though in Iona's was also the merest hint of amusement. She sensed victory. A servant girl appeared, gave a flustered, uncertain exclamation and was gone just as quickly.

Lethal voiced, he warned her, 'Never ever do anything like that again.'

Her eyebrows raised questioningly. She blinked innocently, infuriatingly, 'Whatever do you mean, Jack?'

'I can keep my own life in order, thank you. I don't need a busy-body female taking matters into her own hands.'

'Didn't you like my idea?'

'I didn't care for your methods, on everyone elses behalf as well as my own. You nearly started a war.'

'Oh, you exaggerate, surely,' she scoffed.

His grip tightened. He shook her so her hair tumbled. She spat it out of her mouth, eyes slamming.

'Let go of me, Jack. You're hurting. And I think you're forgetting who I am.'

'And that's another thing,' he shouted. 'When we're alone you can bloody well cut out that nonsense. You're just plain Iona Stanley to me. Always will be.'

'Try telling that to my elders and they'll have you put to death most horribly for blasphemy.'

'No woman is my superior. I won't have it and neither will my people. You'd better believe it. The Coconut King is superior to all . . . especially women.'

'Bah.' She didn't agree.

'Well, you may not like it and I don't say I wholly agree with it myself, but that's the way they think, what they believe. If I cannot be seen to be superior then I must at least appear as an equal. If you cannot concede that then there will be nothing but trouble ahead and I might just as well take them back to their side of the island.'

Iona no longer smiled gloatingly. He spoke sense and he alarmed her by speaking of leaving.

'Can't you see I only did it initially because I wanted to get rid of your women? Then the idea just sort of grew, even took me by surprise, kept spilling out of my mouth. It was jealousy. I wasn't thinking straight.'

Instantly he softened just a little. 'Jealous? Whatever for? Are you that unsure of me? Silly. D'you know, I spent many a miserable hour thinking of you, remembering our very brief time together, believing you dead. I can't put into words the joy I feel at having you back, the one woman I knew I wanted above all others. It was because of loving you that I never took a wife, had so many women who meant less to me than they should have.'

She blinked at him, her eyes fever bright. 'Love *me*, Jack? Aren't you just glad to see me alive because I'm . . . well . . . a white woman, a reminder of civilisation?'

He nodded definitely. 'I love you, Iona. Love you with a passion, even now when I'm mad enough to slap you. I love you fiercely.'

She didn't want him to release her any longer. She never wanted him to ever again. She curled her naked, coral-bangled and silver braceleted arms about his neck, gave a disbelieving little shake of her head. 'Oh, I'm so glad, Jack. So very glad, I could almost squeal with excitement and happiness. I've loved you through all these long years, even when I was Tiku's wife – his seventh wife. I never forgot you . . . always remembered.'

'I think its time to stop living off memories. We're back together – in the most extraordinary circumstances, I'll admit. Shall we share our experiences from now on?'

She nodded with almost indecent eagerness at his formal enquiry, pulled his blond head forward, groaned as his mouth swooped, crushed, hot and hungrily demanding, full of the longing of years.

Clothes did little to hamper them. In a moment his loincloth was gone, her skirt of feathers merely lifted aside. He lifted her, kissing her continuously, her legs going about his waist, his manhood sliding sweetly into her. He cradled her buttocks, held her while Iona raised and fell with exquisite, agonising slowness upon him. Their bodies banged against the door with thud-thud noises, glistening with sweat, groanings filling the air.

From behind the kitchen door the servant girl, Oami, listened and giggled, decided to prepare a tray of wine and delicacies. In a while they would be very hungry, then very sleepy. Tonight, for the first time, the Living God was truly pleased and happy.

But even the servant girl had underestimated their need for each other. Dawn was breaking before they collapsed exhausted and sated on top of Iona's majestic bed. They fell asleep at once, too mind-blown even to think of eating, the snores of both filling the dawn-cooled chamber.

And even then Jack was not done. He woke as the sun appeared, hard for her again, his member huge and uncomfortable between his legs.

Iona woke to find pillows beneath her belly, so that her bottom-mouth and vagina were conveniently offered up to him, and Jack deep within her, holding her wide open by the thighs and thrusting with majestic tenderness at her very core.

She'd never had such an exquisite awakening, and came quickly with a drowsy cry, as he plunged into her wetness, roaring through his climax. Still in her, he collapsed, and was soon snoring in her ear.

The boy and girl stared out across the starlit ocean, in the same place and yet not together, keeping a wary distance.

The boy, Tomo, was one of Iona's 'helpers'. He'd come up onto the high plateau above the village to drown his sorrows with wine. His dearest heart, his beloved Iona, had rejected him, along with rest of her boys. He couldn't understand it. His pride was wounded. His heart broken.

The girl, Sita, from the squat people's tribe, had had a furious row with her parents over this controversial subject of arranged marriages between the two tribes, had come, bringing naught but a pouch of narcotic nuts, to simmer down and be alone. Unfortunately, she'd climbed up to the grassy, treed plateau only to find that someone else had beaten her to it. And, of all people, one of the Tall Ones.

She sat several paces away from him, ignoring him, muttering, 'Marry one like you? Never! Look how you sit; so tall, so arrogant, and not a hair on your lanky body!'

He shot her a hostile glance, not understanding a word, of course, then looked out to sea, snarling, 'Me, marry the likes of her? Hah! She has funny little legs and a squashed up nose. There is nothing graceful about her . . . about any of them. No, I won't do it, won't settle for a woolly haired creature covered in ashes. Not when I've pleasured the Great One herself.'

He drank deeply from his pitcher, remembered his inbred sense of hospitality and grudgingly extended the wine towards the girl with a grunt.

She eyed it suspiciously, moved closer, held out her pouch of nuts in exchange. Equally suspiciously, he took one and held it in his mouth, letting the saliva moisten it to a chewable softness as the girl demonstrated. She drank some wine, then handed back the pitcher, watching him surreptitiously out the corner of her eye.

Maybe he wasn't so bad. Not as repulsive as she first thought. Certainly she liked the way his manhood lay long and slim down his leg, so different from the members of the men in her tribe. Theirs were shorter, had more girth.

The juices from the nut began, insidiously, to work upon him. He was barely aware of the fact. Gave the girl a grudging smile and thumped his slim, hairless chest. 'Me Tomo.'

She quirked an eyebrow. 'Tomo?'

He poined at himself again. 'Tomo.' Then at her. 'You?'

'You?' She shook her head uncomprehendingly.

He took a deep breath, determined to keep his patience. But, heavens, she was slow! He went through the procedure again.

This time there was a spark of understanding in the hazel eyes. 'Ah,' she pointed, 'Tomo. Me Sita. S – i – t

– a.' She said it painstakingly slow and clear, as if conversing with an imbecile.

They fell silent again, looking each other over and chewing on their nuts. They were both thoughtful. A little frown puckered her forehead. He quirked an eyebrow.

Her eyes were on his penis again, her sex growing moist. His gaze had fastened upon her breasts. He couldn't understand why he hadn't noticed them before. They were lovely. Wahwuese women had high, pert, modest breasts when young. But this girl was more like Iona, had full, pendulous breasts, pulled down by their own weight, the nipples large, drawing the eye, calling out to be sucked.

'Would you mind . . .?' he wondered, reaching out experimentally and touching, his senses heightened by the drug that now invaded and fuddled his brain.

She made no objection, reached out a hand herself and ran a finger down the length of his silky, soft member.

Together, they shuffled nearer on their bottoms, no longer needing to stretch, hands given free rein.

They knelt chest to chest, thigh to thigh, hands seeking out all that was foreign and appraising it, shy one moment, bold the next. She rubbed against him, he nuzzled between her breasts, loving the warm softness that all but smothered him.

'I should like to couple with you,' said the girl, full of curiosity.

He knit his brow, not understanding, but was left in no doubt when her little hand tugged awkwardly at his lenghtening slim shaft and rolled it between her generous thighs.

That sent sparks of passion flaring within him. 'I wonder if you'd like to do it, here, now, in the grass? Let me show you some of the tricks the Great One taught me; invade your hot, pungent little body, touch at your very core with the tip of my lengthy shaft.'

She stared at him starry eyed, feeling the snake's

head slithering along her sex, gliding into her. She didn't understand a word but there was a wonderful velvety quality to his voice. She rose and fell upon him, feeling him where no squat man's blade had ever managed to penetrate, was heady with delight.

Gently she fell backwards, arms tight about the boy, into the grass and moss, feeling the full penetration of his shaft, her legs wide flung, inner thighs and mound straining upwards to offer and take all.

He stayed close, as if welded to her, jerking his loins and nuzzling her magnificent breasts, her whole body seeming to cushion him, caress him, enfold him in some delicious spell of wantoness.

He took her speedily and, when they'd both rested and drank some more wine, curled up down the length of her back on his side and entered her again in a lazy, far more leisurely manner, his hand snaking around to her bud so that he might stimulate her there, most gently, most thoroughly and thoughtfully, as Iona had shown him.

Sated, on the verge of sleep, he rested on an elbow and watched her as she lay dreamily, her eyes half closed. There were after all, good points about her. 'I should like to do this again,' he conceded.

She smiled to herself, not quite so definite now in her mind about the obnoxiousness of marriage if it involved such a man. Perhaps she had been a little rash to say 'No' so soon. She should perhaps give it a little more thought.

Chapter Twenty-Six

'Jack, do you trust me?'

'Yes,' he said with deliberate thoughtful slowness. 'Yes, I suppose so. Have I a reason not to?'

'No,' she said quickly, 'Oh no. It's just that I have to ask you to do something. Something demanded of you as Special Chosen One of the Living God . . . a ritual.'

'What sort of ritual?' he wondered, eyebrow quirking, body coming up into a sitting position, warily alert. He'd been lying on a couch on the veranda, watching the sun going down with Iona lounging beside him. It was something they did nearly every afternoon when the activities and business of the day ceased.

'I can't say. It's secret until the event. The elders and officiators like it that way and it's essential to the success of the ritual. But you won't be harmed, I promise you. You know that anyhow – that I'd never do anything to hurt you.'

'Yes . . . well . . .' Jack sounded just a might dubious.

'*Please*, Jack. Do this one little thing for me,' she pleaded softly, voice weedling, smile winning.

'When's it to be?'

'Tonight.'

'Don't want to give a chap time for second thoughts, that it?'

She just smiled.

'What do I have to do?'

'Nothing. Don't worry about a thing. Two handmaidens will come to collect you when the sun finally disappears.'

'What about you?'

'I'll be waiting at the Place of Sacrifice for you, Jack.'

A lone eyebrow shot up high on his forehead at that.

'Oh, and Jack . . .'

'Yes?'

'Have a word with your people, will you, put their minds at ease. They're not used to our ways, might misinterpret certain aspects of the ritual they'll witness. Assure them that you have wholeheartedly consented.'

'I'm not entirely sure that I can,' he said, with an exaggerated frown that remained, despite her reassuringly light laugh.

Curiously, trusting, Jack climbed the mountainside, trying once or twice to strike up some sort of conversation with his two pretty escorts. But they were having none of it and carried out their duties with a solemnity that amused him.

He'd been cloaked in a fine mantle of black feathers, his blond locks combed and braided into a queue at his nape in a style which did much for his already considerable good looks. He'd been given a tangy cordial to drink which was deceptively alcoholic and had his body rubbed with coconut milk and wild flower essence. *That* he'd enjoyed enormously.

Up the ancient hewn stone steps he climbed, thigh muscles groaning a little, his limp barely noticeable during such exertions.

'Nice night for it,' he joked.

Neither girl spoke but he would have sworn he'd seen a spark of amusement in the brown-black eyes of one of them.

Below him squat and tall people were assembled, torches burning, a Wahwuese chant pulsing through the air in time to the drum beat. Communal fires lit the scene, illuminating dark faces, bleached skulls upon poles; shrunken, mummified heads, their bones and brains removed by some fiendish, unknown method to allow for the considerable shrinkage achieved. Jack saw all this, heard the deep, resounding drum beat and felt a shiver course his spine.

On reaching the terrace upon which, long ago, had been constructed the Place of Sacrifice, Jack immediately looked for the reassuring presence of Iona. She wasn't there. Certainly amongst the gowned and masked attendants she wasn't apparent.

He had no time to think, or become overly apprehensive. His handmaidens were removing his cloak, leaving him standing there in front of the vast, torchlit assembly, in nothing but his red pigskin loincloth. They gestured gracefully to the huge slab of stone at centre stage, bade him in well rehearsed unison, 'Please, mount.'

It was an imposing slab of local stone, seven feet long, three feet wide, four feet high off the ground. At its upper corners were protruding chicken effigies fashioned in gold. Not keen to comply and yet feeling obliged to because of his hasty promise to Iona, Jack climbed up, allowed himself to be manoeuvered onto his back. He instantly regretted it. Four muscular men garbed in robes, carrying ropes, appeared from nowhere, had him bound tight to the slab, the ropes anchored at the convenient hooks made by the golden claws of the ornamental chickens. They worked damnably fast, taking Jack completely by surprise.

'Hoi now, what's this,' he demanded to know, worriedly.

One of the handmaidens whispered at his ear. 'Ssh, King Jack. You are safe, don't fear. Lie still. Remember your promise to our Living God. Hers to you.'

He did, but his anxiety remained.

A cloaked and masked figure appeared before the giant skull hewn into the face of the mountain. At first

Jack thought it was Iona, but the actions of the person lead him to doubt this. Facing the altar, back to Jack, the cloaked figure raised a dagger dramatically to the heavens. Jack, tied to the slab, felt instant alarm and panic, actually strained uselessly against his bonds.

'This has gone far—'

His words were cut off by the hand of Arnk, who leant over him in a loose robe of gaudy splendour and snapped in quite theatrical severity, 'Silence in the presence of the Living God!'

Chastened like a schoolboy, he fell quiet, though there remained a defiant set to his mouth. Behind her mask Iona almost giggled. She cut the fruits of passion with the ceremonial knife and then passed them over to a servant for squeezing. Jack watched, deflated with a sigh of relief, began to think that perhaps he had overreacted just a little.

Into a bowl went the juices, something else amber and clear, and a flick of powders with much incanting and intoning from those self-important attendants upon the ceremonial terrace.

Iona took back the brew, placed it in the mouth orifice of a great stone skull and stood before it, quiet and still.

Jack watched her, trying to decide whether it was her or not, and if it was, just what the hell was she doing? He couldn't apply his mind to it though, and was soon faced with other distractions.

Arnk was searching for the end of his loincloth, fingers going back, sides, then down the front of the skimpy garment. He squirmed, her eyes, when they locked with his, full of silent mirth. She found it. He apprehensively held his breath. Then she began to unwind. Jack had never been so embarrassed in his life, didn't think he'd ever be able to forgive Iona for inflicting this upon him. Arnk's gropings of moments before had aroused him despite himself. He was ramrod stiff, his member sprang up to attention the moment the pigskin was finally whisked away with a dramatic flourish.

Over Jack's face washed a look of shock and deep disquiet. On the faces of those who hovered near was amusement, solemnity and, in Arnk's case, appreciation. He was a fine figure of a man. Not a giant like Tiku, but nicely proportioned even so. Very nicely proportioned, she decided, taking another, closer, unabashed perusal of his golden body. Iona was a lucky woman.

Arnk took up the ceremonial metal jug and dripped a few droplets of oil onto Jack's taut belly. He tensed even more. She laid brown hands artfully on him, remembering years of pleasing Tiku, and smoothed in the oil over his belly, his thighs, between his legs. She cupped his balls, circled his penis and glided upwards.

Jack groaned as if in pain. 'This isn't fair.'

And Arnk smiled, showing her teeth, almost laughing.

He grew still more in her hand, squirmed against his bonds vigorously, was stirred greatly despite himself and his other conflicting emotions.

Then, just as cruelly, Arnk let him go, stepped back. His mind protested, *Oh, no no*, in frustration, and he growled out loud, only to be startled into silence by the looming figure in the black cloak and mask. The figure bade him drink, even lifted his head to assist him. Jack gulped and choked a little on the flow, and then knew an almost childish relief and lessening of fear when the mask was removed and Iona revealed. *I'm safe, safe.*

He smiled at her. She stared back at him with serene dignity, all mysterious like a true goddess, even as an attendant lifted the cloak from her shoulders, leaving her naked. She was red fire and the palest, smoothest alabaster.

She climbed up onto the slab, between his twitching legs with their golden hairs, stroked him casually almost, experimentally. He sprang up in response, his body quite beyond his control. Then Iona smiled.

She leant over him, her breasts grazing his chest with the lightest of touches and whispered at his ear, 'This is the final act, Jack. Perform well. For them . . .' her head inclined to the spellbound crowd below '. . . and for me.'

Perform? he wondered, What? How?

She straddled him, came down over him with exquisite slowness and impaled herself. The breath rushed out of him. It seemed to Jack that it was she, not he, who was the performer. He couldn't do much else save lie still and let her do what she would. Even while he couldn't deny that he was enjoying this ceremonial coupling (despite the discomfiture of being watched by well over a thousand people!) he had to admit to a slight petulance of spirit, a resentment at being so used. He liked it, yet hated being powerless: loved her touch and yet knew he'd been drugged into a lethargic kind of acquiesence that infuriated him. He was used. Without will. Manipulated.

She moved faster, her breathing heavy. Up. Down. There was a sublime look upon her face, a glaze to her eyes that enchanted Jack. Iona Stanley was no beauty, yet in that instance she was quite lovely. He adored her, reared up the harder in response to her frantic movements, her approaching crisis, whispered up huskily as if to the heavens rather than her, 'Love you . . . love you . . .'

She cried out, racked by delightful spasms of sensation, hung her head exhaustedly and draped his chest with her abundant red hair. A thrill went through Jack, tipped him over the edge. He thrust up, up, as much as his bindings would allow and came to a climax with a roar that not even a multitude could make him suppress for dignity's sake.

The mixed crowd roared in satisfaction, the drums died down to a gentle, slow rhythmn and Iona slipped off his sweating body, was immediately cloaked. She turned, smiled fondly as her chair arrived and she took her seat. 'It is over now, Jack. You did well. I shall see you back at the lodge.'

He was abandoned, dismissed. Only temporarily,

granted, but abandoned even so. He lay there, naked, sated and sticky wet from lovemaking; he felt an utter fool.

Only a short while later, after climbing down to the village on oddly wobbly legs, Jack flew into the lodge, full of indignation, and demanded some answers from Iona.

She was reclining on a couch before which had been set a low table laden with tempting supper morsels. She looked up, smiling sweetly, unperturbed.

'Now, pray tell, what the hell was that all about?'

'It was the Ritual of Sensation, Jack. Undertaken by very few. You were greatly honoured.'

'Huh!' he scoffed.

'Truly. You knew all emotions tonight. All save jealousy, that is; the Wahwuese won't tolerate that emotion . . . not openly, at least. You knew fear; anger, I expect; joy, I hope; perhaps even some amusement at your extraordinary predicament?'

'Most of those, I admit, though definitely not amusement. But what was the point?'

'Why should there be one? And if there is, why should a Living God divulge it to you?' she said with wry superiority.

He frowned at that, then overcame any resentment and laughed. 'It was all a bloody nonsense and I won't do it ever again, d'you hear?'

'Fear not, Jack. You won't be asked. Where would be the point? The ritual relies upon surprise, upon innocence . . . of a kind. After tonight yours has gone. Only strangers – chosen strangers – can take part in the ritual. For those who know of it could not feel the emotions, would know what was coming next.'

Jack digested that thoughtfully.

'Come. Eat. You deserve it,' said Iona, smirking.

Her meaning wasn't lost upon him. His eyebrows knit. 'And that's another thing, being made to perform like that, in front of all those people. It was . . .'

'Humiliating?'

'Well, no, not exactly.'

'What was it then, Jack?' pressed Iona, trying not to laugh.

'It was bloody undignified, that's what. Not on.'

'I know. But I wouldn't ask you to do anything I haven't done myself. I knew you could see it through with spirit, prove yourself to my people. Now they think you a worthy consort for me, Jack, don't you see?'

He nodded, a little reluctantly, 'Yes . . . yes, I suppose,' then grinned as he moved close to her on the couch, took the succulent piece of chicken she profered specially for him. She smiled to herself, knowing that flattery had smoothed his ruffled feathers with apparent ease.

Chapter Twenty-Seven

*T*wo pairs of eyes peered intently into the night amidst fern fronds, focusing on the torchlit high altar on the terrace above the village. One pair were blue-grey, sparkling full of mischief and the others were brown-black, unfathomable.

They were hidden in the undergrowth on the same level as the ceremony. They were spying. And they were disappointed.

Tig yawned. 'What you reckon they doing, Friend Jack? It just so much mumbling and playing at . . . how you say? Silly buggers? to me.'

'Aye, silly buggers, Tig. That's about the measure of it. Another bloody ritual. A lot of mumbo-jumbo,' said Jack, flatly, as bored as his companion.

Why they'd bothered to steal up on the proceedings and watch unobserved, they couldn't rightly remember now. It had seemed a good idea at the time. Something forbidden. Iona had said it was private, a ceremony to honour the revered of Wahwu's ancestors. Jack had felt certain there was more to it than that, that she was missing something out, misleading him, excluding him. Now he thought perhaps she had just been trying to spare him a night of tedium, of endless incanting and sombre doings.

On his belly beside Tig, Jack stretched down a hand, felt for the pigskin pouch tied at his waist which contained a supply of narcotic nuts. He rationed himself stringently, didn't like to think that they were in any way getting a hold over him, though he had to admit that, in small doses, they *were* something of a habit. It wasn't that he worried overmuch about the effect they had temporarily over him psychologically. No, that came a very poor second to his niggling concern for his teeth. The nuts stained. The more he used them the browner his teeth would become. Vanity it was, then, that had prompted moderation.

Jack handed Tig a nut, popped one into his own mouth and began to chew. The effects of the chewing which followed would likely be far more exciting than anything that was going to happen that night at the Place of Sacrifice.

They chewed, chewed, the centre of the nuts turning to gum in their mouths, its narcotic properties stealing over them subtly. It was like being drunk but more so, images and colours brilliantly highlighted.

They chewed lazily, and watched.

On the terrace Iona and Mam made the offerings of fruit and wine to the Old Ones, piling their succulent gifts high around the great skull. Tomorrow, when the ceremony had been played out, the fruit would be sent down to the village, to the old, the young. Tonight, in a private ceremony, the Living God supposedly became one with exalted ones who had previously trodden her path.

It was a lonely, rather personal vigil that gave little reward for a heavy night's worshipping, and the villagers, accordingly, were given the option of staying at home. They did so, very willingly, seeing no point in standing about watching something that wasn't remotely interesting, miraculous, or sexual of nature.

Beside Iona and Mam in their flowing carmine robes that – Jack had begun to think as the nut's essences seeped into his bloodstream, affecting his brain – clung enticingly to their plump and lovely women's forms, were two male attendants. Jack recognised them with a curl of the lip, his snort rousing the dreamy Tig.

'Playthings,' he sneered derisively. 'Penises in pretty packaging.'

'This penis, Jack, is it another of your quaint English swear words?'

'Oh no. Penis is . . . Well, in your language its something like Shaft-with-a-mind-of-its-own or Woman-pleaser.'

'Ah, I see. I have one of those. Yes. I call mine Pleasure-Giver. While my woman calls it, simply, Joy.'

Jack nodded. 'No doubt very apt.' And was about to elaborate on his theory that Iona's boys had little between their ears save air, when Mia stole up behind him and lay down the length of his body.

'What the . . .!' his head pivoted in surprise. 'How did you find us?'

'I follow you. Miss you. You no come see Mia any longer.'

'I have and want one woman only,' he told her firmly, removing her hand from his upper arm.

'Even when she spend her time in such foolishness? Spend it talking to stone skulls instead of keeping Jack happy?'

Jack smiled, admired her deviousness. He could feel her breasts against his shoulder-blade, was disquieted by the hand that now crept around his torso, down over his waist and didn't stop until it had possessively gripped about the girth of him.

'Now cut that out!' He rolled away from her, nearer his friend who was watching them with interest.

She pouted, plump lips plumping still further. 'Maybe I should kill her, rid you of her, get you back for me . . . me alone.'

A harshness instantly cloaked his sharp features, flinted his grey eyes. 'Never even think it, Mia,' he warned her. 'If anything ever happened to Iona I would be destroyed. There would be no Jack for you then, not even as a friend. I would be finished. Do you understand? I would be so unhappy that I might as well be dead too. Would you want that?'

She frowned, reluctantly gave the faintest shake of her head. 'But its . . . it's not . . .' There wasn't the appropriate word in her language and her fists balled with frustration. Then it came to her, the words that eloquently expressed her feelings and she declared, in a passion:

'Its not damned bloody fair!'

Jack almost smiled, but stopped himself, nodded understandingly, placatingly. 'I know. I know. Life is like that. Never straightforward, never simple.'

Mia was aggrieved by his triteness, though she guessed it was the magic nuts speaking now rather than her Jack. She knelt behind him and wrapped her arms around his chest, her breath hot on his nape.

He shoved her away, too interested in what was happening on the terrace to be bothered with her, ordered Tig, as his second in command, 'Get rid of her. Shut her up.'

'At once,' acknowledged the native, eyes demonically gleeful.

He dragged Mia off, a hand over her mouth, bound her with vine to the trunk of a nearby tree and held his knife to her throat, threatening her, 'Make a sound and I'll slit your nose, woman.'

She hissed, straining at her bonds. 'You no scare me, Tig.'

'No?'

'No!'

He trailed the point of his knife delicately down from throat to breasts, pricking a nipple.

Her breath caught. She tensed, going wet between the legs.

He removed the knife and took her nipple into his mouth instead, sucking violently.

She arched, a thrill running through her.

'Open,' he commanded.

'No,' she snarled, though she wanted him desperately despite her defiance.

He trailed the knife down over her belly, circling her navel, sliding down over her triangle of hair, shaving a path through it with the finely honed blade, knelt before her and forced her legs wide.

Her clitoris peeped from between the slits of her black curled mound. He touched it with the point of his knife, with care, cold steel caressing with great delicacy, making Mia groan with a terrible pleasure, though she didn't dare to squirm, stood rigid, very slightly quivering.

Tig touched himself at the same time, stroking a fat member that was already hard, then abandoned the knife, to plunge his length up into her, lifting the girl clear off the floor with the violence of his assault.

Jack soon forgot about Mia completely, his eyes going back to the altar of the Living God, his hand reaching up and parting the obscuring fronds before his eyes.

'I don't like the way they look at her,' he observed with more than a hint of possessiveness in his voice.

'Certainly their eyes seem hungry as they go over their bodies,' agreed Tig, his interest centred upon the Living God's number one assistant that night, Mam. Iona was beautiful in her own rather odd way, but she was Jack's, out of bounds to Tig, and so he dismissed her almost from his thoughts. But Mam, well, she was quite different, very interesting . . . a very pretty little widow, just crying out, it seemed to him, for love, for fun.

Tig watched her kneel beside the chanting goddess, hand over a ceremonial beaker from which Iona drank. Her rear was round and generous, the simple red robe she wore swishing about it enticingly, accentuating its curves. He felt himself stiffening in his loincloth, standing out like a tentpole.

'I don't like the way they're staring at her . . . her breasts . . . her . . . I'm going . . .'

'Jack?' Tig came up into a crouch, blinked in surprise

and stared after the lurching form of his friend as he crept none too expertly, up behind the pretty boys, who stood removed from the sanctified area near the altar, were, Tig felt derisively, there purely for decoration. He moved quickly and silently after his friend.

What followed can only be described as a brawl. Fists flew, noses bled and Iona's boys lost their poise and grace completely, rolled in the dust, kicked, punched, spat and clawed, trying to prove that they were something more than nice bodies and fair looks. Unfortunately they didn't and, fighting against the likes of Jack and Tig who were all fired up, intoxicated and not above fighting dirty, they were always the underdogs.

Iona could see the commotion going on out the corner of her eye, recognised Jack and his friend. She tried to carry on, frowning, lips thinning with displeasure, noticeably flinched when one of her male attendants landed on his back only a yard from her, with a groan of pain and the wind audibly knocked out of him.

Mam squealed with surprise and even a little fright, then found that even though she tried desperately hard – mindful of her circumstances and the honour done her in being chosen as Iona's assistant for the occasion – she just couldn't quite stop herself giggling.

Tig kicked his bloodied and beaten adversary over the edge of the terrace and the man's yell of pain could be heard growing fainter as he rolled and fell, rolled and fell, down an unknown number of the giant hewn steps.

Jack's man ran off before a similar indignity could be heaped upon him, two fingers pegging his bleeding nose and his vile curses raining down upon Jack in frantic, jabbering Wahwuese.

Iona rose, turned imperiously, furious. 'That was disgraceful, deplorable, unpardonable!' Then focused a cold eye on the chuckling Mam. 'And certainly not in the least amusing.'

Mam put a hand over her mouth but it did no good. Jack swaggered up, dusty, bloody and obviously pleased with himself. He'd been itching to hit one of her boys for days. 'It wasn't meant to amuse or entertain. It was to . . .' He paused, eyebrows quirking as he thought hard. What was it for? For the life of him he couldn't remember now. He'd just felt compelled. He finished by telling Iona with some belligerence. 'Well, I'm not sorry, that's for sure.'

'What are you doing here at all? I should very much like to know,' demanded the Living God.

'We came to watch, to see, to keep an eye on what's ours.'

'Oh you did, did you!' gasped Iona, wide-eyed at such arrogance.

'Yes,' said Jack, soberly.

'Yes,' said Tig, leering at Mam and winking.

She giggled, made much of looking about for a route of escape, then dashed off into the bushes, squealing shrilly with delight when she looked back quickly and saw that Tig was after her, as expected, as desired.

'Oh honestly!' said Iona disgustedly, turning her back on them and Jack and swiftly marching to the edge of the terrace and the steps.

He threw himself after her, tackled her about the ankles, grappled with her as she turned, onto her back, kicking and wriggling, absolutely furious.

He lay atop of her, pinioning her, kissing her until he felt the fury dissolve into spirited acquiesence, heard her reluctant rumble of laughter.

He took her in the dust, quickly, roughly, feeling – thanks to his magic nuts – like a Viking enjoying the spoils after a very satisfactory battle. And like Eric Bloodaxe, he let out a barbaric yell of joy.

Chapter Twenty-Eight

She watched him now, studying him intensely, lovingly, as moments before he had watched her intently with his blue-grey eyes. They'd been making love on the beach, hidden from prying eyes by the smattering of pinnacle rocks, his loins thrusting, her hips lifting hungrily to bring him fully into her.

Still they couldn't quite believe that fate had been so kind, that they had each other now, until death probably. They didn't trust fate. It had a way of playing cruel tricks. It had done so before, after all, and cruelly, too; they'd been saved from death only to be kept apart for many years, on the opposite shores of the same island. The irony was lost on neither of them. So they monopolised each other, kept constantly in the other's presence, watching, ever wary.

As far as sex was concerned – every day was the mating season. They were always hungry. Satisfaction, no matter how devastating, was only ever temporary. They were mad for each other – possession, taste and smell. Their days were heady, crazy, their need obsessional. Having lost each other, it was now as if they were determined to make up for lost time, to lay claim over and over again their sole rights to each other.

Floating on her back out beyond the surf, Iona

watched him, thrilled as always as she knew him to be hers and hers alone. Devoid of mud now (for she had insisted some ten months previously on his re-entry into her life that he should foresake that particularly unbecoming custom so beloved of his cannibal brothers), he cavorted in the waves before her, lean body tanned dark brown, the blond hairs on his torso gleaming. His hair streamed wetly out behind him, golden, bleached, untidy and long enough to sweep his shoulders with ease. Naked, he was quite beautiful, his unaroused body still daunting, dripping wet with the crystal waters.

Iona let her toes find the sandy bottom beneath her and waded ashore. Her russet hair streamed about her naked breasts, runnels of water taken earthwards by gravity, down over her breasts and rounded, golden tanned belly. She replaced her feathered and beaded skirt and relaxed back into the comfortably warm sand.

Exercised and content, Jack flopped down beside her, drips of chill water falling on her hot belly.

'Jack!' she screeched. 'Watch it!'

'Sorry,' he yawned lazily, obviously nothing of the sort, and closed his eyes as he lay back, hands behind his head. 'Hum.'

She smiled at his noise of contentment, turned onto her side and reached out a hand to lay across his ribs.

He opened his eyes. His gaze narrowed against the suns glare, looked up to her. Iona's eyebrow quirked. 'What's that expression for?'

Both her eyebrows raised. 'What expression?'

'That smug-smug I-know-something-you-don't expression.'

'I don't know what you mean,' she trilled.

'Yes you do, I think,' he said with a grin, raising himself on an elbow, eyes probing.

'Let me ask you something then, Jack.'

His shoulders shrugged. 'Ask away.'

'How would you feel about another child? I know

you've several already and I've a couple. Is there room for another?'

His gaze had become brightly intense, a spark of delighted understanding growing there. 'I get the feeling this question is something more than academic. Come on, Iona, out with it, woman. Stop beating about the bush. What have you got to tell Jack? Tell me or I'll wring my hair out all over your hot little body.' As he spoke he had taken her by the shoulders, pinned her down, then straddled her, kneeling over her like some youth indulging in horseplay.

She giggled and writhed, trying to buck him off, like a child herself in that magical moment. 'Stop messing about, Jack. Get off me. Is this any way to treat a pregnant woman?'

'Ah-ha!' he exclaimed with theatrical dramatics, 'Now we come to the truth, my pretty. A baby! I suspected as much. Now you'll have to marry me.'

She laughed, pushed him off and leant over him, planting a soft kiss on his smiling mouth. 'Are you pleased, then?'

'What do you think?'

'I think you're almost as happy as I am.'

'*Almost?* More, woman, *more!* I'm . . . I'm . . . Oh, I don't know, can't think of the word. But I've been thinking of this possibility for a long time – ten months, in fact – hoping. Now the Honourable Jonathan Savage will have an heir at long last.'

'Another heir,' Iona corrected.

'*The* heir,' stated Jack, determinedly, 'For you are the only woman I should ever want to marry.'

'Thank you, Jack. I'm touched. That's a lovely thought. But we both know marriage is quite unnecessary. The Church of England would be glaringly out of place here.'

'But who's to say that we'll always be here? There's always the possibility that a ship might come. It's happened before . . .'

'God forbid that we should have another visitation

from Chinese pirates!' said Iona, shivering. She remembered listening wide-eyed to Jack's particularly colourful retelling of that fearful episode. It was something the men spoke of often when they gathered around the communal campfires. Iona could only feel a kind of selfish relief that the squat people had had to deal with the problem rather than Tiku's. They were farmers, liked an easy, slow-paced life. They would never have succeeded in fighting off a well-armed attack.

'Perhaps it'll be an English ship next time,' said an optimstic Jack. 'A Ship-of-the-Line, a Man-o'-War, or maybe a Merchantman.'

'But . . .' Iona broke off in dismay,

He looked at her enquiringly, concerned. 'My love?'

'Jack, do you mean to leave here if opportunity presents itself?'

'But of course. I want to take you home. Show you off. I'm *so* proud of you.'

'I never think of leaving, Jack. Not now. Once, yes, long ago. But my son's birth changed all that. I realised then that I could never return home, that I wouldn't be accepted, would no longer belong.'

'I'd make them accept us, dammit! Money talks, after all. I'd have influence. They wouldn't dare to say anything against you with me at your side.'

'But we could never stop what they said about us behind our backs, could we? I can just picture the sniggers, the nudges. Shouldn't like it. And I should never get used to wearing Western clothes again. *Never!*'

They both laughed then, a little forced, a shade relieved to have been extricated from any unpleasantness on so happy an occasion. It wasn't the time to talk further of England. Even so, Iona was worried.

Chapter Twenty-Nine

The monsoon was particularly unpredictable in its savagery that year, seemed to go on relentlessly for months on end, destroying, ruining. No sooner had the villagers rebuilt their homes after the typhoon had brought down tidal waves upon them, washing clear away everything low-lying, than the hurricane struck, the unbelievable strength of the winds lifting roofs without effort, uprooting the palms and destroying the young crops. Poorly built dwellings folded in upon themselves and trees sent down a hail of branches or fronds, leaves and twigs.

In the annuls it went down as an inauspicious year.

Her garden still littered with the resultant debris of the storm, Iona sat beneath the veranda of her lodge, a dish of appetisingly segmented fruits and a pitcher of spring water on the bamboo table at her side.

She chewed, listened to the weekly procession of people protesting and quarrelling, and gave judgement. Jack often listened from the sidelines but he rarely interferred. She wasn't a stupid woman by any means, he was of the opinion, proud of her, could give sound, if sometimes unorthodox, rulings in disputes amongst her islanders. Only when his people were in any way involved did he make a point of being there, present but silent, unless she specifically asked for his opinion. She was a peace-loving woman, down to earth. She never did anything that smacked of omnipotence when dealing with her people. Highhandedness had been Tiku's trademark and having lived through some of his less than marvellous dictates, Iona had decided early on that his way wasn't for her. She wanted to be liked, not feared. When she died she wanted to be remembered fondly as a mother of the people, not some powerful, all terrible living deity.

Business was very much the same as normal: someone claimed somebody else's black rooster as his own; somebody was aggrieved that their son hadn't been chosen, in the recent ceremonies, as a servant to the Living God; someone else asked if those whose crops hadn't been destroyed in the last storm would share with those less fortunate and stop hoarding in an uncharitable, un-Wahwuese way.

Iona drank, winced, willed the ache in her belly to stay away until she had concluded her business.

Seeing that Sanga and her fiancé were next in line to talk to Iona, Jack stepped out of the lodge, leant against the totem-like carvings of the door jam. He watched with wary curiosity. Sanga was a minx; there might well be trouble. Above all he wished to spare Iona that at present. Her time was very near, he sensed. She was tired and pale, large with his baby. A smile touched the corners of his mouth, sparked his grey eyes, too, filling them with tenderness. There was little likelihood of the necessity, but he knew he'd have protected her with his life, died for her. She was everything to him. His reason for being. His happiness. He was fearful sometimes that such happiness couldn't last, that it was too intense.

He listened cautiously, ready to intervene if Sanga meant to cause trouble, watching her and warning her with a certain look.

Defiantly her eyes blazed back. She turned her gaze to Iona, spoke to her with loud aggression. 'I will not marry this man. Just will not. I don't love him. He don't love me. I wish this known, understood.'

'Was this match not arranged by your families?'

'It was, though I . . .'

'You love another? Is that what you would say? If so, Sanga, I am already aware of that fact.'

'Yes, I *do* love another. Not your boy Bili, the one who was chosen for me, but his brother, Junga.'

Iona blinked at her, momentarily forgot the niggling pain in her abdomen, queried, 'Junga?' Not Jack? A tall person? A tall person of her own choosing? Without coercion? Iona's smile was radiant. What she had hoped for more than anything was beginning to happen. The two tribes were starting to see each other as people, not strangers for whom they felt an aversion and deep suspicion. They were becoming used to each other to the extent that they saw physical things in the other that they could admire, desire. They were beginning to fall in love, integrating, and most beautifully too.

'Yes, Junga,' said Sanga, defiantly loud.

'Well I'm . . .' Iona never finished, found herself laughing.

'Bili find woman he want, too. She my cousin, Willa.'

'Indeed?' Iona's eyebrows had risen high on her forehead. Two tall people in love with short people! Iona was elated. 'I'm very pleased for you, Sanga. Truly. And I bless both unions.'

Sanga's eyebrows knit in puzzlement. 'But we have gone against your wishes?'

'I'm not going to hand out punishment to people for falling in love, Sanga. That would be cruel indeed, and unnecessary. You have, after all, done what I wanted, fulfilled my deepest wish. Our peoples will be united.'

Sanga frowned, didn't altogether care for the fact that she'd made Iona ecstatically happy. That had never been her aim. It was certainly against her nature.

Iona's servants waved the pair away, Iona clearly finished with them, and most satisfactorily so. Her closest house-servant, Oami, looked at her closely, arched a brow. 'Iona looks tired,' she fussed. 'Iona should rest.'

Iona nodded. 'Yes, you're right. I feel I should lie down . . . just for a while. Jack, would you listen to the last few? Womawhi the Elder will interpret; he prides himself on having learnt a smattering of English.'

'Yes . . . of course. Do you feel well, love?'

'I'm hail and hearty, Jack. Though I fear I've left things a little late, won't make it up the mountain to the midwife in time.'

'The baby's coming?' His voice grew loud with worried agitation.

'Yes, and soon. But you've time enough to listen to these last people. Honestly, don't fret.'

Such words were wasted. He looked stricken, and nothing she might have said could have changed that. She went indoors, Oami supporting her about the shoulders, determined that she wouldn't moan, wouldn't make pained faces in front of him; he looked guilty enough already.

He watched her go, frowning, then took her chair. 'Righty-o then, um . . . Let's see if we can get you sorted out. Who's going to speak? What's your-a . . . problem?'

'Oh, Jack . . . Jack,' Iona moaned, despite her resolutions of earlier. 'Dear God.'

Everything was happening so quickly, so violently.

He said nothing in reply. Was too worried. And, besides, Jack felt that any inanities he might have managed to blurt out in those fraught moments would have been highly inappropriate, would have irritated her greatly. She *was* greatly agitated, his tenderly calming presence, his supportive silence, was the best he could manage.

Iona had taken to her bed, surprised by the speed of events. Oami hovered, trying to be helpful, but inept under the circumstances. She'd never had a baby herself, was, indeed, a virgin still at twenty-three years of age, by choice. Jack had come to the conclusion that she just didn't care for men. Such 'unnaturalness' as he saw it, didn't bother him overmuch though. She was more than devoted to Iona. That was all that mattered.

Jack sat behind Iona, his wretched love resting between his cradling legs, her head against his chest. He stroked back her damp hair from her forehead, sponged her hot face with the fresh, cool water Oami kept bringing in earthenware basins.

Staring knowingly between Iona's spread legs, as if she knew what she was about, Jack thought, comforted, was the Mother of Several, Aya; so called because she had produced no less than twenty-two children in her childbearing years, sixteen of whom had reached maturity, and were still alive and healthy. Aya was old now, a haughty old bird with just a solitary front tooth left in her mouth. Aya had been caught out more than once in all those pregnancies, hadn't been able to get to the mountain pool and know the soothing benefits of the waters and the expertise of the midwife. Now she employed the same basic techniques of midwifery that her mother had used so matter-of-factly upon herself.

It was not a difficult birth, but it racked Iona with the severist, indescribable pain, left her exhausted and panting in those brief moments of reprieve.

Jack cooed, smoothed her hair the more violently as things came to a head, felt a shade ill, and thanked God he'd positioned himself at the head of the bed! He hadn't been present at the births of his other children. Squat women didn't like men hanging around at such times and squat men were quite happy for it to continue to be so.

His deep love for Iona had brought him to her side supportively. Now Jack began to wish himself somewhere else. He didn't like Iona's pain, the stoicism she employed, he felt, for his benefit. It filled him with guilt. He'd brought her to this, him and his almost uncontrollable desire for her. I'm a swine, he thought irrationally. A selfish brute. How any woman could go through such an experience more than once was beyond him.

And then the baby appeared, its head first, then quickly afterwards its slithering little body. Iona heralded its vacation of her body with a long, satisfying cry of joyous relief. Old Aya cackled and took up the infant with sure hands, happy to hold a child again.

It was too much for Jack. The mess; the blood; the multicoloured afterbirth. He moaned, turning grey-green, and fainted, his body slumping sideways.

The howling baby on her belly by then, its cord cut and tied, Iona turned her head sideways, looked into Jack's unconscious face where the mouth gaped, eyes rolling between partially closed lids. 'Jack? Jack! Oh, what an ass!' she scolded, then rolled her eyes comically at Aya and joined the woman in a happy burst of laughter at her lover's expense.

Chapter Thirty

Three days later the women of the village were still laughing because old Aya had told the tale of Jack's unheroic mishap many times over. He bore the giggles, the pointing fingers with good grace, too happy to care.

Around the village, pausing at the communal cooking fires while Iona rested or slept back at the lodge, Jack would unwrap his daughter time after time to show off her perfection to any who showed the remotest, politest interest.

Iona and he had decided to call their daughter Ann. It was a good old English name, yet it wasn't out of place on Wahwu either. It was short, sweet; the villagers nodded agreeably when they heard it for the first time. Ann? Um, yes. Ann was good.

Each time he unwrapped her, freeing tiny limbs to start their experimental thrashing, Jack could only stare in wonder at his partial creation, completely bewitched. She was tiny, pale, bad tempered for most of the time and sported a light cap of strawberry blond fuzz atop her head. To him she was perfect. To everyone else, by the third day, she had begun to lose her novelty value. They'd seen her once, twice, congratulated him, said how fetching she was; they'd cooed, been happy for him and Iona, polite. Now they took avoiding action when they saw Jack coming, prayed that he'd come down to earth and be more his usual self again soon. Temporarily he'd become a bore.

On the afternoon of the fourth day, with Ann fed and asleep in the nursery, Iona drowsed in her chair on the veranda, savouring the blissful quiet that wouldn't last for long. Ann had a wondrous pair of lungs and could be heard half way across the village when she cried in demand of sustenance.

Oami came through the garden, up the steps. 'Iona need anything? Fruit maybe? White meat of chicken to build you up?'

Iona smiled. 'I'm fine, thanks. Want nothing. I'm just trying to collect my wits before the baby wakes. I don't seem to have time to think, let alone anything else.'

Oami lingered, just looking out silently over the village, up at the sky where Frigate birds wheeled screeching. They seemed agitated for some reason.

'I make sacrifice at the altar of Living God. Take your blood rags and burn them. Put ashes in pot in skull eyehole. Blood rags very strong magic. I ask for long life for Ann.'

'That is good, Oami. Thank you. I'm not up to climbing to the terrace just yet.'

'Where King Jack?'

'After I forcibly took the baby from him,' laughed Iona, 'insisting that she be fed and put to bed properly for a change, he didn't know what to do with himself. Then he decided he'd go see how work on the road was progressing, lend a hand. Apparently the navigators have hit a bad patch – lots of rocks, jungle. But I think he'll be back soon. I can't imagine him staying away from Ann for more than an hour or two.'

The road to the cannibal village (where the squat people's elderly and infirm had stayed behind, seeing the undertaking of Jack's expedition in search of the tall people as foolish in the extreme) was lengthening only slowly. So far they'd cleared eighteen miles. But they weren't disheartened. Both peoples worked well together, squabbles few these days.

'I go prepare meal,' decided Oami.

'Um.' Iona barely heard her, lulled by the sun. Her eyes flickered, closed.

The baby's intensifying squeals woke her some time later. Not much later, Iona deduced, tutting, coming reluctantly off her bamboo lounging chair, for the sun was only just dipping beneath the tree line.

She went inside, poured pitchered fruit juice into a beaker on the sideboard and drank thirstily. The birds outside began shrieking again, then Iona could hear voices, some of them calling her name. A commotion was erupting outside. She went to her window, peeped through the louvred slats, the body of people who advanced, invading her garden, making her stare in disbelief and alarm.

White people!

They were flanked by an escort of able-bodied islanders who were cordial but wary in their handling of the Western strangers. They were armed, but the weapons were kept out of sight but at the ready. The islanders plainly assumed that these newcomers were friendly simply because they looked like Iona and Jack – European.

But instinctively Iona didn't like the look of them at all, certainly didn't like the way the men behind their obvious leader ogled the island's gathered maidens.

All at once Iona felt naked too, vulnerable, wanted to cover her body up. She hadn't felt like that in years.

Oami came from the kitchen, wondering why Iona neglected to go to her yelling offspring. Iona almost bumped into her coming out of her closet.

'Oami, a ship's come in,' she explained, rushing by, voice unnaturally high. Iona was neither excited nor pleased by the unexpected occurrence. She was dismayed. A ship meant a means of voyaging back to England, meant that Jack would want to go home.

Several alarm bells went off in her head at once. 'Please, go to Ann, comfort her until I can come.'

'A ship?' Oami ran to the window, looked out. 'Is that good?'

Iona shook her head. 'Somehow I don't think so.'

Jack trudged home wearily with the work party, his hands blistered and back breaking after just a few hours of manual labour. He wasn't used to it, realised with alarm that he'd allowed himself to get a shade out of condition over the last year or so. Life had been easy and he'd been lulled, allowed himself to get lazy. Mentally he made a resolution to get himself back into shape. If he volunteered to work on the road for a spell or two in the future, that should do the trick, he thought. And he'd enjoyed the work. Well, not the work maybe. But certainly the company of the men. They'd chattered and sang until the sun went down, then chattered all along the new, easy to travel road home.

Once or twice he'd tried to take hold of the conversation, talk about his little Ann, but quickly someone had drowned him out with some tale or anecdote. Eventually Tig had jovially taken him by the arm, said what no one else had dared to.

'Jack, my friend, your Ann is a treasure, indeed, but then, so are *all* our children. Can you try, do you think, to talk of something else just for once? You are a man of interesting conversation . . . usually. Some even say you are something of a wit, a man of natural humour. But we have seen little of it lately.'

Jack quirked his eyebrows, puzzled. 'Are you trying to tell me I've been a bit of a bore?'

Tig nodded, smiled kindly. 'Just a bit, my friend.'

Jack gave him a look of mock amazement. 'But why didn't anyone tell me?'

'We didn't want to offend.'

'Offend? Me? No!' he said low and resoundingly.

'But you must admit, Tig, that she is the most perfect baby that you've ever set eyes upon . . .'

Tig shoved him playfully between the shoulder-blades, almost sending him sprawling. 'Shut up, Jack!'

And the rest of the work gang, tall and short, in a mix of English, Wahwuese and the cannibals' tongue, echoed in chorus, 'Shut up, Jack, you silly bugger.'

Another bend in the road brought them in sight of the sea.

'Look there!' someone called, pointing.

They looked, they exclaimed. Jack frowned. A ship – bedraggled by the recent hurricane, no doubt – was riding at anchor out beyond the coral reef. By her lines Jack could tell she was European. A Brigantine. Everyone hurried then, speculation rife as to the nationality, business and true destination of those who made up her company.

As Iona – draping her cloak of black feathers about her shoulders as if it would lend stature and self-assurance – stepped out onto her veranda, her children came ahead of the crowd; Tula disappeared inside to stay with Ann of whom she was inordinately fond and protective, and Ran mounted the step to stand slightly behind his mother, at her right hand. She squeezed his hand, smiled her thanks, then looked to the purposefully advancing strangers.

They showed no fear, no trepidation at being in the midst of such a formidable looking throng. In fact they were almost arrogant in their swaggering approach, their leader mounting the steps to stand at the same height as Iona. Ran took exception, narrowed his eyes, but said nothing, though he itched to, as his mother stalled him in Wahwuese.

Then she smiled a polite greeting to the sombrely dressed man before her. He was in breeches, white linen shirt and plainly cut and buttoned jacket. Fashions, she perceived, hadn't changed so very much in all the years she'd been away from England. His hair was clipped short like a spikey grey skirt that ran around from ear to ear; his pate was bald. For formal occasions he doubtless wore a white wig complete with beribboned queue. He was pot-bellied, bow-legged and sallow skinned. He had no feature that Iona could latch upon as being fetching, becoming or in the least handsome. Nothing made her warm towards him. Indeed, he reminded her of Horace, that fact alone made her dislike him without even knowing him.

'Welcome,' she said stiffly, 'to our island of Wahwu.'

'God's blessings upon you, Daughter of Eve. How come you here, to this Godforsaken, heathen land?'

'I was shipwrecked . . . many years ago now.'

'Rejoice then, daughter, for you are found again, shall be saved.'

She smiled, amused. 'I've no wish to be *saved*. Can't think what you would save me from, frankly. This is my home. These are my people . . . my son,' she said, putting an arm about Ran's shoulder proudly.

A look of unmistakable horror crossed the man's face. 'Madam, for shame! How could you proclaim a heathen's spawn so readily? He is the fruit of sin, of an unholy, unnatural joining of flesh. He is an abomination in the eyes of the Almighty. In God's name, daughter, how could you let such a thing befall you? How could you submit?'

'How could I not?' she said, getting angry now.

Beside her, Ran had tensed, ground his teeth. He knew some English, understood well enough what had been said.

'It is a Christian woman's moral duty to defend her honour. And, if she cannot, to make that sacrifice expected of her,' ranted the man before her, sounding more and more like the sanctimonious Horace with each minute that passed, infuriating her. HIs booming diatribe had the villagers frowning.

'Kill myself do you mean?'

'It would have been unfortunate, but yes. Surely that

was preferable to being made the unwilling slave of a black man, a heathen, a . . . a savage?'

She seemed to deliberate mentally for only a moment, then she said bluntly, 'No.'

The man sucked in his breath with outrage. Iona got the distinct impression that he would have liked to strike her but didn't dare. 'Madam, you cannot mean . . .'

'In future when you wish to speak to me, address me as Great One. I am a Living God here, the spiritual leader of this island.'

More horror on his face. 'There is only one true God, woman, and his son is Jesus Christ who is in heaven!'

'Such things mean nothing here. Christianity has no place.'

'It is my job in life, my mission, to alter that lamentable state of affairs. These Southern Seas have long been neglected by the Christian ministerings of the Church.'

She glared, clamped her mouth shut upon a retort as Jack and the work party hurried into the garden. She'd never been so glad to see anyone, felt that if she continued with her line of conversation any longer with this odious little man that she would declare him hostile, have the islanders deal with him in their own distinctly brutal way. Those who displeased the Living God too greatly seldom lived to lament the mistake. That was the legend; just because no one *had* been put to death in a very long time didn't mean they couldn't be!

Jack's brows knit perturbedly as he saw Iona's thunderous expression, her sparkling eyes. Something had certainly made her mad.

He came up onto the veranda eagerly, took the little man's hand, shook it vigorously in Western Fashion. It was a pudgy hand, cold and damp.

'Sir, I'm delighted to see you . . . you and your friends. Where are you from? What brings you here? Will you come into my lodge and take refreshments . . .?'

Iona snorted audibly then, infuriated that Jack should so blindly, trustingly bestow hospitality on such an obnoxious fellow, should put *her* house at his and his men's disposal. She would put Jack straight on a few things and make her feelings known as soon as opportunity presented itself.

Chapter Thirty-One

Partly she was glad that Jack was doing all the talking; she couldn't trust herself to be civil.

Jack's questions were endless: where were they heading? What business brought them to the South Pacific?

Wilfred Smegson and his small crew aboard the chartered brigantine, *Queen of Sheba* had been on their way to spread the word of God in the isles of New Caledonia (which Cook had discovered in 1774), when the hurricane had struck, torn out a goodly portion of their rigging and blown them to this island.

A missionary of some reputation and long service to his master the Bishop of Ely, Smegson had worked in China and Ceylon before being sent to spread the word of God around the islands and *persuade* the heathens he found in those far flung places to embrace Christian teachings. Missionary activity in the East India Company's territories was now being discouraged under a policy of non-interference in other countries' cultural affairs.

He was zealous to the extreme, some even said fanatical. Certainly Iona sensed it, though he hadn't mentioned his methods for converting the heathen masses straight away. He chattered on, voice booming as if he were giving a sermon, carrying to all who had been invited into the lodge to take refreshments with their guests. Smegson raised his eyebrows eloquently when he found that he was to share the couch and tidbits with a black man. Evidently he did not think that it was their place, would have preferred them kept outside much as Englishmen kept dogs.

Iona smouldered bad-temperedly, all but snarling when Smegson held out his cup to her to be refilled. He spoke to her as she had never spoken to her servants, like a Western female, an inferior. She had forgotten how it felt, detested being reminded. With every word he spoke down to her, sought to put Iona firmly in that place he'd decided she belonged.

She'd disliked Smegson before he'd ever opened his mouth. After listening to him for an hour or more, referring to Jack and herself as his *strayed sheep*, talking of their sins, their unholy union, their mountainous list of shortcomings, she hated him thoroughly. How Jack could go on listening to him politely, curiously, like a well-bred gentleman mindful of his manners, she would never know. She assumed he was just hungry for news of home, would put up with Smegson in order to glean from their guest.

George III had officially been declared mad, was living at Windsor Castle, a pathetic, bearded figure. His son George (Prinny) had been named Regent. Lord Liverpool governed. Life went on much as usual.

Jack lapped up every meagre scrap. Iona listened worriedly, her own enthusiasm for such tidbits of news sorely lacking. She no longer had much interest in England, had not thought of it as home for so long now. But with mounting panic, she watched Jack and surmised that perhaps he still did.

She made her excuses and left them to it, seething as Smegson dismissed her with a negligent wave of the hand. As if she needed his permission to leave!

Her breasts ached, felt uncomfortable and heavy. She went to the nursery, smiled her thanks at Tula and took up the baby.

'You're a good girl for me, Tula. A mother couldn't ask for more in a daughter. Soon, I think, we shall have to start thinking about finding you a husband.'

'Shall we, mother? Shall we still be here?'

Iona's eyebrows raised. 'Yes. Of course. Why should you think otherwise?'

'The ship. Jack. The King always speaks with great fondness of England, talks of it as his home still. I thought that now, now a ship has come, he will go, and you will go, too.'

'Never!' declared Iona hotly, hugging Tula, the baby squealing in protest as it was squashed between them.

Tula sighed, snuggled close while her mother smoothed a palm down her blue-black tresses lovingly, reassuringly. 'I'm so glad, mother.'

Iona smiled, broke free, taking the baby to suckle behind the grass screen in her reception room, so that she could keep an eye on proceedings whilst staying conveniently out of sight.

Her breasts softened, became more comfortable, but her mind knew no such ease. Tula's question wouldn't go away.

Iona wouldn't go, she was adamant. But what of Jack? They never spoke of it. Hadn't, not since that far off conversation when he'd tried to reassure her of her future as his wife, in England, tried to waylay her fears, dash her objections. No other words had ever been spared on the matter, simply because it upset Iona even to think of it, and would surely have started an unpleasant argument.

She hadn't changed her mind; she would stay. But had Jack. Would he go? Go without her?

She wished that Smegson and every one of the rough and ready crew who had accidentally brought him here, had gone to the bottom of the sea when hit by the hurricane, wished them all dead, her island still overlooked, passed by in ignorance.

The captain of the *Queen of Sheba* was talking now, regaling his listeners with the more ferocious moments of the storm. His language was colourful to say the least, four-letter words flying left, right and centre. If Jack's and Iona's rather tame forms of cursing could have been said to originate in the gaming clubs and such like, the captain's came straight from the gutter.

Tig's younger sister, Mara, brought the captain a fruit cocktail to lubricate his tongue and he thanked her with a leer and a slap on her pigskin-draped rump.

She cried out in alarm, such a gesture quite unknown on Wahwu, and instantly Tig was leaping forward, a saw-toothed dagger drawn.

'Whow!' shouted Jack, jumping between them, laughing nervously, palms padding downwards through the air, symbolically begging for calm. 'No harm done. Tig, put the knife away. Captain, don't touch the women here unless they give you permission to do so. And that's unlikely.'

'Yes, I want none of that,' barked Smegson. 'No fornication. Not with soulless, sinful heathens.'

Still grinning with an insolence that belied his words, Captain Overbeck apologised. 'I didn't mean no harm. Were just being friendly, like.'

'Yes, well,' snorted a flustered Jack, regaining his place. 'Least said . . .'

The missionary had decided that they'd heard quite enough of Overbeck's account of the storm and took off on his usual tack.

'I intend to start converting these people without delay. There shall be daily bible reading, scripture lessons, and then, later, baptisms. God will embrace all these people, no matter what colour their skins, no matter their undeniable inferiority. I will teach them Christian ways, turn them away from the bad lives they presently lead. Your knowing something of their language will help enormously in the process of communication, Mister Savage.'

Jack's eyebrows had knit. 'But these people are happy as they are.'

'They are heathens. Must be saved.'

'Saved from what?'

'From themselves. From the lazy, ungodly lives they lead,' snapped Smegson, impatiently. 'I had hoped to meet with more understanding from you, sir, as to my aims and the necessity for them. It is a Christian's duty to spread the word, bring more mortal souls into His flock. I understand that it is perhaps difficult for the female – the one who fancifully calls herself Great One – to grasp these principles, but I had expected more comprehension from an intelligent gentleman like yourself.'

Jack laughed loudly at the man's sneering contempt for Wahwu's Living God. And behind her screen Iona chuckled and shifted the baby to her other breast. Smegson was a fool, a preposterous idiot.

'But,' said Jack, not very helpfully, 'how is learning scriptures and getting themselves baptised going to enrich these peoples lives?'

'Why . . . well, firstly they'll know themselves blessed in the eyes of God. And when they die they'll be comforted by the knowledge that they'll go to heaven.'

'But they have that already. Their existence here is surely blessed. And when they die they're certain of meeting up with their ancestors once more. I don't see as how your Church can offer them anything they haven't got already. I think you're wasting your time, should move on, find yourself another island,' suggested Jack, firmly.

'The road God has chosen for me is not an easy one, sir, but I shall stick to it, do His work as best I'm able and in the face of others' cynism and unhelpfulness. It is what I was put on this earth to do. My mission.'

'I should be remiss as a gentleman if I didn't try to deter you, sir, for you will surely fail here, know naught but despondency.'

'We shall see, sir,' said Smegson with that arrogance that reminded Iona so much of the jumped-up Horace. Horace had always thought he knew better than everyone else, took great delight in being proven right so that he might say, 'There, I told you so' with a sneering look of triumph. But Smegson couldn't be allowed to meddle here, mustn't be given a chance to destroy the fabric of the island's society.

The *Queen of Sheba* and all who sailed on her had to be made to leave.

Nichols, able seaman aboard the *Queen of Sheba* pushed back the slatted bamboo blind in the stuffy communal sleeping quarters and stared shiftily out. All about him, sprawled on the divans, the mat-covered floor, slept his shipmates, some twenty-five men in all. It was a small crew for a brigantine, but they managed, in a grumbling, surly way, knowing that hands were always hard to find because of Smegson. People just didn't like him. He was a hard man, imposing his doctrine on them through the mediatory Captain Overbeck. But they could stand that, humour him, laugh at him behind his back.

He was like a detested headmaster. They knuckled down when they had to, treated him as a joke when they didn't. And they didn't very often, for Smegson had another master besides God – the bottle. He couldn't resist a drink whether it be rum or gin. Whenever the crew wanted a rest from him they left the rum bottle conveniently within his reach. He'd never been known not to succumb to the temptation. Such lapses from the spiritually straight and narrow gave the crew opportunities aplenty to then indulge in their own favourite and basest of pastimes.

Nichols scratched his crotch, watched the servant girl, Oami, cross the garden in the dawn light with a basket of eggs from a nest which the hen had thought craftily hidden but which Oami had found even so.

He hardened below at the sight of her naked breasts bouncing slightly amongst strands of a pearl and coral necklace, and narrowed his eyes lasciviously. He'd get himself some of that, he decided, coldly, unemotionally almost. Soon. It had been three weeks now since the death of Smegson's servant girl, Mai Lin, the slave the missionary had bought at auction on Formosa. Nichols hadn't had a bitch's rear end since then; he felt the depravation acutely.

The girl who crossed the lawn between orchid patches, was taller, older, more robust looking than the delicate little Mai Lin had been, but he felt he'd enjoy her just the same, find some new ways to bring her to heel, have her begging. He liked that in a woman – fear. It excited him. He could see it in their eyes, felt it in their trembling when he touched them. And tremble they should, tremble they did when Nichols singled them out.

Mai Lin had been repeatedly raped by the crew whenever Smegson fell into a drunken stupor. It had gone on for months as they sailed the China Sea, came south to Australia for provisions.

On one particular night when the first violent downpouring of the monsoon kept them below deck, Smegson was drunk and out of the way. Captain Overbeck was on deck, cursing everything and the weather in particular.

Nichols cornered Mai Lin in the companionway as she tried to take the Captain the grog he'd yelled down for. In an instant Nichols had her cowering, turned her, thrust into her as she fell upon the stairs, and made her scream with pain. He'd liked that, laughed, intensified his assault.

When he'd finished, leaving her tiny body bleeding, he turned her back over, ignored her tears, her pleading looks and thrust his flaccid flesh into her mouth. She gagged. He held her, hardening again, thrust against the back of her throat and eventually came again, making her gag and choke. He buttoned up his britches, kicked her and staggered off, unbalanced by the pitching of the ship.

The Captain called again, quite out of humour now. She fled with the half spilt tankard of grog, could expect a beating for being careless.

A week later, after what seemed like endless days of such treatment from Nichols and the rest of the crew, Mai Lin climbed the rigging during a temporary lull in the worsening weather, and took a dive from the yardarm. She called something in Chinese as she plummeted to her death on the deck below. No one heard her. No one on board would have cared anyhow.

When Nichols watched Oami he thought only of the fun he could have, saw her – as he did all women – as an object to be used and abused or otherwise ignored. Tenderness wasn't something that graced anyone aboard the *Queen of Sheba*.

'Suck me, girlie,' demanded Nichols, holding his flaccid member forth, pointing it at the island girl beside him.

She looked reluctant, shook her head, beginning to think that coming into the rain forest with two of her friends and two of Nichols' cronies had been a mistake. She'd been curious about the white man, naïve, thinking them cast in the same mould as King Jack. But they most definitely were not.

'Suck me, I say,' snarled Nichols, grabbing her blue-black tresses and forcing her down, forcing her face close to his pale, rank flesh.

Her friends seemed to be enjoying themselves no better at the hands of his companions.

One man was masturbating between the girlish breasts of a dusky female, the other trying to get a hand beneath the skirt of the third, and seemingly most reluctant of the females.

'No,' she snapped, indignant.

Nichols shook his head in exasperation, a most unpleasant look upon his bristly face. 'God Almighty, these natives ain't no fun at all. They'm enough t'make a full-blooded male ferget 'is manners and 'elp 'isself, heevens that they be.'

'Aye, Nichols, yer dead right. Why waste time wi' the nicities, like, when girls like these don't 'preciate 'em, need nowt better than a good fucking.'

'Yer right, Atkins. Let's ferget the nonsense an' get down t'business.'

They grabbed the young girls and forced them down into the grass, slapping them into a state of semi-meekness, then mounted them, shoving members deep within unprepared, pubescent bodies, pumping away mindlessly until the repetition and lack of response from the frightened females they ravaged led them to change position.

They turned them over, took them from the rear, squeezing breasts so hard and biting dark shoulders that the girls begged them to stop, seemed on the verge of tears, humbled and humiliated.

'No, please, don't . . .'

'Be gentle, I implore!'

The third could only cry softly, her unwilling flesh dragged and abused by a punishing member.

'Be gentle! Be gentle!' laughed the seaman buried deep within her, his loins slapping meatily at her dark, globular buttocks, the mimicked female voice ridiculing. 'No damned heeven lays down conditins t'Billy Atkins.' He snarled, removing his shaft from her woman's passage and forcing it into her tight, unwelcoming anus.

She arched with the shock, a scream erupting from her depths, only to be smothered by his dirty paw clamped over her mouth.

The other men egged him on, jeering. 'That's the way, Atkins. Show her who's boss. Make her bleed and beg fer mercy, boyo.'

When they were finished and the men lazed about drinking rum from a stone jar, the girls stole away.

They were silent, dishevelled, sore and miserable. They cleaned themselves up at a pool beneath a spring and agreed that they would tell no one about what had taken place. They couldn't. It would be just too humiliating. In future they would steer well clear of the rough and smelly whitemen.

Chapter Thirty-Two

Iona put her foot down, would not have the new arrivals stay at her lodge, had them moved to guest accommodation outside the garden precincts, her coolness towards them unmistakable.

They didn't seem to care about any slights she might inflict on them, were plainly thick-skinned.

Abed, on the monstrously gaudy divan that Tiku had had installed in the lodge years before for his own inimitable form of love games, Iona lay restlessly on her back, sighing, turning, turning again.

She couldn't sleep, couldn't stop the worry building within her. She disturbed Jack. He grumbled groggily, flung out an arm that came to rest uncomfortably across her windpipe.

In her head she heard Smegson, his opinionated, fanatical doctrine spurted out at every opportunity, and she thought of Horace, hated Horace. It was as if he'd re-entered her life in another not dissimilar guise. She turned on her side, snuggled closer to the snoring Jack for protection.

Memories of another night, another bed, came flooding into her mind disturbingly.

They had been married at a little church on the outskirts of Norwich and then travelled quickly – as if he must consolidate his position by snatching her from her old home quickly, cleanly, brutally – down to his London town house. There he'd neither asked if she was hungry or thirsty, had simply lead her with unseemly haste upstairs and, slamming the door of the matrimonial bedchamber, ordered her to undress.

Even thinking of it all these years later made Iona seeth with humiliation and a burning indignance that grew rapidly into something more like hate.

He'd loved her no more than she did him. But they might have been friends if he'd been inclined to try. Iona had been relying on it. Friendship, however, was something he reserved exclusively for his cronies. She was just a wife. He either despised women (and Iona knew she fell into this category) or he feared them in a perverse, contrived sort of way, wanted to be dominated.

She'd been shivering, she remembered, had undressed down to her lawn underwear and white silk stockings. But that wasn't enough.

'Get it all off,' Horace had ordered, pouring himself a drink. He offered her nothing.

'But . . . can't I have the lamp turned down just a bit?'

'No.'

She felt cold, and sick inside, trembled. Her hands had shaken as she'd done his bidding. No one had ever seen her naked before. No one. She felt that she could have died from the shame of being exposed in that brutal manner. She hadn't. That would have been more merciful.

He had downed his drink, a sneer on his face, his look shrivelling her inside. She must be ugly, she had thought. Downright ugly for him to stare at her with such distaste.

She had reached out a hand to the linen coverlet of the bed, to her nightgown which had been laid out there in anticipation of the nuptials. He had barked at her, made her jump, then almost laughed at her distress.

'No. No clothes. Get into bed, *wife*.'

From then on she had hated that word. The binding, irrefutable finality of it. *Wife* meant prisoner, obedience, misery. She still didn't care for it now, for the commitment it demanded of one being from another, despite the fact that she deeply loved her Jack.

She blinked up at the dark shadows of the lodge ceiling and wondered whether that was the real reason she never wanted to leave Wahwu. Could it be that she resented the idea of ever being any man's property again, even Jack's? Well, yes, perhaps, maybe. But not entirely. She was bonded to Jack, his mate anyhow. Marriage would have changed nothing, she felt, for Jack was definitely not like Horace. Jack would have loved her and married her for all the right reasons. Not because it was proper in the eyes of Church and Law, legally binding. Not because he wanted to tie her to him like an object of possession. No, Jack would have wed her as a means of affording her protection, of ensuring that she was financially provided for if he should die before her, that her old age was comfortable. Jack loved her and was a kindly man. But none of that mattered a jot anyway, not here on Wahwu. Marriage was unnecessary. It was only if she went back to England that such nonsense would press in upon her, threatening her happiness. So she wouldn't. She was determined. Her decision final once and for all.

She was staying because she wanted to. It was best for her and her children, her only realistic future. And it was best for her peoples . . . all of them. She was their leader, their mediator. If Jack went – and she hated even to give that possibility room for thought – they would need her even more.

Don't go, Jack. Don't go, she prayed, squeezing him tightly with unconscious, desperate possessiveness.

'Are you all right, my love?' he said, sleepily, arms

going about her, warm, strong, covered in a soft down of white blond hair, silvered by the moonlight.

'I felt cold.' Her voice was small.

'Cold?'

'Um.'

'But it's so hot.'

'Cold inside, Jack, not on the surface. Frightened.'

He squeezed her reassuringly. 'Things'll seem better in the morning, when the sun's shining.'

'Will they?' She sounded anything but sure.

'Yes,' he said, scoffingly, as if to say, How could you doubt it?' 'After all, Jack's here, isn't he?'

She elbowed him, 'Bloody fool!' smiled despite herself, trying harder to relax and closed her eyes willing herself to sleep. But Jack was asleep again long before she was, his gentle, even breathing filling the still quiet of their room. He shared her bed, had declined the separate suite of rooms that had been offered him as Coconut King. He wanted to be with her as much as she with him, wanted nothing to distance them. But for how much longer? she wondered. Until he stepped aboard the *Queen of Sheba* and left her!

Her mind went back to brooding over Smegson again, then naturally, Horace, thoughts taking up where they had left off earlier.

She had been an obedient wife then, had done as she was told, going to the marriage bed and lying there beneath the cold sheets while he had yet another drink, undressed and left his clothing in a heap for the servants to clear up in the morning.

He was pale, a little flabby and – although she hadn't of course known it then, being no connosieur of men – less than generously endowed in the wedding tackle department. She hadn't been impressed. Perhaps it had shown in her face, too. Anyhow, his humour hadn't improved. He'd climbed into bed, leaving the lamp burning, and rolled over onto Iona without more ado.

'Open,' he'd demanded, nudging her legs with his knees.

She hadn't wanted to. It was the last thing she wanted. She was revolted. But she knew she had to. Marriage did that to you; stripped you of self-will, self-respect and the authority to say 'no'.

'Turn out the light, Horace, please,' she pleaded, thinking that somehow she might find refuge in the dark.

But he ignored her, forced his way between her legs, forced his horrible, pale, veined *thing* into her unprepared body.

She yelped, bit her lip and focused her eyes on the Royal Worcester mantle clock. He thrust and withdrew, thrust and withdrew, his hand clamped over her mouth when she looked likely to air a protest. And then it was all over, very quickly thankfully.

He fell off her with a grunt, turned his back to her and never said another word that night.

Her eyes still focused on the clock. The hands hadn't even moved, the consummation of their marriage taking less than one minute!

Chapter Thirty-Three

The islanders followed curiously behind their king and goddess, off to see what this pasty-faced, black-garbed stranger was truly all about. They took their lead from Iona as far as attitude went. They'd been watching her, noting her cynicism, her lack of regard for the Westerner, Smegson. She was usually a good judge of character, and so, accordingly, they were skeptical. cool. They'd listen to what the man had to say, but somehow they doubted that he'd be able to offer them anything that could enrich their lives further. They were happy. Jack and Iona repeatedly told the newcomers so, but they were very persistent, acted at such times as if they were deaf.

Iona wore a crimson sarong and in her burnished, flowing hair there were cymbidium orchids of white, shot through with scarlet; one behind her right ear, another tangled in her mane.

Smegson and the crew were assembled at the door of their lodgings, rested, breakfasted and washed, clean and tidy. They looked as if about to set off for church in rural Gloucestershire, so spruced and rustically sombre were they, so noticeably blank of face. There were no smiles, no talking. It made the islanders feel uncomfortable. If this was Christianity, then so far they were unimpressed. Apart from anything else, it looked boring. Nothing was happening. Everyone was glum. No one smiled.

Tig scratched his brown head, eyebrows knitting. Where were the spectacles, he wondered, the entertainment? Where was the god this man Smegson kept harping on about? Would he appear in a puff of smoke and impress them all with his superhuman powers, his tricks and sorcery? Tig watched intently, hopefully, quite willing, in his innocent, very unworldly way, to be won over and convinced, entertained and amazed.

Seats were brought up and Iona and Jack were seated, everyone falling in around them as usual, sitting on the grass, on mats, and watching the missionary.

The baby in Iona's arms gurgled, eliciting a coo from its mother, an attentive smile from his father. Smegson frowned sourly. The elder children lounging at their parents' feet made the Englishman's eyes turn narrower still. Iona had no doubt he thought all her children abominations, the spawn of lust, the damned born outside of Christian wedlock. She stared back her defiance, her mouth compressed into a humourless line.

One of the crew produced a musical pipe, began falteringly to blast out a crude rendition of some hymn. It was difficult to tell at first which one, until Smegson lead in the singing. It was 'Rock of Ages'. It was awful. Smegson was tone deaf.

The islanders looked at each other, put their hands over their ears and rolled their eyes in mock horror.

Iona began to giggle.

'Christ,' said Jack, out the side of his mouth. 'This is murder.'

And then Iona began to laugh, exploded with it, startling Ann, who had just that second dropped off to sleep. She gave a loud yowl, arms thrashing, her protest drowning out Smegson temporarily.

He glared, sang all the louder, his choir trying to do likewise, acting as if nothing was amiss.

Tig turned to Womawhi the Elder, nudged him, serious-faced. 'Why they do that, you think?'

Womawhi was thoughtful, uncertain. 'Maybe it frightens away the bad spirits.'

'Ah,' said Tig, nodding, and striving to look as wise and inscrutable as the old man.

Thankfully the hymn came to an end.

Iona loosened her sarong and put Ann to her breast. It was a sure fire way of halting her squaling. Within moments she dropped contentedly off to sleep again. In the interim, though, Smegson gaped at her – or more precisely at her swollen, generous breast – with eyes-a-popping. When she covered herself, he crossed himself like a Catholic and mumbled, 'Thank you dear Lord. Amen.'

Iona stared back brazenly, eyes sparkling defiance. 'Sir, don't expect me to be ashamed of the breasts, which according to your doctrine, God endowed me with. The baseness is in your mind, not in me.'

'Woman, you offend. You have no modesty,' countered Smegson in recriminatory fashion.

'Tosh!' she spat.

'Oh come on now,' Jack soothed. 'This bickering between you two is getting a might tedious. I've come here to listen to a sermon, to see you try to convince these people, Smegson,' he said, with an expansive gesturing of the arms, encompassing the throng, 'that you can offer them something better than they've already got. If not then I'm going to have to ask you to get back aboard your ship and sail off in search of a flock more in need of saving.'

There came across Smegson's face then what can only be described as a sublimely devious expression, a smile so cloyingly sweet that Iona's lip curled with distaste. It was the face of a man not to be trusted. Jack saw it, too.

'Christianity is not enjoyable or entertaining,' Smegson told them, his voice broadcasting coldly to all. 'It is my duty to convert even the most reluctant and seemingly irredeemable of God's earthly flock . . . by whatever means necessary. They must not be allowed to think that they know better. They must relent, repent of their wicked ways and embrace Mother Church. They *must*. That is my mission in life. I know no peace lest I be a-doing God's work. God gives me strength, He guides me, He gives me the inner strength to realise that I know better than these people what is best for them. They don't have to like something for it to be good for them or beneficial to their souls.'

Iona's eyes were popping. She might well have laughed at him again if she hadn't been so alarmed. He was a fanatic. He might even be mad.

Even as she thought it, Smegson advanced upon her, eyes bright with purpose. She pressed back into her seat instinctively. Ignoring the baby in her arms and the son at her feet, he laid his hand on her head, his fingers digging into her scalp, his other hand doing likewise to a gape-mouthed Jack.

'Let the good work start with you two,' he insisted, eyes going from one to the other. 'Set an example to these people by marrying here and now, so atoning a little for your sins.'

Iona slapped his hand away violently and jumped up, clutching Ann to her. 'Never! You can go bugger yourself!'

Jack stood up too, frowning. He'd come here this day secretly expecting to derive a little amusement out of Smegson's antics before he was cordially invited to continue on his do-gooding way elsewhere. He was angry at Smegson for making Iona angry. And now he was angry at her for so adamantly refusing marriage to him. His pride was pricked. Didn't she love him enough?

'I think it would have been only courteous, Mister Smegson, if you had consulted the pair of us first instead of dropping it on us now . . . without warning. People don't like being rushed, or surprised. Iona maybe needs time to get used to the idea.'

'My thoughts on marraige are quite clear – I won't!

Besides, in the eyes of the Church, Mister Smegson, I have a husband already, presumably still alive and residing in Sydney Australia.' There, she thought, smugly, try and work you way around that one, you sanctimonious smart ass!

Still reeling disgustedly from her earlier, colourful outburst, Smegson lashed out with a tongue full of hatred. 'Then you are doubly damned, woman, for you are a fornicator *and* an adultress. Worse still, you show no remorse, no shame.'

'In other words, I'm beyond saving? Yes? Well, in that case,' she declared, not giving Smegson time to answer, 'I shall leave you to try your luck with the others, shan't waste your time further. I certainly won't waste my own.'

Jack made as if to follow, but she turned on him, voice angry, and, to his consternation, shouted at him, 'Stay! I don't want anyone about me. Not *anyone*.'

It was like a punch in the stomach. He stopped in his tracks, wounded.

'Perhaps there is another couple willing to consolidate their union in the eyes of God?' wondered Smegson, unperturbed by Iona's departure. She was an obvious trouble-maker anyhow. They'd do better without her.

'For God's sake, give it a rest,' thundered Jack. 'For a man of God, who's supposed to advocate peace and love to your fellow man, you aren't half causing some disharmony and strife. Give our people a straightforward service with no embellishments and let them make up their minds about you, let them see what the day-to-day church is all about.'

'Very well.'

Smegson did so. And Jack sat through every tedious, long minute of it. Many of the islanders didn't. Some fell asleep and curled up where they were on their mats. Some yawned, stood up, stretched and wandered off.

Jack watched Smegson, thought of Iona's violent rejection and fumed within. Then his eyes, driven by boredom, perused the missionary's choirboys' for want of something better to do, and he grew uneasy. They were armed. He hadn't noticed before, the unobtrusive flintlocks hidden, save their wooden stocks, down the breeches of the men, their coats acting like a curtain that kept them concealed, until just then when one of them had reached up to scratch his head. His coat had flapped and the firearm was revealed. Then Jack had quickly checked the others. Yes, he'd have vouched that they were all carrying a piece.

So, he thought, that's how Smegson imposes his beliefs on others, converts even the most reluctant. Any show of dissent or rebellion against the *mission* and the heavy mob were brought in, doubtless to persuade in a most unchristian spate of brutality, to change minds, open eyes that didn't want to see, and clear ears that had played conveniently deaf.

If the people of Wahwu didn't respond of their own free will, they were to be 'encouraged'. And what were they expecting Jack to do? Turn a blind eye to such goings-on because he was English like themselves? Did they think that these people meant as little to him as that?

According to the missionary the islanders were savages, heathens, an inferior race without the acceptable shade of Anglo-Saxon skin. They only mattered if they embraced God. Were important only as numbers to impress the Bishop of Ely. If they didn't become a Christian statistic then they remained worthless, less than the dirt beneath Smegson's feet.

If Smegson had his way then Wahwu would be turned into some ridiculous imitation of an English parish. The islanders would be made to wear clothes . . . proper clothes. They would be made to learn to read and write so that they could study the Bible. They would be made to work. Not to just feed and cloth themselves, but because it would keep them out of mischief, ungodly ways. And they'd most likely be made to work for the mission in exchange for poor wages, harvesting the island's abundant natural resources, raping the land, depleting and destroying it before they realised. And by then it would be too late. The people and the island would be exploited, spoilt, would forget their old way of life, not know how to continue without, and therefore become dependant on, the Church.

If I was a cynical person, thought Jack wrily, and knew he indeed was, then I'd say they planned it that way, were out to make a killing in all departments. Islanders' souls, island resources, overall control – they'd have it all.

The moment the sermons and hymn cacophony finished Jack was up and out of his seat. Smegson leapt forward, trying to waylay him. Jack was too quick, determined, wouldn't stop. He turned his head, spoke even as he strode away, not caring if he appeared rude. Besides, Smegson had a very thick skin. 'No, I can't stop. No time. I'll speak to you later.'

He wanted to go to Iona, demand to know what she truly felt for him, why marriage would have been so repugnant. But first he had to think. There were urgent matters afoot. Things to settle. He would figure out how, then meet a Council of islanders to discuss evicting their unwelcomed guests.

Chapter Thirty-Four

He sat on a densely vegetated ledge high up in the hills for a long time, thinking, and finally thought he had the answer.

They – the island's menfolk and himself – would arm themselves with knives, clubs, the guns from the Chinese pirates which had been carefully stored away for many years, the powder kegs kept dry. And they would simply pick their moment, take Smegson and his cohorts by surprise and politely request that they leave forthwith. And, to make certain that they did go, Jack and the rest would escort them right out to their ship, see them aboard. Yes, that would solve their immediate problem. Though he couldn't guarantee that Smegson wouldn't come back, try again, or – more likely – inform interested parties for a fee in some Far East or Australasian port that Wahwu existed, supply the degrees of longitude and latitude by which it could be found. That was a worrying prospect. But there was nothing Jack could do about it. It was inevitable anyhow. He just hoped it would be later rather than sooner.

Once he'd felt European still, had longed to voyage home, to his proper home. But now, suddenly, he realised that was no longer the case. Home was here, now. Wahwu was the centre of his universe and Iona the most important person in it.

And then he thought, knocking himself on the head and feeling a chump, what a slow fool I've been. Of course she doesn't want marriage. In her head that's all tied up with that pathetic specimen of a husband she was lumbered with, with England, with . . . going home. God, yes, she thinks I'll leave, that I'll force her, if she's my wife, to go too.

He tutted at his lack of foresight in this matter, at the lack of communication between them, too. Smegson's turning up with the means of transport back to civilisation must have worried her sick. Yet there had been no real cause. He'd never go home now, knew it with certainty, would die with her on Wahwu.

He realised he should have told her that, for when last they'd broached the subject, returning to England had still been a fancy. He should have told her, yes, but in all honesty he couldn't say when his mind had changed, when he'd felt that commitment to her, their children and their people was for ever.

Perhaps he just knew for certain today.

He stood up, brushed the dirt from the seat of his red pigskin loincloth and started back down the hill to the village, his lopsided gait making the steep descent difficult and ungainly to behold.

Ahead Jack heard a smothered squeal in the lush undergrowth, he slowed. Caution was always advisable under such circumstances, he knew. It might well be a wild piglet calling to the sow; certainly since they'd been introduced to this side of the island beyond the volcano – which had hitherto acted as a natural barrier – they'd bred like wildfire.

Prudently, Jack darted behind the trunk of a palm and observed. He had his knife tucked into the hip folds of his loincloth, would kill the piglet and carry it home to Iona as a kind of peace offering if opportunity presented itself.

But it was no piglet.

Out of the undergrowth one of Smegson's sailor/choirboys was dragging a girl, one of the squat peoples' children. It was she who squealed, who tried to do so again now but the man's white and hairy hand clamped the tighter over her lips. There was wild fear in her brown eyes, reluctance in every step she fought not to take with her abductor. Most of the time he had to drag and carry her.

Stunned, Jack's mind got itself back into gear and worked frantically.

She might have been curious and too trusting when the crewman from the *Queen of Sheba* waylaid her, she might even have been flattered and perhaps found him attractive. But she certainly wasn't willing now, and went with him very much against her will.

Once in the clearing the burly man prized her down to the ground instantly and started trying to strip her clothes off. She didn't wear much – just a little pigskin strip of skirt. In a moment it was snatched away. She struggled, fought with nails, feet and knees, redoubled her efforts when he unbuttoned his fly, exposing his rigid member.

Jack crept up on them silently from behind, had yanked back the man's hair and slit his white throat even before his mind had had a chance to wonder at the look which came over the girls face, the glint in her eyes as she'd spied Jack over her attacker's shoulder.

Helped by Jack and the girl, the body was shoved contemptuously sideways, blood gushing from the gaping, horrible wound that went almost from ear to ear.

'I no tease. Honest, King Jack. Only smile. I not understand why he act so,' cried the girl, tears streaming down her face, washing a path through the spatters of blood. 'I no want this.'

Jack smiled kindly, hugged her. She was one of those children who might just be his. No one was certain. 'It's all right. It's not your fault. King Jack understands. These men are bad.'

As if to emphasise the point, Jack kicked the corpse unceremoniously into the undergrowth where the island's animal population could finish it off.

She covered herself again, then Jack took up the trembling child-woman and started down the hill once more, more ungainly in his passage than ever. Her hands went about his neck, her face snuggled against his chest. Relief overwhelmed her, that and a feeling of absolute safety in Jack's arms.

'Let's get you home, Little One, and get you cleaned up before your mother sees you. Otherwise she'll be unduly alarmed.'

She nodded, glad to let Jack take charge.

It was dark before they stole into the lodge. Purposefully, Jack and the girl had waited, hiding on the outskirts of the village, wanting to get to the lodge without being seen, without questions being asked by the wrong people.

Iona was waiting anxiously, had been worrying all afternoon, regretting her angry outburst.

The instant he came stealthily through the door she had embarked upon some kind of conciliatory explanation, but it had faltered at the sight of the bloodied girl pulled along in his wake. 'Jack, I'm sorry. I . . . Good God, whatever's happened?'

'She's been attacked by one of Smegson's men. He's dead. Up on the hill.'

'Dead?' Instantly there was worry in her eyes. Obviously Jack and killed him, had been in danger himself, perhaps.

He nodded, dismissively. 'Aye, but don't worry about that. This child needs some attention.'

Iona ran forward, put her arm about the girl and brought her further into the room. 'Are you hurt, lamb?'

'Not badly. Just bruised, I think. And a might shocked,' opinioned Jack.

'Let's get you cleaned up then,' soothed Iona, leading the girl to the couch more often used by visitors for informal reclining at the Living God's numerous yearly functions. 'A sponge and water, please, Oami.' the servant hastily disappeared.

Then Iona turned to Jack, spoke in English over the girl's head. 'Something has to be done about those men, Jack. They're bad; I can feel it, sense it. They'll do nothing but harm here. We *must* make them leave.'

Jack's head was nodding even before she'd finished.

'I agree. That's what I've been doing most of the afternoon. Thinking. But I don't think that sending them packing is the answer any longer. They'll come back because they're the persistent type, probably with reinforcements, more muscle power to make us toe the line.'

'Us? Would you still be here then, Jack? I thought . . . well, you said, if a ship came . . .'

'That was a long time ago. Leastways it feels a long time. Much has happened since I thought along those lines. My priorities have changed.'

'Yes?' She was desperately hopeful.

'Yes, I'm staying. I feel too much like you now to do otherwise. I love you far too dearly to make you unhappy by taking you back to England. And I don't long for it any more . . . not like I did. It wasn't *that* wonderful, not like this.'

'Oh Jack, thank God,' said Iona, raggedly, 'I've been so worried, so afraid. And I'm sorry about today, about saying 'no' to marriage. It was hurtful. I hate the thought of hurting you. If you still want marriage, I'll do it . . . for you.'

He laughed at her not quite concealing his reluctance.

His possible daughter saw herself as being in the way and, as Oami re-entered carrying a basin and sponge, thoughtfully extricated herself from the space between them and went to have herself cleaned up in another corner of the lodge.

Jack and Iona hardly noticed her leave. In that instance there was only the two of them and the world stopped still. They saw nothing else, heard nothing else

– not Ann awakening in the nursery and beginning to growl, not the roosting island birds creating a din in the treetops then going quiet again just as quickly, not the iron pots clattering out back in the yard where most of the cooking was done.

'No,' said Jack, covering the distance between them. 'No marriage. You are right. It would be hypocrisy, not to mention bigamy.'

She smiled broadly, thankful for his lightness, fell into his arms and buried her head against his chest. He stroked her hair, over and over again, loving the feel of it, its springy silkiness. There was no need to say anything else.

Chapter Thirty-Five

A Council was hastily convened, warriors, elders and wise women stealing into the lodge through shadowy gardens that would have more usually been lit by torches and lanterns for such a gathering. But this was not usual; this was serious business and very clandestine.

The Council didn't sit in session for long, were quick to reach a unanimous decision once Jack had spoken, told them of that afternoon's attack on one of their own.

They all agreed: Smegson and his men must be got rid of. Tig stood up and addressed the lamplit faces, half in shadow, grave and determined. He told them that he and his men (because there was no denying that they were the most war-loving of the islanders), would see to it, immediately, if that was the wish of the others.

Gazes shifted, locked, moved on, heads nodded. Yes, let it be now, tonight. The sooner the better.

The Council dispersed.

Jack waylaid Tig in the garden, Iona dogging his heels. 'I shall come with you? Its only fitting for I am King.'

Tig shook his head. 'No, Friend Jack. Not this time. This is squat people's business . . . *cannibal business*. I owe you . . . for the pig. Remember?'

Jack looked at him, disquieted, eyebrows quirking. He knew what the warrior was referring to but it wasn't that which worried him. It was the use of the term 'cannibal' and the emphasis placed upon it.

Iona watched him, saw the look of troubled understanding dawning. She was bemused.

Jack nodded, resigned. 'Very well, Tig. Do it. I, along with Mia and Sanga – who know well enough, I think, how to dispose of unwanted vessels – shall paddle out a canoe and hole and fire the ship.

The said women were instantly at his side, leaving their impatiently hovering groups, faces beaming, ready, hands symbolically on the hilts of their daggers, minds doubtless already working fiendishly at a plan. As ever, when given a task by their beloved Jack, they looked gleeful, their enthusiasm somehow out of all proportion to the job.

'And what about me?' said Iona, belligerently. 'What am I to do? If we're pulling rank here, Jack Savage, then let me remind you that I'm the Living God, most definitely your superior.'

He frowned, turned to his co-saboteurs, 'Go ahead. I'll catch you up,' then took Iona by the shoulders, spoke to her with a gentle authority that infuriated her. 'Look, love, its not many days since you birthed Ann. You've recovered well, I know,' he said quickly when she opened her mouth to start arguing, 'but you need more time . . . peace, tranquillity. You need to devote yourself to the nursing of our child. She's most important, surely . . . to both of us.'

Her lips pursed. He'd got the upper hand, blast him, was making sense, being logical. She couldn't argue against it. It was maddening. 'Oh, all right then,' she snorted.

'I knew I could rely upon you to be sensible. Go back inside, look after the children, and lock the door.'

'Only if you'll kiss me,' she bargained.

His eyes rolled in exasperation, lips thinned. Grudingly almost he complied, but then artfully she worked upon him, pressed to him, snaked arms about him, mingled her breath with his. He almost groaned when she moved away first, his fingers holding on, losing their grip and then missing her touch.

He smiled at her standing on the veranda where black cockerels roosted above on the exposed beams, and told her with assurance, 'I won't be too long, I promise.'

She waved, was certain of it, of him.

In their hut (one of the most basic in the village, and a fact that hadn't escaped the indignant and offended missionary) Smegson and his men drank and grumbled, drank and ate. The hut was poor, compared to the lodge where the fornicator, who dared to call herself a god, lived in perpetual sin with a supposed gentleman who was no gentleman at all to Semgson's way of thinking. That would all have to change. So would the standard of food which the villagers brought them as if on an afterthought. It was haphazard in quality, scrappy for the most part and suspiciously like leftovers to look at. When they took over they wanted good food, four times a day, cooked for them personally, and they wanted half a dozen islanders to keep their quarters clean and in order for them, once they'd taken up residence in the new, desired dwelling Smegson was planning in his head.

All these things and more he jabbered about as he downed just 'one more' snifter of rum. He'd had so many now he'd lost count.

It was his only vice, he told himself leniently. God would understand. As usual when he drank he ranted. His crew had become used to it, didn't mind his out-of-control habit because it gave them a chance to drink, too, to relax. When Smegson drank, he forgot discipline, overlooked their behaviour as well as his own. As long as they agreed with whatever he was sounding off about and uttered the odd 'definitely, here-here' and 'Oh, I absolutely agree', in the right places, they were all but ignored. Certainly Smegson never asked their opinion on anything, wanted no exchange of views. His were the only views he cared for, his the only conversation he found interesting. Indeed, his crew knew that if they hadn't been there tonight, Smegson would just as happily have talked to no one. He often did.

'They need to be whipped into shape, literally. Lack discipline. All savages are the same – African niggers, slanty-eyed Chinamen, those crafty bloody Indians with their permanent, untrustworthy smiles. I've dealt with them all. Put the fear of God into them, I say, and beat 'em regular. It's the only way. We'll start tomorrow, men. Yes, tomorrow. No point in delaying. I'll have them reciting Psalm nineteen by Sunday, or they'll know His displeasure.'

'Oh, aye, Mister Smegson, right you are,' said Captain Overbeck, then whispered to the man beside him, who was licking chicken grease from his fingers, 'Where's Nichols?'

'He went off after some girl after service today. Winked at her and guessed that she were accommodating, like, when she smiled back at him.'

'Been gone a long time.'

'Must be having fun, then. Might try a spot of winking and wenching meself tomorrow.'

'Just be careful,' said Overbeck, Nichols already forgotten, his mind wandering off, on to something else.

'. . . and they shall be put to work, too,' Smegson rambled on, drunkenly swaying in his seat. 'There is sloth here, idle hands for the Devil's work. It must be stamped out. Stamp out the Devil. Yes, stamp it out. And *her* especially; she'll have to go. Heathen idolatory. Wickedness. She's a false goddess, a Jezebel.'

One of Overbeck's crew sniggered as Smegson's diatribe went into shouting mode.

And then the door to their hut burst open and an intimidating throng of bubbly-haired savages outnumbered them, overwhelmed them, Tig at their head brandishing a club, a saw-edged knife and a gleeful smile.

'What's this then?' barked Smegson in righteous fury. 'How dare you burst in here, you damned heathens, you black devils! Get out!'

His face smeared with ashes and mud, his broad cheekbones accentuated by two bright white daubs of paint, Tig stared back at him with proud contempt. 'We are Red Devils, not black. And we do not like your God, Smeg-son.'

With everyone save Smegson reclining on the grass-matted floor of their furnitureless abode, the Englishmen never had a chance, senses slowed by drink, weapons discarded about the place, they know not where. Certainly not on their persons.

Screaming, they were dragged up off their backsides and out into the night. Smegson turned furious, fear crazed eyes towards the dark and distant shape of the Living God's lodge, shouted frantically at the top of his considerable voice, 'Help us, Savage. Help!'

As if in an awful, final denial of his pleaded request, the lights in the lodge's reception room were extinguished. The village remained quiet.

The Englishmen were never spoken of again. It was as if they had never existed. Howls and screams had been heard far off, cooking fires seen through the black, criss-crossed trunks of palm trees, but only Tig and his band of warriors knew for certain what had befallen them and they weren't saying. It was done, over, no longer important.

There were those who guessed, though, of course, guessed accurately too. For a long while afterwards Jack found himself unconsciously thinking *cannibal* instead of *squat person*, though he never so much as intimated, was too glad, too happy to disturb the quiet waters.

Life returned to normal, the only excitement in the islander's lives caused by the unpredictability of nature . . . and man. Nothing changed. Everything stayed comfortingly, reassuringly the same. There were feuds, love affairs, betrayals, disagreements and the odd theft which were severely punished. But there were no more outsiders.

The Gods – their Gods – did indeed smile down upon them.

Chapter Thirty-Six

On August 23rd 1910 the frigate HMS *Iron Acton*, powered by steam and sail, sighted an island in the hazy distance of first light, an island that shouldn't be there.

Maps were scanned, scanned again. Heads were scratched. The Captain was called to the bridge. His ginger eyebrows knit. He called for the map, scrutinised it.

'Perhaps its a mirage,' someone quipped.

The Captain frowned. 'Is our position correct?'

'Yes, sir. We checked, rechecked before deciding to rouse you from your bed.'

'Then the map's wrong.' He stabbed the compasses into it. 'There should be an island . . . right there.'

'But—'

'No buts about it. She's there. Our maps are wrong, they need updating.'

'Shall we land, sir?'

'I think we will, Lieutenant. Don't know about anyone else but I'm mighty curious.'

Orders were given, the ship's course changed.

They were spotted long before they dropped anchor and started rowing ashore in the long boat. They were all in formal dress, spotless white uniforms respelendant with braid and, where applicable, ribbons and medals. Captain Wilson stood in the prow, tall and stiffly self-assured, gazing ahead with a typically English demeanour – all over-the-top fearlessness and national pride, looking, Leiutenant Cruikshank thought with a secret smile of amusement, much as Captain Cook must have done as he approached what had once been called the Sandwich Islands but were now known as Hawaii. And look what had happened to him! He felt his Navy issue revolver at his waist reassuringly.

Also in the long boat were fourteen able seamen to do the rowing, a sub-leiutenant and two midshipmen. They were all discreetly armed though, to be honest, none of them expected to encounter anything out of the ordinary once ashore. Likelihood was that the island – and it was very small indeed as far as South Sea Islands went – wasn't inhabited. And if it was, then it had probably been claimed as sovereign territory by some other seafaring nation, then forgotten about because of its lack of geographical or ecological importance.

'Look here, sir,' called out one of the oarsmen, 'Right below us in the shallows . . . a wreck.'

The Captain stared, kneeling in the prow and leaning far out over the side to get a better look.

Lying there in the crystal waters, perhaps some five fathoms below them, he calculated, was the scuppered remains of a barque. No, a brig, he decided, counting the jagged coral encrusted stumps of what had once been its masts.

'You're right, Rawlins, Well done. Well spotted. That means the island has definitely been visited before.'

'It also means, doesn't it, sir,' said Wilfred Cruikshank, 'that they probably never left.'

The Captain nodded thoughtfully.

Alerted some time ago and carried down to the water's edge in the ceremonial chair once used by the Living

God, King Ran waited, eyes narrowing as he peered with failing sight out to sea.

He was so old now that he seldom walked anywhere, took full advantage of his regal status and had himself carried. Once he had been huge, ever bigger than his father, Tiku, but his appetite had begun to fail round about his seventy-eighth summer and since then he'd slimmed down to a less considerable seventeen stone, his dark, wrinkled skin hanging on him a little, like a suit that was too big for the wearer.

Ranked behind him his children, (who were very old men and women themselves) grandchildren, great grandchildren and even great, great, great grandchildren, were a veritable army backing him up. His wife, Alaba of the squat people, had died a long time ago, leaving him a sad and somewhat lonely widower. He'd married again. Indeed, he'd had three wives at different times, one of whom still lived, but it was Alaba whom he always remembered with the greatest affection.

Some said Ran was one hundred and seven years old. He wasn't the oldest man on the island, though. That honour went to his half-brother, Jin-Jon, son of Tiku and Mam, who had been born in 1799, he was one hundred and ten.

Behind his family were all the other families descended from the Living God, Iona, and the Coconut King, Jack; from Tig, Mara, Mia, Tula and all the rest. They filled the beach, raven locked, brown curly haired, auburn brown and golden brown. Skin shades varied, too. Dark brown, light brown, coffee, golden. And their clothes had changed, though they were always on that old familiar theme – Red pigskin and black cockerel feathers. Now people who were neither squat nor tall, wore combinations of both old tribes' cultural fashion. Everything was mixed up. There were very few tall people any longer, not many who were noticeably short. Marriage between the two tribes, as Iona had long ago encouraged, had seen to that. And the injection of European blood through her and Jack and their daughter, Ann, had made them a truly mixed race, a strong race, all so similar in their ways but all a little different to behold.

Ann had lived to be ninety-two or-three (no one was ever totally sure), had had nine children with her husband, Togo, a squat people's warrior, fathered by that prolific sire, Tig. Their descendants were noticeably golden brown of skin and hair.

Ran knew what he was going to do, faced with these new outsiders. He was primed, such an eventuality planned for long ago by Iona and Jack. They had decided that the islanders would have to put on a united, strong show for any who might come, that that was the only way to deal with the British, Dutch, Portuguese or Spanish. Those were the nationalities they were expecting because those were the great seafaring nations. Always had been. The Americans had been dismissed because they were so insular after their War of Independence and so isolated by the vast oceans surrounding them. And if Chinese came, in any way resembling the ones who had come before, they knew exactly how they would deal with them; quickly and violently.

So everything was prepared.

King Jack had spent the latter years of his life perfecting the making of paper from a variety of the island's many trees. He'd travelled the whole island in search of the best woods for pulping, using the ever-lenghtening network of roads, which successive generations of navigators kept on building.

Iona travelled with him when duties would allow, visiting villages that had sprung up in geographically suitable spots along their route, settling disputes, attending weddings. Her revered presence was the icing on the cake, so to speak, on such momentous occasions, it supposedly brought good luck.

Upon the paper the history of the island was set down in English and a polyglot version so that all could study and retain in memory, their ancestors' lore; could read of Rantavitiku and his son; the coming of Iona and Jack from the ferocity of the seas around their shores; the coming together of the tribes and the failure of a devil called Smegson to impose Christianity upon them. That period in the weighty annuls ended with the simple line:

'The Great warrior, Tig, rid the island of them and their ship was sunk.'

It was simply put. It said nothing, yet it stated everything that the islander's (and outsiders who might come) needed to know. The wider truth, after all, was in their heads, need not be put down on paper. They knew; the knowledge was part of them, had always been there, handed down from one generation to the next.

Afterwards, had come a period of calm, a period of subtle change. The three languages had become one. Iona had called the resulting tongue Outlandish, and the tag had stuck, for many could recall stories from Tiku's other wives, and Mam in particular, of a little dance that Iona had once done for the Living God, Tiku.

Jack Savage's journals had made the first references around then to the Outlandish language.

The most important entry for 1865 read:

'This year our beloved Iona died peacefully in her bed.' (She had been celebrating the birth of her twenty-fifth great grandchild that day with Jack, went to bed tired and happy and never woke again). 'She was a wise woman, a good leader. King Jack's heart was crushed by the pain of it and, before the moon had gone from crescent to full face, he too was dead, gone to join her.'

Ran, strong and notably clever, was elected King but there never was another Living God. It was explained in the journals thus:

'It was decided by Council during the last years of Iona's divine protection, that Living Gods were of the past, that the Council, with the elected king at their head were all that the island needed. Iona was in full agreement with them, said that she had never felt anything but mortal in all the years she'd donned the mantle of office. Said, too, that absolute power was bad.

Another period of calm followed. Then great rejoicing, feasting and giving of presents when King Ran celebrated fifty years as their ruler. To mark the occasion to the degree that they thought worthy, the Council of islanders decreed that henceforth the island should be known as Outlandia in honour of Ran and his mother. Approval was unanimous, for Wahwu had not been a name that belonged to, and encompassed everyone. Certainly the squat people had felt little allegiance to it. Outlandia was the natural choice, especially as it had already given name to their shared language.

Now, many years on, that was all history, fuzzy in many an islander's mind. Many of the younger ones couldn't remember the island ever being called anything else. To them it had always been Outlandia, and Iona and Jack were remembered in somewhat mythological terms, fact elaborated into fiction, like Robin Hood and Maid Marian, King Arthur and Guinevere.

'There's definitely people on the shore now, sir,' said Cruikshank, with deliberate understatement.

'Let's cross fingers that they're friendly, then,' hoped the Captain. 'And try not to look so damned unfriendly, Jones; you could sour milk.'

'Sorry, sir. I'm nervous,' apologised the midshipman.

'We're all nervous. But men of the British Navy don't show it. That's rule number one, always.'

'Yes, sir.'

They were over the coral reef now, the breakers carrying them in the last several hundred yards recklessly fast. From HMS *Iron Acton* the two hundred or so men remaining on board, crowded the rails to watch. They covered the distance in mere seconds, were powerless to control their little vessel to any great extent, could only steer it. The Captain tried to look calm, confident, in charge, but even he failed when the nose of the long boat dug into the sloping beach of white sand and he was thrown forward. He caught at the prow, saved himself from being thrown out, but lost his splendid hat.

Ran's bearers lifted him up in his comfortable chair and repositioned him so that he was directly in front of the boat. By the time he'd settled, made himself comfortable and summoned a boy to cool him with a fan of palm fronds, Captain Wilson and the party were wading ashore, Wilson retrieving and shaking the surplus tide from his hat. He looked at it disgustedly, tucked the now useless thing under his arm and hoped it would be overlooked. He'd aimed to impress, knew that he'd failed. And somehow, he wasn't quite certain how, he knew he was never to get the upper hand in this encounter.

Ran rose from his chair, towered over them, huge and dark, ancient and impressive, remembering the advice that had been given him by his mother and her man.

Captain Wilson was tall enough – nearly six foot – but the native was much taller, perhaps six foot six, perhaps even more. Looking up continually put him at an instant disadvantage. Ran's bearing underlined it. The rest of Wilson's men were mesmerised by him.

'Welcome,' Ran said, deliberately forsaking his usual Outlandish for pure, perfect English. He liked surprising people, loved the astounded looks on their faces now as he continued, clipped, clear, without pause or hesitation. 'Twice welcome to the Kingdom of Outlandia. Those who come in peace need not fear us. I am Ran, elected King of these people, protector of this sovereign isle. You are welcome to visit with us *for a while.*'

The emphasis wasn't lost on Wilson.

'Um . . . thank you. That is most kind,' he said,

255

stiffly, and a little confused. He'd been to many of the South Sea islands during his twenty years as a sailor, most of them spent in this part of the world, but he'd never come across any island name that didn't sound every bit the part – Tonga, Tahiti, Honolulu. But never Outlandia. It was contrived. Theatrical. Like something fanciful out of a play by Shakespeare. It was romantic, archaic. Surely it couldn't be, in any way imaginable, a native creation? They just wouldn't come up with words like that.

Ran was pleased. He liked the way things were going, especially the uncomfortable uncertainty of the white man's face. It made him feel more confident, more powerful, and more benevolent and kindly, too. He had the upper hand, he knew, felt sure he could keep it. Extreme old age had made him wise and very wily.

'Outlandia?' questioned Wilson, voice politely quiet.

'Yes. Outlandia. Once upon a time this half of the island was called Wahwu by the tall tribe who lived here, while hidden from the squat people who lived on the other side of the island, beyond the volcano. They had no name for their island, weren't intellectual enough to worry about thinking of one. Then one day the two tribes came together. A name was thought of which was acceptable to both,' explained Ran, even as he evaded the main point.

Wilson listened in growing amazement. Where had this man picked up a word like 'intellectual'? Where were the white people who had had such an obvious influence? Was that *their* ship scuppered out in the bay? He looked totally confused now.

Ran smiled indulgently, enjoying the game. 'I shall explain. Come to our village, my guests, and all questions will be answered. Only first I have a question for you. Have you any missionaries on board that ship which brought you across the sea?'

'Missionaries?' Wilson's eyebrows knit. 'Heavens, no! We are a naval vessel, in the service of his Brittanic Majesty, King Edward the Seventh.'

'Edward now, is it? Not George?'

'No . . .' Wilson was about to say 'sir', thought better of it, '. . . Your Majesty. There hasn't been a George since before Victoria and William. George the Fourth.'

Ran shook his head. 'No, not him. The last ship that sailed here came during the reign of the mad one . . . the one whose son was Regent. I remember hearing that.'

'George the Third! Good God,' gasped the Captain. 'That was long ago'. Ran was old indeed, the oldest man Wilson had ever met.

Ran nodded, smiling. 'Come. Without missionaries you are *very* welcome. Without missionaries you shall stay as my guests at the royal lodge. And you shall hear a tale to end all tales, I Ran, guarantee it. You shall hear of the Living God and the Coconut King and sample our hospitality,' said Ran, knowing that he had the better of them, enjoying himself. Of course there were things that he would never tell, things that would be conveniently changed. He would make them see that Outlandia was strong enough to be left alone, that she'd stand for no unwelcomed meddling in her affairs. Though that wasn't to say that Ran wanted no contact with a friendly, powerful nation like Britain. He did. He would nurture it carefully, craftily, move Outlandia – figuratively speaking – under Brittania's mantle and enjoy her maternal protection whilst remaining independent. That's what had been suggested many years before and he could see the wisdom in it, was clever enough to know how to manipulate such things. After all, that was why he had been chosen as King.

Ran's chair was turned around. The sea of bodies parted and the procession moved back towards the trees and the road to the village.

'Will the men on your ship also join us?' wondered the King.

Wilson shrugged vaguely, uncommitted, hadn't made up his mind. 'Perhaps later.'

'They will be safe,' reassured Ran. 'You are guests. Invited. You are safe.'

'Thank you,' Wilson smiled, 'I never doubted it.'

'Good.' Ran watched the hat that the Captain was unconsciously toying with, liked the braid, the brass. 'It's a fine hat.'

Wilson looked it over dubiously. 'This? It's ruined.'

'Then might you make a gift of it, do you think?' wondered Ran.

'But wouldn't you rather have a new one? I can send for one from the ship. One that isn't wet.'

Ran laughed. 'I like that one.'

'Then it's yours.'

Ran crammed it on his head, adjusted the angle and looked to his wrinkled old wife, who walked at his side, for an opinion. She laughed. Then he laughed, pleased by her response.

He lifted the long string of pearls from around his neck, offered them to Wilson.

The man was taken aback. 'I couldn't, Your Majesty. Really.'

'Of course you can. I know their worth, man, have been well schooled upon the things Western people value and what comes cheap.'

'But it isn't a fair swap.'

'To whom? And am I grumbling? Take the necklace. I'm sure your wife would never forgive you if you didn't. To me the swap is fair,' said Ran, jovially.

He was no fool. He wanted Wilson on his side, the Royal Navy on his side, good King Edward on his side. He sensed already that he had them. A string of pearls was a small price to pay for the introductions.

Wilson accepted the gift, thrilled to think them his, kept them in his hands while he walked briskly beside the King, their warmth beguiling him.

Ran smiled to himself, quietly content, felt that his mother would have been proud of him and this day's work.

* * *

The fires burned, the wine and magic nuts were passed around. Seated on finely carved chairs in a semi-circle that had King Ran at its apex in a chair far larger and more ornate than all the rest, Wilson and his fellow officers, resplendent in their white dress-uniforms, not wanting to offend by refusing such odd bounty, chewed as vigorously as the natives, allowing no grimace of distaste to cross their faces. The men had been well briefed before being allowed ashore.

Silhouetted against the orange fireglow, a dozen and more island girls snaked across their field of vision, wearing nothing but black feathered and red pigskin skirts that draped their hips and barely covered their groins.

A drum started and the girls sang, voices light, full of charm and amusement, 'I'm dancing the Outlandish Ootalana in a land I call Outlandia,' in a tongue discernibly English. As they sang, so they moved, slowly, languidly, girating their hips, raising their arms so that their pert breasts were lifted amongst necklaces of shell and coral.

The alluring sight, the pulsating beats from the drum, made the row of meticulously turned out officers hot about the collar. Ran observed this and smiled, observed, too, how several of them were bulging appreciatievely in their tailored trousers.

The dance grew more erotic, the drum beat intense and the girls dropped to their knees, swayed back and forth, arms in the air, displaying dark sex-lips and peeping tongues of clitoris for the British Navy's delectation.

Wilson chewed the harder on his nut, mesmerised despite himself. He was not a very sexual being, the Navy was his life nowadays and romance a thing of the very distant past, killed off when he'd married the miserable, unaccommodating Mrs Wilson. But tonight he was stirred greatly, found the dormant snake at his loins raising its head for the first time in a long time.

The dance grew to fever pitch, the girl's movements

wholly suggestive and enticing as they shook themselves, thrusting forth their pelvises, or else waggling a near naked and darkly globular backside.

The men clutched the arms of their chairs white knuckled, the nuts fogging their brains, overwhelming them with a feeling of unreality and well being.

Suddenly the music stopped, the girls stood poised. The officers were disconcerted and disappointed, thinking the entertainment at an end.

King Ran explained. 'Now they will choose partners for the final act. It is deemed good manners to go willingly when chosen and perform well for the enjoyment of others . . . for those who only watch.'

Wilson looked confused. 'I don't quite see.'

'All will become clear,' Ran assured, smile patronising. He clapped his hands and, with squeals of playful delight, the girls ran forward, took the hand of the man they'd selected and pulled him up from his seat. Disappointingly, Wilson found that he had been left behind, somehow rejected, along with old Midshipman Evans who was due to retire when they arrived home in Portsmouth.

The girls dragged the men into the grass clearing before the fires, holding tight to their hands. The men felt foolish, didn't know what was expected of them. They dreaded that they might be obliged to dance. The drum started beating again and the girls started unbuttoning shirts and flies with sensuous slowness, bodies moving liquidly, enticingly, before the disarranged gentlemen whose trousers now lay bunched around their ankles along with their crisp white underpants; their collective members wagged in different stages of arousal, all sizes and colours, slim, huge, red-headed, blue-veined.

Then the girls snaked their arms around the necks of their chosen partners, rubbed hard-nippled breasts against muscular, pale chests, raised themsevles and wrapped their legs around the men's hips. Instinctively the men clutched at their partners buttocks, supporting them, impaling them, staggering on the spot as they were worked upon, tight sexes enveloping them, driving down on them.

There were cries of unexpected joy from the men, mind-blown that they should be treated so wonderfully, followed by exclamations of unbelievable pleasure as, one by one, they were brought to grinding climaxes by the accomplished troupe of dancers.

By this time Wilson's disappointment was acute and he found it difficult to conceal. It might have killed him, for he was no longer a young man, but he'd almost have welcomed dying in order to perform like his men.

Ran leant sideways, patted his hand. 'Never mind, Wilson my friend. As leader of your men it is my duty as host to see that your comfort is pandered to. We cannot leave you in *that* sorry state, now can we?' laughed the King, prodding a finger at the lump in the Captain's trousers. 'You shall relieve yourself in private with a woman from my own household. 'Tis only fitting. You, like me, should not have to perform before others.'

'Really, there's no need to go to any trouble,' declined Wilson, suddenly alarmed by the prosepct of being obliged to couple with one of the King's matronly concubines.

'Nonsense! You are my guest. You must have every comfort,' said Ran decisively, signalling to a female at his right hand shoulder.

She stepped forward, smiling enchantingly at Wilson, a vision of coffee coloured loveliness. 'This is Julee,' said Ran, 'I think she will make you happy.'

Wilson couldn't believe his eyes. Just looking at her luscious curves, her high, dark nippled breasts, her tiny waist and flaring hips, was enough to make him go off in his trousers.

She reached out a hand and Wilson was up and out of his seat like a shot, as sprightly as a schoolboy about to experience his first sexual encounter rather than one of his last.

Ran watched him being willingly led away, a spark of merriment in his old eyes. Mentally he congratulated himself and his people for their wiliness in a job well done. Outlandia had thoroughly seduced the Englishmen.

As Wilson followed behind the beautiful Julee, breathing in her perfume and ogling her uncontrollably, he was thinking along not dissimilar lines.

Mentally he sighed, if only I need never go home. Could stay here forever.

King Edward VII died in the Winter of 1910 and his son George V succeeded him. An invitation to the Coronation was delivered by naval vessel out of Sydney, Australia. Ran, unfortunately, was too old and too fearful of the sea to go. It was something he bitterly regretted until the end of his days. He died in 1911.

However, the great, great granddaughter of Ann Savage, who was elected queen on the death of Towimara – who had succeeded Ran – travelled by ship to Australia and then by BOAC Aeroplane to London, England, to attend the Coronation of Queen Elizabeth II in 1953.

She was seventy-six years old, weighed seventeen stone and sat proudly in her alloted seat under the splendidly vaulted ceiling of Westminster Abbey's choir.

Queen Mimiona thought the ceremony wonderful, the chorused shouts of *'Vivat! Vivat Regina!'* stirring indeed.

Her English was pretty good and she could follow the service with ease, but often her gaze wandered up from the book to the one who was called Archbishop of Canterbury and the white gowned, impeccably groomed woman who sat in an ancient chair under the considerable weight of a golden, jewel-encrusted crown.

Queen Mimiona was impressed by the jewels, not to say dazzled, wondered whether perhaps this new queen, Elizabeth, might want to swap some of the choicest gems for a bag or two of flawless pearls?

Afterwards, when the newly crowned queen was driven back to her palace in a magnificent coach, Mimiona followed behind with the Prime Minister of some South African Commonwealth country and two Foreign Ambassadors in a gleaming black Landau. They didn't have much to say, were too excited despite their grandness, and Mimiona was too busy waving to the crowds, thinking that it was a pity about the rain.

The British Pathe News team thought her colourful enough to warrant a mention on their newsreel, and spent one minute following her with their cameras while mention was made of her beaded dress, her numerous strings of pearls and her flamboyantly styled black hat resplendent with a complete cockerel's tail compliment of gleaming blue-black feathers.

Outlandia prospers still . . . in its own way.

BLACK lace

NO LADY
Saskia Hope

30 year-old Kate dumps her boyfriend, walks out of her job and sets off in search of sexual adventure. Set against the rugged terrain of the Pyrenees, the love-making is as rough as the landscape. Only a sense of danger can satisfy her longing for erotic encounters beyond the boundaries of ordinary experience.

ISBN 0 352 32857 6

WEB OF DESIRE
Sophie Danson

High-flying executive Marcie is gradually drawn away from the normality of her married life. Strange messages begin to appear on her computer, summoning her to sinister and fetishistic sexual liaisons with strangers whose identity remains secret. She's given glimpses of the world of The Omega Network, where her every desire is known and fulfilled.

ISBN 0 352 32856 8

BLUE HOTEL
Cherri Pickford

Hotelier Ramon can't understand why best-selling author Floy Pennington has come to stay at his quiet hotel in the rural idyll of the English countryside. Her exhibitionist tendencies are driving him crazy, as are her increasingly wanton encounters with the hotel's other guests.

ISBN 0 352 32858 4

CASSANDRA'S CONFLICT
Fredrica Alleyn

Behind the respectable facade of a house in present-day Hampstead lies a world of decadent indulgence and darkly bizarre eroticism. The sternly attractive Baron and his beautiful but cruel wife are playing games with the young Cassandra, employed as a nanny in their sumptuous household. Games where only the Baron knows the rules, and where there can only be one winner.

ISBN 0 352 32859 2

THE CAPTIVE FLESH
Cleo Cordell

Marietta and Claudine, French aristocrats saved from pirates, learn their invitation to stay at the opulent Algerian mansion of their rescuer, Kasim, requires something in return; their complete surrender to the ecstasy of pleasure in pain. Kasim's decadent orgies also require the services of the handsome blonde slave, Gabriel – perfect in his male beauty. Together in their slavery, they savour delights at the depths of shame.

ISBN 0 352 32872 X

PLEASURE HUNT
Sophie Danson

Sexual adventurer Olympia Deschamps is determined to become a member of the Legion D'Amour – the most exclusive society of French libertines who pride themselves on their capacity for limitless erotic pleasure. Set in Paris – Europe's most romantic city – Olympia's sense of unbridled hedonism finds release in an extraordinary variety of libidinous challenges.

ISBN 0 352 32880 0

ODALISQUE
Fleur Reynolds

A tale of family intrigue and depravity set against the glittering backdrop of the designer set. Auralie and Jeanine are cousins, both young, glamorous and wealthy. Catering to the business classes with their design consultancy and exclusive hotel, this facade of respectability conceals a reality of bitter rivalry and unnatural love.

ISBN 0 352 32887 8

OUTLAW LOVER
Saskia Hope

Fee Cambridge lives in an upper level deluxe pleasuredome of technologically advanced comfort. The pirates live in the harsh outer reaches of the decaying 21st century city where lawlessness abounds in a sexual underworld. Bored with her predictable husband and pampered lifestyle, Fee ventures into the wild side of town, finding an urban outlaw who becomes her lover. Leading a double life of piracy and privilege, will her taste for adventure get her too deep into danger?

ISBN 0 352 32909 2

AVALON NIGHTS
Sophie Danson

On a stormy night in Camelot, a shape-shifting sorceress weaves a potent spell. Enthralled by her magical powers, each knight of the Round Table – King Arthur included – must tell the tale of his most lustful conquest. Virtuous knights, brave and true, recount before the gathering ribald deeds more befitting licentious knaves. Before the evening is done, the sorceress must complete a mystic quest for the grail of ultimate pleasure.

ISBN 0 352 32910 6

THE SENSES BEJEWELLED
Cleo Cordell

Willing captives Marietta and Claudine are settling into an opulent life at Kasim's harem. But 18th century Alergia can be a hostile place. When the women are kidnapped by Kasim's sworn enemy, they face indignities that will test the boundaries of erotic experience. Marietta is reunited with her slave lover Gabriel, whose heart she previously broke. Will Kasim win back his cherished concubines? This is the sequel to *The Captive Flesh*.

ISBN 0 352 32904 1

GEMINI HEAT
Portia Da Costa

As the metropolis sizzles in freak early summer temperatures, twin sisters Deana and Delia find themselves cooking up a heatwave of their own. Jackson de Guile, master of power dynamics and wealthy connoisseur of fine things, draws them both into a web of luxuriously decadent debauchery. Sooner or later, one of them has to make a life-changing decision.

ISBN 0 352 32912 2

March '94

VIRTUOSO
Katrina Vincenzi

Mika and Serena, darlings of classical music's jet-set, inhabit a world of secluded passion. The reason? Since Mika's tragic accident which put a stop to his meteoric rise to fame as a solo violinist, he cannot face the world, and together they lead a decadent, reclusive existence. But Serena is determined to change things. The potent force of her ravenous sensuality cannot be ignored, as she rekindles Mika's zest for love and life through unexpected means. But together they share a dark secret.

ISBN 0 352 32912 2

MOON OF DESIRE
Sophie Danson

When Soraya Chilton is posted to the ancient and mysterious city of Ragzburg on a mission for the Foreign Office, strange things begin to happen to her. Wild, sexual urges overwhelm her at the coming of each full moon. Will her boyfriend, Anton, be her saviour – or her victim? What price will she have to pay to lift the curse of unquenchable lust that courses through her veins?

ISBN 0 352 32911 4 *April '94*

FIONA'S FATE
Fredrica Alleyn

When Fiona Sheldon is kidnapped by the infamous Trimarchi brothers, along with her friend Bethany, she finds herself acting in ways her husband Duncan would be shocked by. For it is he who owes the brothers money and is more concerned to free his voluptuous mistress than his shy and quiet wife. Alesandro Trimarchi makes full use of this opportunity to discover the true extent of Fiona's suppressed, but powerful, sexuality.

ISBN 0 352 32913 0 *April '94*

HANDMAIDEN OF PALMYRA
Fleur Reynolds

3rd century Palmyra: a lush oasis in the Syrian desert. The beautiful and fiercely independent Samoya takes her place in the temple of Antioch as an apprentice priestess. Decadent bachelor Prince Alif has other plans for her and sends his scheming sister to bring her to his Bacchanalian wedding feast. Embarking on a journey across the desert, Samoya encounters Marcus, the battle-hardened centurion who will unearth the core of her desires and change the course of her destiny.

ISBN 0 352 32919 X *May '94*

OUTLAW FANTASY
Saskia Hope

For Fee Cambridge, playing with fire had become a full time job. Helping her pirate lover to escape his lawless lifestyle had its rewards as well as its drawbacks. On the outer reaches of the 21st century metropolis the Amazenes are on the prowl; fierce warrior women who have some unfinished business with Fee's lover. Will she be able to stop him straying back to the wrong side of the tracks? This is the sequel to *Outlaw Lover*.

ISBN 0 352 32920 3 *May '94*

Three special, longer length Black Lace summer sizzlers to be published in June 1994.

THE SILKEN CAGE
Sophie Danson

When University lecturer, Maria Treharne, inherits her aunt's mansion in Cornwall, she finds herself the subject of strange and unexpected attention. Her new dwelling resides on much-prized land; sacred, some would say. Anthony Pendorran has waited a long time for the mistress to arrive at Brackwater Tor. Now she's here, his lust can be quenched as their longing for each other has a hunger beyond the realm of the physical. Using the craft of goddess worship and sexual magnetism, Maria finds allies and foes in this savage and beautiful landscape.

ISBN 0 352 32928 9

RIVER OF SECRETS
Saskia Hope & Georgia Angelis

When intrepid female reporter Sydney Johnson takes over someone else's assignment up the Amazon river, the planned exploration seems straightforward enough. But the crew's photographer seems to be keeping some very shady company and the handsome botanist is proving to be a distraction with a difference. Sydney soon realises this mission to find a lost Inca city has a hidden agenda. Everyone is behaving so strangely, so sexually, and the tropical humidity is reaching fever pitch as if a mysterious force is working its magic over the expedition. Echoing with primeval sounds, the jungle holds both dangers and delights for Sydney in this Indiana Jones-esque story of lust and adventure.

ISBN 0 352 32925 4

VELVET CLAWS
Cleo Cordell

It's the 19th century; a time of exploration and discovery and young, spirited Gwendoline Farnshawe is determined not to be left behind in the parlour when the handsome and celebrated anthropologist, Jonathan Kimberton, is planning his latest expedition to Africa. Rebelling against Victorian society's expectation of a young woman and lured by the mystery and exotic climate of this exciting continent, Gwendoline sets sail with her entourage bound for a land of unknown pleasures.

ISBN 0 352 32926 2

BLACK lace

WE NEED YOUR HELP . . .
to plan the future of women's erotic fiction –

– and no stamp required!

Yours are the only opinions that matter.
Black Lace is a new and exciting venture: the first series of books devoted to erotic fiction by women for women.

We're going to do our best to provide the brightest, best-written, bonk-filled books you can buy. And we'd like your help in these early stages. Tell us what you want to read.

THE BLACK LACE QUESTIONNAIRE

SECTION ONE: ABOUT YOU

1.1 Sex (*we presume you are female, but so as not to discriminate*) are you?
　　Male　☐　　Female　☐

1.2 Age
　　under 21　☐　　21–30　☐
　　31–40　　☐　　41–50　☐
　　51–60　　☐　　over 60　☐

1.3 At what age did you leave full-time education?
　　still in education　☐　　16 or younger　☐
　　17–19　　　　　　☐　　20 or older　　☐

1.4 Occupation _____

1.5 Annual household income
- under £10,000 ☐
- £10–£20,000 ☐
- £20–£30,000 ☐
- £30–£40,000 ☐
- over £40,000 ☐

1.6 We are perfectly happy for you to remain anonymous; but if you would like us to send you a free booklist of Nexus books for men and Black Lace books for Women, please insert your name and address

_____
_____
_____
_____

SECTION TWO: ABOUT BUYING BLACK LACE BOOKS

2.1 How did you acquire this copy
- I bought it myself ☐
- My partner bought it ☐
- I borrowed/found it ☐

2.2 How did you find out about Black Lace books?
- I saw them in a shop ☐
- I saw them advertised in a magazine ☐
- I saw the London Underground posters ☐
- I read about them in _____
- Other _____

2.3 Please tick the following statements you agree with:
- I would be less embarrassed about buying Black Lace books if the cover pictures were less explicit ☐
- I think that in general the pictures on Black Lace books are about right ☐
- I think Black Lace cover pictures should be as explicit as possible ☐

2.4 Would you read a Black Lace book in a public place – on a train for instance?
- Yes ☐
- No ☐

SECTION THREE: ABOUT THIS BLACK LACE BOOK

3.1 Do you think the sex content in this book is:
   Too much ☐   About right ☐
   Not enough ☐

3.2 Do you think the writing style in this book is:
   Too unreal/escapist ☐   About right ☐
   Too down to earth ☐

3.3 Do you think the story in this book is:
   Too complicated ☐   About right ☐
   Too boring/simple ☐

3.4 Do you think the cover of this book is:
   Too explicit ☐   About right ☐
   Not explicit enough ☐

Here's a space for any other comments:

SECTION FOUR: ABOUT OTHER BLACK LACE BOOKS

4.1 How many Black Lace books have you read? ☐

4.2 If more than one, which one did you prefer?

4.3 Why?

SECTION FIVE: ABOUT YOUR IDEAL EROTIC NOVEL

We want to publish the books you want to read – so this is your chance to tell us exactly what your ideal erotic novel would be like.

5.1 Using a scale of 1 to 5 (1 = no interest at all, 5 = your ideal), please rate the following possible settings for an erotic novel:
- Medieval/barbarian/sword 'n' sorcery ☐
- Renaissance/Elizabethan/Restoration ☐
- Victorian/Edwardian ☐
- 1920s & 1930s – the Jazz Age ☐
- Present day ☐
- Future/Science Fiction ☐

5.2 Using the same scale of 1 to 5, please rate the following themes you may find in an erotic novel:
- Submissive male/dominant female ☐
- Submissive female/dominant male ☐
- Lesbianism ☐
- Bondage/fetishism ☐
- Romantic love ☐
- Experimental sex e.g. anal/watersports/sex toys ☐
- Gay male sex ☐
- Group sex ☐

Using the same scale of 1 to 5, please rate the following styles in which an erotic novel could be written:
- Realistic, down to earth, set in real life ☐
- Escapist fantasy, but just about believable ☐
- Completely unreal, impressionistic, dreamlike ☐

5.3 Would you prefer your ideal erotic novel to be written from the viewpoint of the main male characters or the main female characters?
- Male ☐   Female ☐
- Both ☐

5.4 What would your ideal Black Lace heroine be like? Tick as many as you like:

- Dominant ☐
- Extroverted ☐
- Independent ☐
- Adventurous ☐
- Intellectual ☐
- Professional ☐
- Submissive ☐
- Ordinary ☐
- Glamorous ☐
- Contemporary ☐
- Bisexual ☐
- Naive ☐
- Introverted ☐
- Kinky ☐
- Anything else? ☐

_____

5.5 What would your ideal male lead character be like? Again, tick as many as you like:

- Rugged ☐
- Athletic ☐
- Sophisticated ☐
- Retiring ☐
- Outdoor-type ☐
- Executive-type ☐
- Ordinary ☐
- Kinky ☐
- Hunky ☐
- Sexually dominant ☐
- Sexually submissive ☐
- Caring ☐
- Cruel ☐
- Debonair ☐
- Naive ☐
- Intellectual ☐
- Professional ☐
- Romantic ☐
- Anything else? ☐

_____

5.6 Is there one particular setting or subject matter that your ideal erotic novel would contain?

_____

SECTION SIX: LAST WORDS

6.1 What do you like best about Black Lace books?

_____

6.2 What do you most dislike about Black Lace books?

_____

6.3 In what way, if any, would you like to change Black Lace covers?

_____

6.4 Here's a space for any other comments!

_____
_____
_____
_____

Thank you for completing this questionnaire. Now tear it out of the book – carefully! – put it in an envelope and send it to:

> **Black Lace**
> **FREEPOST**
> **London**
> **W10 5BR**

No stamp is required!